SEA OF REGRET

Carolyn J. Rose

SEA OF REGRET

Carolyn J. Rose

Sea of Regret

ISBN: 978-0-9837359-5-3

Cover design by Dorion D. Rose, Broken Cork Photography

Interior design for print edition by Boulevard Photografica/Patty G. Henderson

Digital editions (epub and mobi) produced by Booknook.biz

Thanks to Sharnelle Fee at the Wildlife Center of the North Coast in Astoria, Oregon. Once again she allowed me to visit her facility, get the answers to dozens of questions about rescuing and rehabilitating injured birds and animals, and hang out with an inquisitive pelican. Any mistakes are mine, all mine. A portion of the profit from this book and from *An Uncertain Refuge* helps support the work of WCNC.
http://www.coastwildlife.org/Home.html

And thanks to Lois Reibach who bid on two of my books at Left Coast Crime in 2011 and won naming rights for a character in a future story. Lois, you rock! I hope the librarian of fictional Castaway Beach lives up to your expectations.

And here's to Rob Nettleton and Dee Towner for good advice.

CHAPTER 1

When it was over, Kate Dalton vowed to abolish the phrase "if only" from her vocabulary and make peace with what they did to survive. But on that June morning when the black car thundered down the road, reviewing her regrets was as much a part of the morning routine as sipping a second cup of coffee at her desk in the corner of the farmhouse kitchen.

She was updating records on sick and injured birds and animals brought to Evie Hopkins' rehab center when she heard the sharp crunch of tires on gravel and the ping and rattle of stones against metal. Spinning her chair about and peering through the window on the far side of the living room, she spotted a car, long and wide, glinting in the sunlight like obsidian. Its horn blasted, sharp and ominous. Geese erupted from the shadow of the house, hissing, honking, and beating their wings in a flurry of feathers. A doe sprang from a snarl of tall grass at the edge of the tattered lawn and bounded into the woods.

1

Kate set her coffee aside and stepped through the open door onto the screened-in porch. This was not a regular visitor driving a car she hadn't seen before. Regulars—volunteers and the occasional student or wildlife expert—knew better than to blast their horns and startle fragile creatures. They also approached at a cautious speed along the potholed lane from the highway. She and Jackson shoveled on just enough gravel to prevent chuckholes from swallowing vehicles, but not so much that the road encouraged speed or invited sightseers. The scraggly grass in front of the old barn a quarter mile from the house was crisscrossed with the tracks of those who turned around and turned back.

Wheels thudding into ruts, the gleaming car jounced to the center of the parking area, sliding in behind Evie's timeworn pickup in a billow of dust. The horn blasted again, but the driver's door didn't open.

Kate frowned. Not someone bringing an injured creature found on the beach or along the highway. In the past year, she'd seen many rescuers arrive at Evie's place north of Castaway Beach. First-timers often hurtled from their cars and raced to the house. But those who had come before, who knew the odds might be against survival, moved more deliberately, as if weighed down by the fact of mortality. None blew their horns and waited for curb service.

Was Evie expecting this person?

She hadn't said anything at breakfast when they discussed plans for the day. Jackson's agenda included driving Way-Ray to school and picking up supplies, including more fencing material. Kate's dance card was full with deskwork, filling out the

2

daily report that made it easier to complete state and federal forms, calling volunteers to set the schedule for July, then helping Jackson. Evie had her usual tasks—feeding, washing, medicating, checking wounds, changing bandages, cleaning cages, draining and refilling the small pools birds paddled in.

Had she forgotten she was speaking at a club or school?

Kate checked the calendar tacked to the wall above her desk. The square for this June day was blank, as white as the car outside was black.

Black as an executioner's hood. Black as a hearse.

Kate shivered, rubbed the scar on her right leg, and, with reflex born of last summer's violence, surveyed the kitchen for available weapons—knives, a cast-iron skillet heavy enough to drop a steer, a kettle releasing wavering wisps of steam, and a barbecue fork with four-inch tines. Jackson's guns were upstairs, locked away where Way-Ray and his friends couldn't get at them if curiosity spurred reckless action. Kate had memorized the combination to the gun safe because Jackson asked her to, and she knew how to load, aim, and fire, but she hoped there would never be a reason to do that. Unlocking the cabinet and loading a gun was admitting a situation had spun out of control.

The horn blasted again. Three vicious bursts.

This person was angry.

No, beyond angry.

Enraged.

Kate shaded her eyes and squinted, but tinted windows obscured the driver's face. He was tall and bulky though—that much she could make out—and

3

he had broad hands, one gripping the wheel, the other in a fist thumping the dashboard.

Telling herself her fears were overblown, Kate retreated to the kitchen and took the cordless phone from its cradle. If he got out of the car looking for more than a verbal fight, she'd call Jackson and the police. With the leather thong on the handle of a barbecue fork hooked around a button on the back pocket of her shorts for added insurance, she started for the door again.

"Keep your shirt on," Evie shouted from one of the enclosures beyond the house. "I'll be there in a minute."

Her voice held more resignation than annoyance and Kate wondered again if Evie was expecting this person. She paused halfway across the porch, hidden from the drive by wisteria vines and the deep shadows of the trees surrounding the house. If this was someone Evie had crossed swords with in the past, she might prefer to handle this encounter on her own. Evie sometimes seemed to yearn for conflict, even thrive on it. Kate often wondered if she felt that deflecting or diluting a disagreement was a sign of aging and weakness.

A gate clanged and Evie strode along the edge of the pasture. Her khaki shorts flapped around bony knees and sweat and dirt streaked her faded green T-shirt. Two buckets swung from each hand. Without glancing at the house, she set them on a concrete pad beside the porch, kicked off a pair of low black rubber boots, and toed into flip-flops. Squaring her shoulders, she walked to the car.

Intrigued by body language that spoke of an unfortunate history with this visitor, Kate watched from the shadows. She felt only the faintest twinge

4

of guilt about spying. Her SUV was in the driveway and Evie must know she was in the house, see that the windows were open, realize Kate couldn't help but hear. And Evie hadn't called out as she passed, inquiring in her cynical way whether Kate was too busy or too special to leave her desk and see what this person wanted.

That was odd. Out of character.

Unless Evie didn't want this person to know Kate was here. Unless Evie wanted an unseen witness, or even someone to come to her aid.

Who was this visitor?

Kate stepped closer to the screen as Evie halted a few yards from the car's snout and planted her fists on the juts of her hipbones. Evie's face was turned away, but Kate reviewed the range of Evie's expressions and settled on one somewhere between barely contained annoyance and nearly exhausted patience.

The car's engine revved and then died with the quavering mewl of a belt in need of adjustment. The driver's door swung open and a tall man got out. He sidestepped a foot or so from the car, but didn't close the door and almost seemed to use it as a shield.

Despite the unseasonable late spring heat, he wore a navy blue blazer with gold buttons, a white shirt, and a crimson tie.

Patriotic? Or conservative in his tastes?

The blazer was too large in the shoulders and too tight in the chest and across the swell of his gut. His brown hair was streaked and tousled and his face tanned, but that did little to soften the nose that curved like a raptor's beak and a nearly lipless mouth.

5

"Mother," he said in freeze-dried tone.

"Paul." A statement of fact without emotional content.

Paul?

Kate blinked. This was Evie's son.

Not long after Kate came to live here last summer he called to warn her that she'd made a big mistake paying the back taxes on this property. He swore she'd be sorry she got involved in a situation that wasn't her business.

Kate thought he meant she would lose her investment. Evie's wildlife rehab center existed at the whim of those willing to open their wallets and donations had dried up. But after a killer shot Kate and Evie when he came to claim Way-Ray, the orphaned boy Kate had vowed to protect, publicity released a river of cash. Smugly, Kate had told Paul she'd already been repaid and, in her new role as administrator for the center, had set aside funds for the next year's tax bill.

"Good luck with that budget and your job," Paul Hopkins sneered. "My mother has a knack for squandering money and alienating people. She's obsessed. You'll see. In a year you'll be sorry you ever met her."

That year was nearly up. So far his prediction hadn't come true.

Yes, Evie wasn't great at managing money—perhaps because she'd never had much to manage—but Kate kept a tight grip on the financial reins. Yes, Evie was a hard-nosed boss who didn't suffer fools gladly, but Kate praised volunteers and kept them focused on tasks instead of the taskmaster. And yes, Evie was obsessed with saving every creature she could, but she recognized when a case was

6

hopeless. When death won the battle, she sucked up her grief and went on. If she brooded or second guessed, she did it in the privacy of her room.

"I don't suppose you drove out here to see the owl enclosure we just finished," Evie said.

Paul gripped the top of the door. "You can't do what you're planning, Mother. You can't give this property away. It's my inheritance."

Evie raised her chin and pulled her shoulders back. "Seems to me an inheritance isn't yours until you inherit it. By law this place is mine until I sell it, give it away, forfeit it, or draw my last breath."

"This land was in father's family for more than a hundred years. He intended that I have it. I earned it. I worked on this farm every day until I went to college."

"Worked? What you did was chores to the lowest standard and not one bit more." Evie waved that argument aside. "And since when did you give a shit what your father intended? He sent you to college because he *intended* that you help him run this farm, make it more productive."

"I never promised him I would do that."

"Oh, I know, Paul. I learned how careful you are not to give your word." Evie aimed a knotted forefinger at him. "In all your years, even when you could barely put two syllables together, you never *promised* one damn thing. It wasn't until after your father died and I wore myself down to my bones waiting for you to make time to lend me a hand that I peeled away all your carefully constructed sentences and saw there was no intention underneath except the intention to make your life more comfortable. I guess that's how you got so

7

good at convincing people to buy more house than they can afford, how you got to be such a success."

She spat out the last word as if it was as bitter as the dark dust inside a puffball.

"You're right, I'm a success." He said the word with pride. "I work hard and I earn my money, not like those freeloaders you have living here."

Kate gritted her teeth. Freeloaders? Yes, they paid no rent, but she and Jackson worked hard—and for damn little pay—to keep this place going. They were a team, a family. Driving her fingernails into her palms, Kate fought to keep from rushing out and setting the record straight.

"I'll take my freeloaders over your so-called friends any day," Evie said. "If I leave this place to you, I won't be cold in my grave before you turn it over to those developers you're so tight with. You'll count your cash while they bulldoze the meadows and log off the trees, while they build a road down to that scrap of beach where the seal pups rest, while they cram so many houses to the acre there's no room to breathe."

Her shoulders trembled. "You don't care about this farm. All you care about—all you ever cared about—is money."

She turned her back on him, her face the color of his tie, her mouth open, her chest heaving. Jamming her fists in her pockets, she trudged toward the house.

Kate wanted to run to her side, but knew that would infuriate and embarrass her. Evie seldom revealed her emotions and when she did, it was wise not to acknowledge that you'd had a glimpse behind the curtain of her stubborn pride.

"You're standing in the way of progress. I'll put a stop to your plan. Don't think I won't," Paul warned in a tight voice. "You're getting crazier every day. I'll go to court to prove you're not in your right mind if I have to."

Evie wheeled on him. "You can go to hell for all I care. Progress be damned. My intention is that the work I'm doing will go on after I die and that it will go on right here." She stomped her foot. "On this piece of the earth."

"We'll see." He straightened his tie. "We'll see whether this place is still running when Christmas rolls around. Long before that you might be begging me to take it off your hands."

Begging? Not likely, Kate thought. Not Evie.

Paul threw himself into the car, fired up the engine, and backed in a wide arc across the parking area, stones spraying from his wheels and spattering around Evie.

She stood like a pillar of stone, chin high, making no move to dodge the assault. But when the car was out of sight, she slumped, ducked her head, and wiped her eyes on the sleeve of her T-shirt.

Kate stepped to the stove and poured hot water into two mugs, then dropped in tea bags. She unhooked the barbecue fork from her shorts, took one mug to her desk, picked up her pen, and studied the form on top of the heap. When Evie got herself together, when she felt she was in control and in charge again, then she'd seek company.

And in a few moments she did, striding through the door, washing her hands, and snatching up the mug by the stove. "I guess you heard that."

Kate set the pen down and spun her chair about. "Some of it."

9

Evie snorted. "You heard every word and you know it."

"Okay, I did. I figured if you wanted a private conversation you'd tell me to get lost. I also thought you might want me as a witness. If that wasn't your intention, then I'm guilty of eavesdropping."

Hooking a chair with her foot, Evie sagged into it and sucked at her tea. "I wish Paul knew what guilt felt like. Well, maybe not guilt, but sensitivity, empathy, sympathy. But he never did, even from the time he was just learning to walk."

She dug a sugar cookie from the jar at the center of the table, dunked it in her tea, and stuffed it in her mouth. "I had him late, when I was sure I'd never conceive. And he was the only one."

She scrubbed at her face with her hands. "Anyway, times were hard. We lived close to the bone. I was always busy with the milk and the garden and the house. I thought the way he behaved was just normal, the way kids are, self-centered and all."

Kate nodded. Young children *were* self-centered. Some carried that into adulthood and occasionally to frightening extremes. If Evie had another child, would Paul's personality be different? If she hadn't been so busy with the burdens of the farm, could she have made a stronger connection with her son and altered the course of his life and actions?

Evie released a bitter laugh. "We used to think it was cute, the way he'd shake his pink piggy bank, the way he'd wheedle change from our pockets and stuff it into that slot and count it every Sunday evening."

She dunked another cookie and crammed it between her lips as if it might soak up the bile in

10

her gut. "I thought he'd grow out of it, or some girl would change him. But he never met a woman he loved as much as he loves himself and those dollars." She sighed, took a third cookie from the jar and dipped just the edge. "Or maybe he never met one he was willing to share his money with."

Or one who had plenty of money to share with him. "Will he go to court to stop you from changing your will?"

"He's probably making plans to do that right now." Teeth snapping together, she chewed off the rim of the cookie. "His developer friends will push him. They won't want to see a prime site like this taken off the board for a bunch of birds."

Kate dunked her teabag, then shoved the mug aside, stomach roiling. "Can he win?"

"My lawyer says he can't. But there's no way to know until a judge hands down a decision."

If Paul won, if the land passed to him, the wildlife rehabilitation center would shut down when Evie died. Bulldozers would level the house, the first house Kate ever thought of as a real home. They'd level the cages and enclosures. Way-Ray would be frantic.

Don't think about that. Concentrate on trying to prevent it.

"What did he mean by what he said—that you'd beg him to take this place?"

"I don't know. I can't even imagine."

With a sharp grunt, Evie stood, drained her tea, then tossed the tea bag into a plastic bowl of banana peels and strawberry hulls bound for the compost heap by the garden. "Could be an empty threat, just something he said because I got in his face. There's no need to tell the boy about this."

11

Kate nodded. Way-Ray didn't handle uncertainty well and occasionally acted out. Knowing they could never make up for his mother's murder and the abuse he suffered at the hands of his uncle, she and Jackson and Evie had spent the past ten months setting boundaries, creating structure, helping him find ways to burn off energy and express anger without yelling or hitting.

He'd made tremendous progress. But there had been setbacks, black moods and harsh words followed by tears and apologies that revealed his inner turmoil and how far he was from making peace with the past and with himself.

"Jackson doesn't need to know either," Evie said. "He doesn't need any extra grief while he's hurting so bad."

Kate nodded again. Jackson drove himself hard last fall while she was healing, racing the rain to get a new roof on the house, running wiring, replacing rusted-out plumbing, and expanding the supply shed to house two washers, two dryers, and a mammoth freezer for fish. With the coming of warm weather and her ability to shoulder some of the load, his limp hadn't improved as she hoped it might. She often heard him cursing his bad leg or wincing at the pain that shot along it and up his back. Yet he kept working, putting up fences, building shelters and enclosures.

In the evenings, after Way-Ray was in bed, she massaged Jackson's tight muscles and put hot and cold packs on his back. And she worried. Worried about the amount of medication his doctor prescribed. Worried when he took it and worried more when he didn't. Worried that he'd trade pills for liquor and wander back into the numbing alcoholic wasteland he emerged from a year ago.

"We gotta convince him to have that surgery," Evie said. "Before it's too late."

Too late to save his leg? Or too late to save him from the bottle? "He won't listen."

"Seems like not one of us out here has a talent for taking advice." Evie hefted the heavy iron skillet. "We're the kind that needs to have sense knocked into us on a regular basis."

She set the skillet down with a clang and strode through the doorway. "Gotta get a move on."

For a long moment Kate gazed after her, thinking about Paul's threats, wondering what he might do and how that might change their lives.

CHAPTER 2

Half an hour later, Kate licked an ice cream cone and leaned against the thick slanting glass of the display case in Rhea Whitaker's shop. As usual after sharing a burden with her friend, she felt both relief and guilt.

Relief because now she wasn't carrying the burden alone.

Guilt for the same reason.

She'd been raised to be independent and self-sufficient, to keep things to herself, to preserve privacy and reputation. But that was BC as Rhea called it, before she came to the coast. Now she had a friend, and friendship meant the give-and-take of confidences. Besides, although she promised Evie she wouldn't tell Way-Ray or Jackson about Paul's visit, Rhea hadn't been included in that request and Kate hadn't mentioned Evie's omission.

And besides that, even if she had agreed to withhold information from Rhea, information would have found its way to her. The same grapevine that delivered news to Paul about Evie's consultation with an attorney would pulse with messages about

14

his visit to his mother. Someone would have seen him headed that way and would report that news to someone else who would speculate about his purpose. They'd form opinions about the reception he received and send them out along the tendrils of an invisible vine that wound through every home and business in Castaway Beach.

In her ice cream parlor at the center of town, Rhea was on the main stem of the grapevine. If Kate hadn't hustled to unload about Paul's visit before the vine delivered, Rhea would have been furious and charged Kate with violating the first rule of friendship—sharing everything, or at least vital or juicy stuff.

A dribble of melted butter pecan ice cream crept over the lip of the sugar cone. Kate caught it with the tip of her tongue and watched Rhea muscle a tub of chocolate ripple into a slot in the long freezer case. When she resigned as head housekeeper and assistant manager at the Wade in the Waves Motel, Rhea planned to stay home and ride herd on her sons, care for her ailing mother-in-law, and help her husband with his painting business.

She was home for three days and reorganizing the kitchen drawers for the second time when Kyle and Sean brought word about a fight in the ice cream parlor. It was a skirmish that needed no embellishment to become legend. Screaming accusations about incidents that went back twenty years, the owners flung ice cream, cones, and toppings. When a customer got pelted with a barrage of peanuts, Chief Lowell crossed the street from the police station to intervene. He took a scoop of strawberry ripple in the eye, then took the shop owners away in handcuffs.

About the time the last smears were wiped from the walls and dry-cleaned from Lowell's uniform, the owners pleaded to charges of assault on an officer and filed for both divorce and bankruptcy. To no one's surprise, Rhea said she needed something to keep her busy and bought the business.

"I wish I could tell you Paul's all bark and no bite." Rhea twisted a straying wisp of springy black hair and secured it with a bright green butterfly clip, then poured herself a mug of coffee, dug a spoonful of French vanilla from a tub, and stirred it into the inky brew. "But I have a feeling this time he's going for Evie's throat and he won't fight fair. It's better if Way-Ray and Jackson know there's something out there before it gets ugly."

"I'm with you." Kate nibbled a fat pecan from the sloping ice cream atop her cone. "But Evie says—"

"Evie isn't thinking this through." Rhea patted the empty pocket of her blue smock, the pocket where she once carried a pack of cigarettes and a lighter, then shook her head and sipped her coffee. "If there's one lesson we all learned from last summer's shitstorm, it's to get the crap out in the yard so it doesn't blow up in the basement and bring the house down."

Kate nodded. Way-Ray and Jackson might not hear about the situation today or tomorrow, but before long the grapevine would deliver a mutated version of events.

"You want me to go talk with her?"

"Yes. But no. She'll be mad at both of us if you do."

"Most days mad is where Evie starts from." Rhea laughed and circled a finger by the side of her head.

16

"Not mad like a smidge off kilter, a half-step over the line into Crazytown. Mad like fired up."

Evie herself often admitted to that, sometimes in a joking way and sometimes not. "A little madness helps when you shoulder the load she's got. Never knowing what kinds of creatures might turn up or how many or what's wrong with them or whether there's anything she can do. That's the worst part, when it's not just one or two, but when it's a die-off because the water's too warm or too cold or there's some kind of algae or—"

Rhea pressed her palms against the air at her sides. "You get any more worked up and I'll have to send out for more ice cream to cool you down. When it comes to fur and feathers, Evie's a saint. But don't forget that when they were alive, lots of saints weren't the most popular people in town."

Kate hauled in a breath and licked at her cone. "Yeah, she doesn't always work and play well with others. And once she sets her course the best thing the rest of us can do is get out of the way."

"She and Paul have that in common," Rhea observed. "Although I doubt Evie would admit to it if you pulled out her fingernails with a pliers."

"What's he like? I mean, other than avaricious?"

"Focused, determined. He gets that from both Evie and his father. He's not the friendliest sort—his father wasn't, either—and no one would ever accuse him of sending out too many Christmas cards. But his clients like the hard bargains he drives even if folks on the other side of the deals don't. He's made a good living selling real estate and turning properties around for a profit. Lots of folks would be content with the pile he's accumulated."

But Paul wasn't.

17

Why?

Did his acquisitive nature stem from a hole in his soul, a need he couldn't fill, perhaps couldn't even name?

Kate nibbled at the rim of her cone, wondering if the answer to that lay in his childhood, in the way he was brought up. Had he always been in love with money for its own sake, or did it represent a degree of security he craved? Evie and her husband had eked out a living but not much more. Paul must have compared his life to the lives of relatives and kids he met in school. He must have longed for toys and television. As an only child growing up miles from town, he must have longed for friends.

Kate thought about her own childhood, the austere parents who restricted her possessions and opportunities and the shadow that cast over her friendships. Like many children, she'd wanted to fit in, but her parents' philosophy about serviceable clothing and serious study, and their rules about having friends over and visiting at their homes, made her the square peg in a world of round holes. Kate doubted that Evie intentionally set Paul up to be a pariah but, given her own daily struggles, she might not have noticed his growing isolation and loneliness.

"Did you know him well when he was a kid? Isn't he a third cousin or something?"

"Or something." Rhea shrugged. "I'd see him at the family reunion every summer, but he kinda got lost in the shuffle. And with a family our size it was a hell of a big shuffle—more than a hundred of us for an all-day picnic at that state park down the coast."

Rhea slid her coffee mug into a sink behind the counter and used the corner of her smock to wipe a smudge. "My mom and Evie were tight—peas in a pod, hard workers and neither of them minced words—they ramrodded the events. But Mom died around the time Evie's husband passed and that was the end of the gatherings."

"Do you miss them?"

"To quote you, 'Yes. But no.' Somebody always got their nose out of joint over a cake recipe or the brand of mayonnaise in the potato salad. And the kids ran wild, in and out of the surf, no one keeping track of who was where. It's a wonder we didn't lose two or three every season."

She glanced at the clock. "Speaking of kids, Way-Ray will be out of school in an hour. You'd better get home and bring Evie around to reality before the poop makes contact with the oscillating device."

Kate grinned and gobbled down the last of her cone. "I'll try, but if you're smart, you'll hedge your bet and put some money on the poop."

Rhea nodded. "Yeah, no matter how you lay it out, Evie will take it the wrong way."

"I didn't say you were wrong." Kate gripped the chain link fence and peered through the diamond-shaped holes as Evie filled a metal tub with a hose—fresh water for a small flock of recuperating ducks. "And I didn't say I'm right. I said I thought it over and it seems there will be a lot less grief if we head off the gossip and tell Jackson and Way-Ray what's going on."

"There's nothing going on!" Evie flailed her arms. Water sang off the rim and sides of the tub.

"Not yet, there isn't. But I heard what Paul said. And I heard you say you can't even imagine what he might do."

Evie said nothing and Kate let the last words hang there, let Evie work on conjuring possibilities.

Water reached a mark two inches from the top and Evie turned off the spigot, let herself out through the gate, and pulled the hose after her. The bravest of the ducks, a green-winged teal, jumped to the rim and stirred the water with the stub of its bill—all that remained after an encounter with who-knew-what. A female wood duck with one wing bandaged tight against its side overshot the rim and landed in the tub, showering the others.

"Maybe it was just an empty threat." Kate rubbed the scar on her leg. "Maybe I'm worrying over nothing. But forewarned is forearmed."

Evie coiled the hose, then glanced at the broken birds splashing in the tub. Her fingers touched her side, the place where a bullet sliced along her ribs last summer. Kate could almost feel her remembering that bloody day beside the old barn.

Evie said "We'll sit them down after dinner. Wouldn't hurt to fix up something they like to fill their bellies. Make this go down a little easier."

"How come we had all of my favorites at once?" Way-Ray rinsed his plate and slid it into the dishwasher. "We hardly never do that unless I get a good report card."

20

"Your favorite foods are Kate's least favorites." Jackson shuttled platters to the counter and ran through the menu. "Hot dogs and fries and corn on the cob and chocolate-covered doughnuts." He grunted, grinned at Kate, and belched. "Except for that salad, it was a real-man meal."

"What you said!" Way-Ray crowed. "A man meal."

Jackson raised his hand above his head for a high-five and Way-Ray jumped to slap it, tapping his fingertips against Jackson's wrist, his fine brown hair lifting like wings as he dropped to the floor. He'd grown three inches since last summer and put on close to twenty pounds. Smacking Jackson's hand, once an impossible feat, was almost within reach. His goal was to make it happen before he turned eleven in September.

"Well, you worked hard today. You deserved a treat." Using two hands, Kate lifted the skillet she'd used to cook the hot dogs—the same one she thought about as a weapon that morning—and poured grease into a can. "But I prefer a meal with more color. This one was mostly brown and yellow and white."

"And red," Way-Ray said. "You forgot about the ketchup on the fries."

Evie snorted a laugh and handed him her plate. Then her fingers pinched at her napkin and she gazed across the living room and out the window at the spot where Paul had parked.

"Ketchup isn't a vegetable." Kate returned the bottle to the refrigerator along with the mustard Way-Ray and Jackson used to stripe their hot dogs, competing to see who could make the best design without breaking the bright yellow ribbon squeezed

21

from the container. "Neither is mustard. That's my position on condiments and I'm sticking to it."

"Well, you're prejudiced," Way-Ray insisted. "Potatoes and corn are vegetables, but you don't like them just because they're not green."

"Definitely prejudiced." Jackson leaned against the counter, taking the weight off his bad leg—as far as he'd go in front of Way-Ray. Kate urged him to be honest about his pain and the occasional weakness in the muscles, but he insisted that Way-Ray needed to have no doubt he was strong enough to protect them should someone like his abusive uncle appear. On an emotional level, there was no arguing with that.

"I'm not prejudiced." Kate shook the placemats over the trash can. "I'm not even sure you can apply that word to food. What I am is concerned about nutrition."

"Sure, hide behind the banner of a balanced diet." Jackson wiped down the skillet, handling it as if it weighed no more than a coffee mug. "I say you're clearly prejudiced."

"We learned about that in school." Way-Ray jammed silverware into the dishwasher's compartments. "We learned how people don't like other people because of the color of their skin or where they come from or where they go to church or how they talk or even what they wear."

Evie coughed and lifted a finger to point to the driveway. Kate nodded. This was as good an opening as any. "People are prejudiced about lots of other things, too, like the way others live their lives and spend their money. And the causes they believe in."

"Causes?" Way-Ray scratched his head with a fork and gawked. "Like Santa Causes?"

Kate rolled her eyes but shot him a smile, rewarding his heavy-handed humor. Three weeks ago he and Rhea's younger son announced they'd abandoned dreams of being race car drivers, firefighters, astronauts, or soldiers. They had definitely and finally—or so they claimed—settled on careers as stand-up comics. Since that day, Sean had been grounded twice for spiking his comedic efforts with offensive language—a good portion of which he didn't understand. So far Way-Ray's forays into humor had been of the goofy variety.

"Causes like rescuing birds and animals." Evie, possessing only a limited sense of humor and tolerance for jokes, especially lame ones, got to the point. "You might hear some people talking about me in town this summer, saying I'm crazy for rescuing birds, for wasting time and money, for standing in the way of progress."

Jackson set the skillet on the back burner with a dull clang and turned to study her, his eyes like a winter sky. "Some people? Meaning your son and the developers he hangs with?"

"Yes." Evie pressed her lips together. "Paul came out here this morning."

"That damn golf course scheme." Jackson raised his gaze to Kate, his hands rolling into tight fists. "He wants to be dealt a hand in that game. And this place is his buy in."

"You don't get dealt a hand in golf," Way-Ray said. "Dealing is for cards. Everybody knows that."

Evie shot him a laser-eyed glare that could bring down a low-flying plane and pointed at his usual chair. "Sit."

Way-Ray mimed hooking himself around the neck and being dragged to his seat. Jackson hesitated, his gaze locked on Kate. When she sat, he followed suit, but kept his chair half turned toward the door. "What kind of a low-ball offer did he make for this place?"

"He didn't make—" Evie threw her napkin at the trash can. "See this is what I didn't want, you getting riled. But Kate saw it the other way around so I'll let her tell it. Tide's going out. I'll hike down to the beach and make sure there aren't any stranded critters."

She scraped her chair back and stomped out, not a slump to her shoulders or a bow to her back. Only the tufts of white hair on her head and the ropy veins in her arms and legs signified that she was halfway through her seventies.

"Well?" Jackson asked after the porch door swung shut.

"Well?" Way-Ray repeated, mimicking Jackson's tone.

Kate took a deep breath. "Paul didn't come to make an offer. He found out that Evie's planning to make a new will and leave this property to the rehab center corporation when she dies and—"

"Dies!" Way-Ray paled and half stood, gripping the table. "Is Evie sick? Is she dying?"

"No." Kate laid her hand over his and felt the stickiness of chocolate icing on his fingers. "She's fine."

Way-Ray frowned. "If she's not sick, then why is she making a will?"

"People do that so they can control what happens to their property," Jackson said. "They decide what they want to do with all their stuff and they leave instructions."

24

Way-Ray's eyes darkened. "My mother made a will." He dropped back into his chair, panting, his voice shrill. "And then my uncle killed her and T.D. the detective guy. Is Paul gonna kill Evie?"

Kate gripped his hand tighter. The horror of the previous summer swept over her like wildfire and she hunched her shoulders and closed her eyes for a second. "Of course not. Paul's not the kind—"

She halted, realizing she had only heard about Paul from others, seen him from a distance, and overheard his harsh words to Evie. She opened her eyes and gazed into Way-Ray's. "Paul grew up here and he's Evie's son after all, so he thinks this farm should be his when she dies."

Way-Ray chewed at his lower lip. "But she's not gonna die?"

"Some day she will." Jackson covered his other hand. "Nobody lives forever. That's just the way nature is. You know that."

"But Evie's not going to die for a long time, right?"

"Not for years and years," Kate agreed. "Not until you're all grown up and working at a comedy club in New York or Los Angeles."

"We'll bring her to see you," Jackson said. "And tell her when to laugh in case she doesn't get your jokes."

"She's not good at getting jokes." Way-Ray rolled his eyes. "But we can stay here, right? Paul can't make us move, can he? When I was little, some mean man made my mom move 'cause she didn't have enough money to pay the rent."

"Lucky thing we don't pay rent. We do chores instead." Jackson grinned. "So as long as you keep doing yours, we won't get evicted."

25

Way-Ray pulled his hands free and rubbed a knuckle against his teeth. "But if Evie dies *before* I'm all grown up, will we have to move?"

Kate longed to lie and assure him that wouldn't happen, but after the anguish caused by a tangle of lies last summer, wouldn't do it. "I hope not. I hope we can keep the rehab center going. But it might come down to what a judge decides."

"He's taking her to court? That greedy—" Jackson caught himself, blew air between his lips, thumped a fist on the table.

"Ooooow. You almost said a swear word and got trash duty for a week." Way-Ray thumped his fist on top of Jackson's, then scratched his head. "What's taking her to court mean?"

"It means hiring a lawyer to go in front of a judge and explain her side of things and why Paul is wrong," Kate said. "Going to court will cost her a lot of money, money she'd rather spend helping birds and animals."

Way-Ray delivered a series of punches to the air. "But she'd win. She'd beat him bad 'cause this is her place and she can do what she wants with it. So why is she all worried?"

Kate winced. Sticking to the truth made for some long and painful conversations. "Well, Paul's angry. And when people get angry they sometimes say they're going to do things that they, um, might never do."

"What things?" Jackson's eyes narrowed. "Did he threaten her?"

"In a vague way." Kate fluttered her fingers. "He said he'd tell the judge she's crazy."

"Evie's not crazy," Way-Ray scoffed.

26

"And proving crazy in court is tough," Jackson said. "What else?"

"He said that long before Christmas she'd be begging him to take this place off her hands."

Way-Ray leaped to his feet, knocking over his chair. "He's not going to hurt the birds and the animals is he?" He clutched the arm his uncle broke last summer. "Or me?"

"No." Jackson stood and slung an arm around Way-Ray's shoulders. "Paul Hopkins is a coward. He won't hurt anything or anyone because he's afraid he'll get hurt himself."

"If he hurts Evie, I'll hurt him." Way-Ray raised his arms and flexed the muscles. "I'll hurt him so bad you won't even hafta shoot him."

Before Kate could say anything, he bolted for the door. "I'm gonna go tell her she can count on me to protect her."

"Evie will calm him down," Jackson said. "And running down to the cove will take the edge off."

"I hope so. I worry when he defaults to violence as the answer. I see his father stabbing Amanda and coming at me with that knife."

"I know." Jackson dropped into Way-Ray's chair and drew her against his chest. "But Wayne Jessop has less of a hold over him every day. He hasn't been in a fight at school for months." He stroked her hair. "For somebody who didn't know squat about being a mother when you took him on, you're doing a damn good job."

Kate allowed herself a few seconds of pride and contentment before she opened the door to anxiety once more. "Is that true that Paul's a coward?"

27

"As yellow as a dandelion." Jackson gazed out the window in the direction of town. "But some of his friends are a whole different breed."

CHAPTER 3

Kate stared up at the clouds she'd sponge-painted on the sloping sky-blue ceiling. A year ago that ceiling was dirty white and splotched with brown water stains and the walls were covered with wallpaper faded, gouged, and dangling loose in long strips. Now the same sky blue as the ceiling, the walls were decorated with framed photographs of Way-Ray, Jackson, Rhea, and others who had become her family. The floorboards, scraped and sanded, had a gloss like honey, and lamps cast warm light across the triangles of bright color in the quilt on the bed she shared with Jackson.

She loved this room. But at the same time she felt she shouldn't allow herself to do that. Her parents brought her up to choose the plain, the simple, the durable, to eschew anything that smacked of frivolity or luxury, and to form no attachments to material things. Like messages on a malfunctioning answering machine, their words kept playing back in her mind. Try as she might, she couldn't turn off the recording or mute the sound. And she couldn't quite ignore the message.

If her parents were still alive, they'd say she shouldn't make an emotional investment in this room—in any room—because that displayed vanity and weakness of character. They'd tell her that, in the grand scheme of things, the work of the wildlife rehab center was pointless. Creatures they labored to help were doomed by nature to live short and often brutal lives and Evie shouldn't interfere with the natural order.

Kate smiled, remembering Evie's response to that philosophy on the first day they met. "That's a bullshit excuse for ignoring man-made problems."

Bullshit excuse or not, Kate's parents would have turned their backs on this place.

But this was the place where she and Way-Ray healed and bonded, where she let herself fall in love with Jackson.

Someday, yes, they might leave here. They'd talked in a vague way about moving to town when Way-Ray was in high school and got involved in more activities, when Jackson completed his long to-do list, when Kate got reporting forms and spreadsheets in order and wanted a fresh challenge and a salary that would let her save for Way-Ray's future. But those discussions had included coming to the farmhouse on weekends and occasional evenings and whenever Evie needed help. They assumed she would be here carrying on her work.

Assumption!

Kate knew the saying about assumption, knew how people broke up the word "assume" to point out the pitfalls of taking something for granted.

30

She couldn't allow Paul and a pack of developers to take this from Evie. Couldn't allow them to make life-altering decisions for her and the rest of them.

She plumped up her pillows, rolled onto her side, and peered at the little she could see of Jackson's face. What she referred to as "a tome on Rome" was propped on his chest, canted toward his eyes. After a day of wrestling with forms, arranging and rearranging schedules, ordering supplies, setting up educational talks at parks and schools, training new volunteers, and keeping up the house and garden, Kate dove into fiction, the lighter the better— mysteries, thrillers, and even chick lit. Jackson preferred history, chronicles of real events— although he admitted that because it came down to who lived to tell the tale and how that tale was told, there might be a great deal of fiction in accounts of battles and political maneuvering.

Kate never asked, but she imagined that when he was deep in the past, standing with the Spartans at Thermopylae, swarming through the Balkans with the Huns, or marching with Roman legions across Britain, his left leg felt whole and strong.

Even after nearly a year, she was still self-conscious about looking at or touching the jagged scars that wrapped around his leg like snakes, writhing when he moved. Way-Ray, on the other hand, thought they were cool, and often ran his fingers across them and begged Jackson to tell him about the logging accident that caused them. Jackson always did, delivering the story in a matter-of-fact tone, glossing over the hours it took for help to arrive, and downplaying the facts that doctors first thought he wouldn't survive surgery, then

31

wanted to remove his leg. After that, who could blame Jackson for delaying surgery on his spine?

Fingering the scar on her thigh, she remembered Evie saying that twice doctors thought they lost her on the operating table, remembered Rhea claiming she would limp for a long time, that she and Jackson would be a matching pair. She smiled, thinking maybe it was because they didn't match in other ways that they were a pair.

Wiggling closer, she watched his eyes, waiting until his gaze reached the bottom of the page. "What if I went to talk to Paul?"

Jackson barked a brief laugh and turned the page.

"If what he wants is money, then maybe we could find a way to raise the value of this place and pay him so he'll leave Evie alone."

Jackson snorted again and marked his place with a callused forefinger. "What this place is worth as it stands is nothing compared to what it will be worth if it's developed."

Another symptom of Kate's frugal childhood and her years working for non-profit agencies. She tended to think in terms of what was enough, of sharing what was in the pot instead of playing to win everything from the others at the table. "But development could be a long way out—years, maybe—and there's no guarantee that it will even happen. There are sure to be environmental concerns. And other issues. Like zoning."

"Yes, but Paul's friends are experts on greasing the skids. Get enough grease on the skids and enough momentum . . ."

He let Kate imagine the rest. Nothing would stop the project. The future of this property would be as bleak as Evie had described. "Tell me about Paul's friends."

Jackson slid a thin plastic ruler into the book and slipped it into a cubbyhole in the headboard he'd built from lumber salvaged at remodeling and rebuilding sites around Castaway Beach. "Well, first off, they're not friends by any definition I ever used. If politics makes for strange bedfellows, the pursuit of money does the same."

"How strange *are* these bedfellows?"

He rubbed the scar that crossed his right palm. "Some are just regular folks who recognize change is inevitable. They have a few thousand spare dollars to invest and this lets them invest it close to home, make a profit, and tell themselves they're helping the local economy." He flexed his shoulders. "Let's use a different image—the ocean. Those regular folks are small fry, sardines, or minnows. They're influenced and intimidated by bigger fish."

Kate imagined a school of tiny fish, silvery bodies veering as one from a looming shadow. "And who are those bigger fish?"

"Well, they're the ones who bring more bucks to the table or more political weight or more all-around force of personality—they're movers and shakers, mostly from this part of the state. Some have held office or are thinking they want to and they're building a base of support. They sit on committees to find answers for problems—problems some of the rest of us might not even realize *are* problems—and they talk a lot about job creation."

He drew the outline of a fish in the air, an outline a yard long. "Let's call them barracudas. They're opportunistic and more dangerous when they work together."

Kate thought of what she knew about barracudas. They had long bodies and sharp teeth. They were attracted to shiny objects. "Paul's definitely a barracuda."

"And he's dangerous. But he's not in the same league with a great white shark."

Kate flashed on an image of a mouth curved into a horrible grin, of flat black eyes, remorseless, almost disinterested. "There are sharks?"

"Kate, if there's money involved, there are *always* sharks." Jackson twirled a strand of her hair around his index finger. "The whiff of financial opportunity is like chum in the water. If there's enough money to be made, we'll have a feeding frenzy."

Kate remembered videos she'd seen of sharks attacking seals, tearing out chunks of flesh. Sharks were killing machines. Biting. Swallowing. Moving on to the next kill.

She shivered "How many sharks are circling this golf course project?"

"Two. That I know of. One's a local shark—he's got a weekend place in Castaway Beach, a ranch over on the east side of the state, townhouses here and there. I don't know much about the other shark except he's bigger and from New Mexico."

She recalled the stark landscape she and Way-Ray drove through last summer. A shark that survived in a parched land must be fearsome indeed. "How did Paul hook up with him?"

"Probably through shark number one. It's like a club at the top of the financial food chain. When it's to their advantage, they hunt together."

Kate shivered again. "But sometimes sharks turn on each other, don't they?"

"Yes." He flashed a wolfish smile. "And sometimes they eat barracudas."

"Good." She ran her fingertips along his jaw, marveling again at how his face could seem so homely or so handsome. He was like the agates Way-Ray and Sean found on the beach. They looked almost like any other rock until sand and tide polished them, until a sunbeam lit them through a sheen of water. Like those agates, Jackson had a translucent quality to him, a glow. "How do you know all this?"

"People underestimate me. They forget I've been sober for almost a year and they talk around me like they used to when my brain was pickled. I pretend I don't hear, don't care, or don't understand." He tapped his forehead. "And then I file it away and connect the dots."

"And what's the picture?"

"When they started it was just an upscale condo complex and restaurant on the edge of town. But then the sharks got interested and more investors lined up behind them and plans got bigger—pools, gyms, spas, boutiques. A few days ago I heard talk about a golf course and tennis courts and they started using the word 'exclusive'. With the economy in the tank, a project like that will look damn good to a lot of people—guys who work construction, kids wanting summer jobs, mothers who need to work part-time. The local barracudas will play on that to build public support."

"But what about all those people who turned out to help Evie last summer, the ones who gave money and volunteered when she was broke and an inch from having to shut down?"

35

"Some of them will stick with her—the ones from out-of-town and the ones who have a decent income and can afford to volunteer and the ones who always pull for the underdog." He shook his head. "The rest, well, they'll feel sorry for the poor little birds and animals, they'll say it's too bad they can't keep the rescue operation going, but they'll forget all about it a few paychecks down the road."

Kate felt as if she was being sucked under by a wave of despair. "Suppose Evie gives up plans to change her will, then there would be no reason for Paul to take her to court, would there? She could stay here as long as she lives, right?"

"Probably. But Evie's no spring chicken."

"She's as healthy as a horse." Kate pulled away and locked her gaze on his, willing him to agree. "She could live another twenty years."

"Or she could die in harness tomorrow. She's never seen a doctor that I know of except for last year when they put a couple of stitches in her side. Her blood pressure and cholesterol could be off the charts."

With a grunt, he shifted on the pillows. "But let's suppose she sets aside plans to change her will. And let's suppose she's in great health and stays that way for years—maybe a decade, maybe longer. That means their plans are in check instead of on the fast track."

He paused and Kate filled in the space. "So Paul will try to speed things along. By making a case for her being incompetent or crazy? You said it was hard to prove that."

"It is. But Evie can be her own worst enemy. Some of her past financial decisions were foolhardy and if she gets mad and pops off to a judge like she's prone to do, well, he might decide Paul has a point. And then . . ."

Kate pounded her pillows, feeling she'd lost a battle she hadn't been aware she was in. "You make it sound hopeless."

"Not at all." Jackson pulled her against the hard plane of his chest and kissed her forehead. "Paul wants a quick win and a court battle isn't it. If Evie gets a sharp lawyer, it could drag on for years. I think Paul will try some less-that-legal methods first. That could be his downfall."

"Less-than-legal methods. Like what?" She felt a cold knot of nausea in her stomach. "Will he . . . will he try to hurt the birds . . . or us?"

"Not while I'm still breathing."

Kate felt a frisson of fear and a ping of hope. Jackson didn't swim in financial or political waters, but he was also a shark. "What can you do?"

"I don't know yet." He reached up and turned off his lamp. "I won't know until he makes his first move."

Kate let herself relax against him. "But we're going to make plans, right? Figure out some options?"

"It doesn't hurt to anticipate." He ran his fingers along her spine from her neck to her hips, then back up, this time beneath her T-shirt. "It's like hunting."

Kate shivered and wriggled against him. She'd had half a dozen lovers over the years, but never dropped her emotional guard, always kept a degree of control and distance. Bit by bit, Jackson made her understand that she was safe with him. She could have as much control—or as little—as she wanted. Control, he said, wasn't like electrical

37

current. It didn't have to alternate in equal degrees. Neither did it have to flow just one way. Control was like water that could be released or dammed or diverted. It could wash in and out like the tide. It could even evaporate.

Relinquishing control still felt risky, even dangerous, but that made being with him more exciting.

"When you're hunting, you sharpen all your senses. You listen and you watch, and you get to know all the habits and peculiarities of what you're going after." His fingers traced her ribs. "And sometimes, as difficult as it is, you have to hold still and let the creature you're hunting make a move toward you."

"Why?"

"First," he breathed into her ear, "so you can get a better look and decide if it's really worth trying to bring it home."

Kate shivered again. "And second?"

He pulled her closer, his lips against hers. "So there's a better chance she can't get away."

CHAPTER 4

Every day, nerves winding tighter, Kate waited for Paul's first move.

But every day it didn't come.

Three days into the waiting, Evie announced she planned to delay revising her will for a few months. In a tone that was both brusque and hesitant, she said she wasn't abandoning her plans, just giving Paul time to cool off. "He's good at his job. He'll find another property for the developers," she said with a hopeful expression. "A real estate commission on a piece of property big enough for a resort and golf course has to amount to a lot of money."

"That's a pipe dream," Jackson told Kate that evening as they ripped out the rotted window frame in Way-Ray's room. "The minute Paul mentioned it to the sharks, this site made the top of the list. And it's a no-brainer that getting everything he can squeeze out of this land is miles ahead of a commission on another site. No matter how long Evie waits, that leopard won't change his spots."

He jammed the pry bar under the edge of the molding. Rusted nails screeched in protest, then gave it up. With a soft tearing, the molding gave way, showering them with flakes of old paint and crumbling splinters of wood that smelled like dust and dead spiders. Jackson braced the molding across a sawhorse, pounded the nails out, and set the wood aside.

"But people *do* change," Kate said.

"Yes. But mostly to survive, or when someone forces them to, or when it hurts too much not to." He paused and smiled at her, his eyes soft. "Or because they have a chance at what they want most only if they give up what stands in the way."

Meaning her. Meaning his tortured love affair with alcohol.

Kate trailed her fingers along his arm. She had changed, too. She had shed a lifetime of self-protective rules and restrictions to raise Way-Ray, to be with Jackson.

He lowered one eyelid in a slow wink, then turned back to the molding.

"I feel like Evie would have a better chance if she goes for it now." Kneeling, Kate gathered the nails into a paper bag. "The longer she puts off changing her will, the more time Paul has to build a case for her being crazy, or incompetent."

She stood and lowered her voice. "I think sometimes she suspects that she's not always on an even keel."

Jackson drew air between his teeth. "But woe to the person who mentions that."

"Exactly."

He set the pry bar under the next piece of molding. "Well, it's Evie's land and, whether she's

40

playing with a full deck or not, what she decides to do with it—and when she decides to do that—is up to her."

"So we stay out of it," Kate agreed, understanding what Evie hadn't said—probably never would say—about delaying her decision. She longed for her son to recognize the value in her work, a value that couldn't be tallied in dollars and cents.

School let out and Way-Ray and Sean, after a weekend of celebrating their final grades and promotions with a pizza-and-pop-fueled videogame marathon, signed on for what they called "Bird Poop Boot Camp" run by Drill Sergeant Evie. If Sean wasn't already at the breakfast table because he stayed over, Rhea dropped him off around eight and the two boys ate enormous bowls of cereal before stuffing their feet into rubber boots and their hands into rubber gloves and setting out to clean cages and enclosures.

Their least favorite was the one that housed the brown pelicans. Over the winter, volunteers had brought in dozens of starving birds. Some had already been released, but others were still gaining weight and strength.

"They eat and eat and eat," Sean told Kate.

"Then they poop and poop and poop," Way-Ray added.

One morning, as they slurped up the dregs of their cereal, the boys bemoaned their tender age—too young to paint houses or work at the ice cream shop like Sean's brother Kyle, or to hold any other "real" summer job—and speculated about whether they could make their chores easier by toilet training the pelicans.

Sean thought the birds might learn to use a litter box like cats. Way-Ray thought it might take the birds a long time to learn and they might be released before they got the hang of it. Still, he felt it was worth a try until Kate pointed out the litter wasn't cheap and there were no funds in the budget to buy it.

"I bet we could use sand." Sean shoved wispy blond hair from his eyes. "We'll take the wheelbarrow down to the top of the beach trail and carry up buckets of sand and fill the wheelbarrow and bring it back and put the sand in a big box Jackson can build and then we'll never have to scrub again, just rake the sand and shovel up the clumps like in a cat box."

Jackson glanced at the page of summer chores secured to the side of the refrigerator with magnets shaped like slugs, groaned, and poured more coffee. "If you can wait until October, I'll have about ten spare minutes to get right on that project."

Way-Ray hoisted his cereal bowl and swallowed the slurry in the bottom, then wiped his milk mustache on the sleeve of his T-shirt. "There are a lot of pelicans so we probably need a whole bunch of boxes."

Jackson glanced at the calendar again. "Make it November."

"There's a stack of old boards behind the book lady's house where they tore down that old shed," Sean said. "Maybe we can build the boxes ourselves."

"Maybe." Way-Ray wrinkled his nose. "But sand's awful heavy. And the trail down to the beach is all

42

twisty and bumpy and steep. It might take all day to get enough for just one box."

Sean scrunched up his face, thinking hard. "Okay, well sand's all over the place and it's free. We can get my mom to take her car down on the beach in town and load up the trunk easy."

"Is it legal to take sand from the beach in town?" Kate asked.

Sean shrugged and scratched his head with the handle of his spoon. "Well, the sand in the cove is Evie's, so it's okay to take that."

"Not all of it," Jackson said. "The wet sand part belongs to the state."

"We're just gonna dig the dry stuff." Sean rolled his eyes. "The wet stuff's way too heavy. Besides, I take sand all the time on accident. It comes home in my shoes and stuff."

"Yeah," Way-Ray agreed. "My shoes get full, too. And Curtis hasn't arrested me yet."

"Well, he'll arrest you if you start carting off tons of it," Kate warned. "He'll charge you with causing erosion of public lands and put you in a jail cell with really hard beds, icky food, and no pizza or ice cream or TV."

The boys looked at each other, grimacing as they contemplated the horror of that. Sean recovered first. "I'm not scared of Curtis. He's hardly much older than my cousin Jerry. And how's Curtis gonna catch us? No one can see Evie's beach unless they're out in a boat or up on the trail looking down or on the rocks right before you jump off."

"Yeah," Way-Ray agreed. "And if someone was up on the trail or on those rocks, we'd see them."

"Yeah, and then we'd pretend we were just building a sand castle or something until they went away."

"You wouldn't see someone watching from the trail if you were so busy you didn't look," Kate said.

"Or if he was camouflaged," Jackson added.

"Camouflaged?" Sean smacked his head with his palm. "That's dumb. Camouflage is like green and brown like the woods, or tan and brown and white like sand. How do you get camouflaged like the bushes and grassy stuff and rocks on that trail?"

"You couldn't use regular camouflage," Way-Ray said. "You'd have to put on rockouflage."

"Rockouflage, yeah. Or grassouflage."

The two boys high-fived each other and repeated the words with delight, then expanded the joke, making up words like roadouflage, floorouflage, bath-tubouflage, and carpetouflage. All the while they hooted and screeched like baboons.

"You brought it up." Kate carried her coffee cup to the sink, patting Jackson on the head as she passed. "Now that's all we'll hear for the rest of the day."

Jackson stood and turned his back on the boys. "They don't know that there are all kinds of camouflage. I bet I could hide up there on the hillside above that cove and they'd never see me, even if they had binoculars. Even if they used Way-Ray's telescope."

The boys fell silent for a few seconds, then spoke as one. "How much you wanna bet?"

Jackson winked at Kate. "How much have you got?"

Way-Ray counted on his fingers. "Eleven dollars. And two dimes."

44

"I got two dollars." Sean rammed his hand into the pocket of his blue jean cutoffs, drew out a collection of coins, and counted, his lips moving. "And sixty-seven cents."

"You're on," Jackson said. "We'll do it this afternoon when the sun is in that cove so when you lose you can't say there wasn't enough light."

"Deal," Way-Ray said. "You're gonna lose big time."

"Maybe we should bet him double or nothing," Sean suggested.

Way-Ray pondered that for a few seconds. "Where are we gonna get the double?"

"We don't need the double. We're not gonna lose."

"But what—"

The jangle of the phone on Kate's desk brought an end to the discussion. "Go on, you two. Go scrub cages."

The boys scooped up their gear from the porch and trundled out, the smack of gloves on boots punctuating plans for what they'd do with their winnings. Kate stepped to her desk and picked up the phone on the third ring. "Castaway Beach Wildlife Rehab Center."

"I'm not coming out there today," a woman's agitated voice proclaimed. "It's too dangerous with those rabid animals roaming around."

"Rabid animals?" Kate recognized the caller as one of their regular volunteers, Melinda Cummings, a high-maintenance woman as nervous around birds and animals as they were when she was in the vicinity. She had her own ideas about how things should be done and announced that Evie was cranky and her standards ridiculous. Kate had found a niche for her—organizing and inventorying supplies and writing thank you notes. "What rabid animals?"

Jackson halted in the doorway and then limped to Kate's side, his face creased with concern. Kate tipped the phone so he could hear.

"That coyote," Melinda said. "The raccoons. And those bats that Evie's trying to cure with grape juice and vinegar and herbs."

Jackson shook his head and mouthed, "Paul."

Kate felt a wave of sickness sweep over her. "There is no cure for rabies, Melinda. Evie knows that better than anyone. She would nev—"

"Don't lie to me, Kate Dalton. Everyone says she's mixed up a big vat of purple juice that smells like rotten eggs."

"Everyone?"

"Everyone in the post office. And the café. Evie Hopkins has gone clear around the bend. She's a menace to us all."

"Evie isn't—"

"When you get bit, don't say I didn't warn you. I know for a fact Chief Lowell and Curtis are on the way out there right now."

The wave of sickness ebbed and Kate drew in a long breath. Chief Lowell was a rational, no-nonsense man. Curtis might get swept up by rumor and speculation, but Sam Lowell would see this for what it was—a malicious attempt to frighten people and defame the rehab center.

"People are calling the newspaper. And the health department. Child welfare, too."

Kate gripped the edge of the desk. She'd been granted custody of Way-Ray subject to regular reviews, but the adoption his mother had wanted

46

was still on hold, paperwork clogged in the legal pipeline. "There are no rabid—"

"If that boy gets bit and has to have those shots, then maybe then you'll stop defending that crazy old woman."

Jackson growled and snatched the phone, but Melinda hung up before he could speak. "That witch." He slammed the phone into the cradle. "That gossipmongering—"

Kate put a finger across his lips. "She's all that, but she did us a favor. She gave us an early warning."

"Five whole minutes."

"That's enough."

Ignoring his frown, she handed him her cell phone and nodded to the door. "Go tell Evie to change into something that doesn't smell like fish and has more fabric than holes. Call Rhea on the way. I'm sure she's figured out this is just a rumor, but I don't want her worrying about Sean. Ask her to keep her eyes and ears open and see if she can track this crap back to the person who started it."

"It's Paul."

"It's got to be. But I'd like to know for sure." Kate slid into her chair, jiggled the mouse to wake up the computer, and brought up a list of names, phone numbers, and e-mail addresses. "In the meantime I'll call that reporter we love to hate and use the embers that Paul is fanning to build a blaze of publicity. We'll fight fire with fire."

CHAPTER 5

Stepping out from the shadow of the house and into a pool of late morning sunlight, Marnie Phillips tugged at the jacket of one of trademark red outfits, brushed her hair with her fingers, and raised her chin. When she reached the spot her photographer pointed to, she faced the camera and tipped the microphone toward Evie. "Do you think spreading a rumor about rabies could be more than a prank? Could it be part of a conspiracy to shut you down?"

Jackson, watching with Kate from the shade beneath the eaves, sucked air through his teeth. "Goes right for the throat, doesn't she?"

Kate crossed her fingers, hoping Evie wouldn't be rattled and deviate from the plan they made while Jackson walked through the house and around the property with Sam Lowell, letting the police chief peer into every room, cage, and enclosure. They agreed to downplay the rumor, agreed that they wouldn't express suspicions about the source. They also recognized that they couldn't control the spin the media put on this.

Evie, showered and wearing clean khaki shorts and a pale green cotton shirt from Kate's closet, frowned and veered away from the bait Marnie dangled. "Conspiracy is a big, scary word. It's the kind of word that can keep folks from thinking as hard as they should about accuracy and logic. It can set off a chain reaction that's hard to stop."

Marnie's lips twitched and she tilted the microphone away from Evie. Wrapping her fingers around Marnie's wrist, Evie tilted it back. "I think—I hope—this is a case of someone spreading a rumor just to see how far it can go and how big it can get. Maybe it was a kid who was bored and wanted a little excitement."

"He got plenty of that." Jackson shifted his weight from his bad leg and leaned against the side of the porch. "Haven't been this many reporters and TV trucks in town since last summer."

Kate nodded, surveying vehicles packed into the parking area and reporters in line waiting to interview Evie. Sean and Way-Ray, having driven the geese off into the pasture, darted among the TV vans as if they were on a carnival midway, peering at equipment and pretending to interview each other with wooden spoons standing in for microphones.

Marnie twitched her lips. From experience, Kate knew that expression meant she would try again to validate her theory. "So you don't think this was a malicious attempt to undermine your work here?"

Kate willed Evie not to lose patience, especially not during her first interview, and especially not with Marnie.

"No. I can't think why anyone would want to destroy what we've built and the work we're doing," Evie said with what sounded like genuine

49

innocence. "More likely the rumor was started by some kid who needed more attention or thought it would be funny. Maybe he knew better, but got egged on by his friends."

"Good line." Jackson laughed. "I'll bet Paul's blood pressure spikes fifty points when he hears that."

"If he *gets* it." From her years at the domestic violence shelter, Kate knew that people's perceptions of themselves and their motivations could be skewed many degrees from reality. If Paul's pestering for coins had been as much an attempt to get his parents' attention and fill his heart as it was an attempt to fill his pockets, would he recognize that, acknowledge it? Many people didn't—they lacked the capacity for self-awareness and examination or they steeled themselves against self-knowledge because it was too painful and disruptive.

Despite her anger, Kate felt a surge of sadness for that little boy, alone out here on the farm with a stack of coins shaken from his bank. If he reached out, would Evie meet him halfway? Or would she turn her back?

"Rabies is nothing to mess around with." Evie looked straight into the camera lens. "And even though it was a false report that brought you out here, it gives me an opportunity to do a little educating. The public should be aware that rabies is out there and everyone should know how a rabid animal acts." She beckoned to Kate. "But folks should also know that the majority of animals are not infected. We printed up a fact sheet with symptoms and advice."

Kate waved the sheaf of pages she'd created on the computer, customizing information found on line with phone numbers for local emergency services, the state wildlife department, and county health officials. Way-Ray and Sean dashed to snatch up the fliers and hand them out. Jackson, who had made it clear they weren't to answer any questions or supply information, watched their progress, ready to step in if a reporter corralled them.

"So there are no cases of rabies at our facility," Evie recapped. "And as far as I know, there hasn't been a case in this county for two years. I'm sorry you came all this way chasing a lie, but I'm always happy to have reporters visit and get a look at what we do here."

With a grim smile, Marnie wrapped up the interview, then shoved her microphone at her photographer and stalked toward Kate and Jackson.

"Uh oh," Jackson muttered. "That's her look of steely determination. Think you can stick to that honest and truthful vow you made last summer?"

Kate winced, recalling the price of becoming ensnared in a web of escalating lies meant to protect Way-Ray from the horrible truth about his father and mother. Rhea was right about the need to get crap out in the yard so it didn't blow up in the basement, but they had no proof Paul was behind this. Mention his name, or even hint at it, and he was perfectly capable of dragging them to court and demanding damages. Beyond that, he could claim the attack on his character was evidence that Evie wasn't sane.

"I'm not going to lie. I'll just be vague and play dumb."

Jackson snorted. "Good luck with that dumb part. I think I hear a plumbing project calling my name."

51

"Coward," Kate whispered.

"Yup. That's one scary woman." He turned and limped up the porch steps.

Marnie halted in front of Kate, screening her view of Evie. "There's more to this, isn't there? Somebody's trying to shut you down, aren't they?"

Denying that outright would pique Marnie's interest and increase her suspicions. For all her primping and polish, Marnie was a shrewd reporter with a sharp mind. When she set out to get a story, she got it—one way or another.

Kate handed the question back. "Why would someone want to do that?"

"A hundred reasons. Maybe Evie Hopkins pissed off one too many people. It's not like she's Miss Congeniality."

Kate flashed on an image of Evie with a banner draped across a swimsuit, every knotted vein in her legs popping, her face in a tight scowl. "Evie tells it like she sees it, if that's what you mean."

"And tells everyone else they've got it wrong."

"She's passionate about this project."

"Passionate? She's *possessed* by this project."

Possessed.

Wouldn't Paul love it if a reporter used that word on the air?

Kate forced a laugh. "And I'm possessed by the need to eat butter pecan ice cream four times a week."

Marnie's eyes narrowed. "That's not the same and you know it."

Kate shrugged.

Marnie fluffed her bangs and twisted a filigreed bracelet so it lined up with the others on her slim wrist. "Way-Ray's growing like a weed. He seems to like it here."

"He loves it," Kate agreed. "We all do."

Marnie pointed to the roof and the new screens on the porch, her carmine nails flashing. "The place looks much better than when I was out here last year."

Kate nodded slowly, thinking about what Marnie left unsaid, about the reporter's relentless pursuit of a story that exposed Kate's protective lies and caused Way-Ray to flee, about the report that brought the killer who beat the boy into a coma and shot Evie and Kate.

"You've put a lot of work into it," Marnie said. "It would be hard on all of you if . . ."

She let that thought swing between them like a hypnotist's watch. As Evie had earlier, Kate shifted her focus. "Is there anything you'd like to see while you're here? Anything else I can tell you about? We've been getting a lot of hungry Common Murres in the past week. Evie says that could mean another dead zone off the coast."

"I'll tell our environmental reporter." Marnie waved the subject aside, bracelets clacking. "Call if you decide you need me."

"Need you?"

"If you want to name names and turn the light on the cockroach behind this."

"It was all I could do to keep my mouth shut and my face still," Kate told Jackson and Evie when the last reporter left and the boys went in search of raspberries on the bushes along the edge of the

53

garden. "The idea of siccing her on Paul made me want to turn cartwheels. She'd tear him apart with those fingernails of hers."

"If he didn't see her coming and slide away." Jackson pulled a pitcher of lemonade from the refrigerator and poured a glass for each of them. "She's got no story unless she comes up with solid proof that he started this rumor *and* that he did it with malicious intent."

"That will be just about impossible to get." Evie slumped into a chair and stared at her glass. "If there's one thing Paul's good at it's covering his ass."

When Rhea arrived to pick up Sean that evening, she made the same assessment. "There's always been talk about Paul and some of his deals, but nothing's ever stuck to him and I doubt there's glue to attach this mess, either."

She shot an apologetic glance at Evie who winced, hunched into her wing chair, and picked at a spot on her shorts.

Rhea snagged a beer from the refrigerator, flopped into a rocker, and gazed around the living room, a space Kate often referred to as "the land before picking up was invented." Video games cluttered the top of the coffee table and shoes clustered beneath it. A small pyramid of cola cans was under construction beside the sofa. T-shirts were stuffed between the cushions and others dangled from a lampshade. Socks, cookie crumbs, and fragments of potato chips were everywhere.

"You have a real flair for decorating," Rhea said. "I love what you've done with this room."

"Nothing to it." Kate kicked aside a balled-up corn chip bag and dropped onto the sofa. "Once I gave up reminding, nagging, and doing it myself, it all fell into place."

"That's sarcasm." Way-Ray, sprawled on the threadbare carpet in front of the television set, nudged Sean and looked up from the controls of a video game. "We shouldn't hafta clean up if Jackson doesn't."

Jackson adjusted his bad leg and leaned back another few inches in an aging recliner with silver tape on the arms and stuffing exploding from the seams. "And I shouldn't have to pick up my stuff if Evie doesn't pick up hers."

"Sure, blame the old lady," Evie groused. "Messy living room, soaring food prices, federal debt, global warming. Dump it all in my lap." Her smile crumpled and she drew her legs up and huddled deeper into the chair. "Don't forget the way my son turned out."

Rhea rolled her eyes. "Here we go, speeding down the parkway to Pity City."

"I don't want your pity," Evie insisted. "What's done is done. I'm just saying I could have been a better mother."

"So could I. But most days our kids aren't playing on the same team. *Their* goal is to make sure we don't reach *our* goal and to wear us down in the process."

Rhea took a long swallow of beer and poked Sean's ankle with the toe of her tennis shoe. "Tomorrow you and Way-Ray get all these cans to the recycling bin, organize your video games in the

55

cabinet under the TV, wash the socks and T-shirts, wipe off the coffee table, and then get the vacuum cleaner in here and suck up all these crumbs. Be sure you get under the sofa. And down between the cushions."

"That will take all day," Sean groaned. "What if we just borrow one of the goats from that place down the highway where they make that cheese? Goats eat lots of stuff."

"Yeah. If we got a really hungry goat, we'd hardly ever have to clean at all," Way-Ray said. "He'd probably even eat some of those cruddy socks. And we'd never have to take the stuff out to the compost heap, either."

"A goat grazing in the house," Kate mused. "Now there's a vision of paradise."

"See what I mean," Rhea told Evie. "I specifically said they should get the vacuum cleaner and now we've got a goat instead. They're not only not on our team, they're playing a whole different game."

"That's just stupid," Way-Ray said. "What kind of a game can you play with a goat?"

"How about baahahahball," Jackson offered.

The boys shook their heads, then exploded in laughter, butting heads and repeating, "baahahahball."

"It wasn't *that* funny," Jackson grumbled.

"It doesn't have to be funny," Rhea said. "In fact, it's funnier if it isn't funny."

Evie smiled, but then chewed at her thumbnail. "I can't remember Paul ever laughing—at least not like that."

"Well things were different out here then." Rhea nodded toward Sean and Way-Ray. "It must have

56

been pretty lonely for him. And it's easier to laugh when you're not the only one doing it."

Evie turned to Kate. "My husband wasn't the type to find humor in much of anything. He never laughed at himself or forgave anyone who did." She knotted her fists in the outsized brown T-shirt she put on once the reporters left. "And when it came to child rearing, his philosophy was that Paul should speak when he was spoken to and stick to the point."

Kate nodded, remembering the long silences of her own childhood and the times she'd been told she'd said quite enough when she was certain she hadn't.

"But you can't change any of that now." Rhea slipped a hand into the pocket of her smock and came up with a red and white mint.

"You're going to have that with beer?" Jackson asked.

Rhea blinked at the mint as if she'd never seen it before. "Damn. I miss my cigarettes." She jammed the candy back into her pocket and sucked at her beer. "Anyway, what I dug up about who started that rumor is essentially zilch."

Jackson arched his brows. "That much?"

Rhea put her hand over her heart. "Yeah, I'm stunned myself. I expected at least six people to offer signed affidavits that they heard it from . . ." She glanced at Way-Ray and Sean. ". . . from you know who."

"She means Paul," Sean told Way-Ray.

"I know," he replied.

Rhea kicked at their shoes and they turned to look at her. "We don't use that name outside of this house. Outside of this group. Got it?"

The boys nodded.

"I mean it," Rhea warned. "You're facing a lifetime without ice cream if you cross me on this and tell anyone."

They gaped, then nodded again and resumed their game.

"So we've got nothing?" Kate asked.

"Well, I always suspected the gossip mill in this town ran overtime at double speed, and now I have confirmation of that."

Rhea slid a sheaf of folded papers from her smock pocket and tossed it on the coffee table. Kate picked up the pages and unfolded them. Each page was divided into numbered columns.

"The first column has the names of the people I talked to," Rhea said. "The second column is the person they think they heard the rumor from first. The third column is the person they think might have told the person they heard it from, and so on."

Kate ran her finger down the second column, seeing mostly notations like "everybody" and "can't remember" and "somebody or other." Melinda Cummings' name also figured prominently.

"As you can see, there are probably earthworms with keener senses of observation and better memories that a lot of these folks. And it didn't help that the ones who heard it from Melinda 'knew' it had to be true because she volunteers out here and 'isn't the kind of person who just makes stuff up.' This rumor moved faster than you-know-what through a goose."

"She means shit," Sean told Way-Ray in a low voice.

Rhea nudged his ankle again. "And she also means to fine you a dollar when you get home."

"But you say it sometimes." Sean rolled his eyes at Way-Ray. "Why can't I?"

"You can when you're eighteen. Or on the day after you drive me to an early grave by asking questions you already know the answer to."

Sean set the game control aside. "And *that* means she's getting really, really grouchy and it's time to go outside for a while."

Way-Ray jumped to his feet and dashed for the door. "Let's take the leftover broccoli and see how fast it goes through a goose."

"Cool. I'll get the oven timer." Sean took off in pursuit.

"Those poor geese," Kate said.

"The geese survived the injuries that got them here," Jackson said. "They drove off that fox last winter. They can take care of themselves."

"Maybe better than the rest of us." Evie pointed at the papers Kate held. "So nobody knows a thing."

Rhea laughed. "More like everybody knows everything. Three people even swore they saw that rabid coyote themselves, frothing at the mouth and standing by your mailbox out on the highway. Lois Reibach over at the library was the only ray of light. She got rumorized by eighteen people, told them it sounded like a load of hooey, and didn't pass the crap on to a single one."

"I always did like Lois," Evie said. "I'll call and thank her in the morning."

For a long moment no one said a thing, then Jackson thumped his fists on the arms of his chair. "I gotta give him credit. That rumor started like spontaneous combustion and spread like wildfire in a drought."

"But we stamped it out," Kate said. "We shut him down."

"Yeah. This round is a draw."

"I guess a draw's better than a loss." Rhea raised her bottle. "Here's to winning the next round."

CHAPTER 6

Way-Ray put his cereal bowl on the counter and turned to face Kate and Jackson. "It's already July. How long until I can get another name?"

As always when this topic came up, Kate resisted the urge to ease her frustration by gnawing at the skin around her thumbnail. Last fall, when she registered him for school, she fought with an officious secretary who insisted paperwork carry his legal last name, that of his abusive father: Jessop. Kate went around the woman and persuaded the principal and teachers to use Blake—his mother's maiden name, the one he'd carried since he was a toddler.

In September, Way-Ray informed her he wanted to use his mother's name and be Wayland Raymond Blake "forever and ever," but over the winter he claimed he wanted a name no one ever had before. He and Sean made up lists of unpronounceable words laced with odd vowel and consonant combinations that sounded like a cat choking up a hairball.

Back in April, he tried out Jackson's last name and asked if he'd be Jackson's son if he and Kate got married. She told him Jackson was proud to think of him that way, but they'd leave that legal hurdle until they came to it. Way-Ray hadn't mentioned taking her name and that was fine. After all, it was her parents' and it came with all their baggage. As for marriage, well, Jackson had made it clear he was willing when she was ready, but for now she subscribed to Evie's philosophy: No point in rushing to fix what ain't broke.

"You'll get a new name soon," she told Way-Ray, crossing her fingers.

"How soon? Like before school starts again?"

"Soon like Kate doesn't know for sure." Jackson swallowed the last of his coffee and set the mug aside. "Lawyers and judges can take a long time to get things done."

"Because they're careful." Kate shot Jackson a sharp glance to remind him they'd agreed to trim back on their biases and balance statements to allow Way-Ray to weigh facts and draw his own conclusions. "Lawyers have to get all the words and the sentences just right and turn in all the papers the judge needs."

"Because the judge would be mad if they didn't, right? Like you get mad when I don't pick up my dirty clothes or make my bed the way I'm supposed to."

"I don't get mad. Sometimes I get a little—"

"Eggggzzassperated!" Way-Ray tucked his thumbs in his armpits and flapped his elbows. "Like a chicken when it has to lay a great big egg and finds the other chickens messed up its nest."

Jackson roared with laughter.

"Don't encourage him." Kate swatted Jackson's shoulder. "He'll be cackling all day and I'll be—"

"Extra exasperated." Jackson choked out the words.

"Egggstra egggzzassperated, Way-Ray crowed, flapping and strutting his way around the table.

"The word has an *X* in it, Way-Ray, and no *G* or *Z*," Jackson said. "It comes from Latin. It means to irritate or roughen."

Kate gawked. "Are you making that up?"

Jackson shook his head. "I looked it up once. Can't remember why."

Way-Ray added more footwork to his flapping, rubbing the soles of his ratty sneakers across dull green linoleum worn patternless except for the area beneath the table. Scuffed trails led from door to door, sink to refrigerator, table to stove. "What's Latin?"

"The language of ancient Rome."

"Ancient like a long time ago?"

"Yes."

Kate grinned, collected her plate and mug and carried them to the dishwasher. Jackson had set off an avalanche of questions and would have to outrun it or be buried beneath it. Whether Way-Ray asked from a desire to learn or a desire to, well, exasperate, the end result was the same—an adult either driven to the verge of gibbering lunacy by nonsensical queries or stampeded into a serious conversation he or she wasn't prepared to have.

"A long time like before I was born?" Way-Ray pulled out his chair and sat beside Jackson, getting comfortable for the interrogation. "Or a long time longer than that?"

"Much longer than that." Jackson picked up his empty mug, scowled at it, and set it back down. "The Roman Empire fell apart hundreds and hundreds of years ago. People still learn Latin—scholars and historians who want to read old manuscripts and translate them."

"Where do they get old manuscripts?"

"Sometimes they find them, but a lot of old manuscripts are in libraries."

"Like the one in town?"

Jackson smiled. "No, like college libraries and the one at the Vatican."

"The what-ican?" Way-Ray raised his brows. "Is that something like a pelican?"

Choking on a chuckle, Kate wiped crumbs from the counter. It was as worn as the linoleum, the wood-look surface gouged and dotted with stains no amount of scrubbing or liberal use of "miracle" kitchen cleaner could erase. The sink was in much the same condition, chipped and yellowed. The faucets were corroded and leaked. They'd talked of renovating this winter, but if the fate of the house was uncertain . . .

Don't think about that!

She turned her attention to Jackson and Way-Ray.

"—isn't a bird. It's a religious state in the middle of Rome. It's where the Pope lives."

"I know about the Pope. He wears a white thing that looks like a dress but isn't and he's got a ring people kiss." Way-Ray raised his hands and lowered them again. "And he blesses people."

"Right." Jackson gave Kate a smug smile, the smile of a man who believes he's outrun the

64

avalanche and provided an educational experience as well. "It sounds like you know a lot about him."

"He was on TV," Way-Ray said, as if that explained it all. He picked at a glop of jelly on the table. "Evie says he's missing the boat when it comes to birth control."

Gotcha! Kate slapped a hand over her mouth to hold back a laugh. *Think fast, Jackson, the avalanche is on top of you.*

Jackson's smile collapsed. Doomed, he picked up his mug once more and peered into its depths as if hoping a Saint Bernard might emerge and drag him to the safety of a lodge with a roaring fire.

Way-Ray abandoned the jelly glop and rested his chin in his hand. "What's birth control? And why do you hafta be on a boat to use it?"

Flashing Jackson a smug smile of her own, Kate fled for the relative safety of the garden where the worst she might encounter would be prickly weeds, bees, spiders, or a snake.

She was hoeing her way down a row of corn when she heard Evie yell from the trailer that served as a makeshift hospital. "Jackson, if you turned off the power while I'm bandaging this owl I'm going to skin you alive."

In a moment, Jackson shouted from the house. "The power's out here, too. I'll check the breakers."

Way-Ray darted down the porch steps and raced to the garden. "The lights are all off and the TV doesn't work and the water won't run in the sink."

Kate laid the hoe down and peeled off her gardening gloves. "Are you sure?"

"Duh." He unlatched the gate and swung it open. "I turned the faucets and nothing came out. It just kinda coughed and rattled."

"Hmmm. Let's go see." She strode past him. "Close that gate tight so the geese don't get in and eat my crops down to the ground."

"On it." The gate slammed into place and Way-Ray shot by her.

Jackson met them at the edge of the porch. "Breaker box is fine. There's no juice coming in."

Kate turned to look at the power lines strung along the edge of the pasture and through the woods to the highway. "What about the water? Why is that off?"

"It takes power to run the pump to bring it up from the well."

"So we hafta drink soda," Way-Ray crowed.

"Warm soda," Jackson said. "Guess who didn't put any in the refrigerator like he said he would yesterday."

"I was gonna," Way-Ray protested. "But then Sean and me—"

Kate made a "time out" sign with her hands. "We'll discuss that—and correct your grammar— later. After the power is back on." She turned to Jackson. "Do you think they're working on the lines along the highway?"

"On Saturday?" He shaded his eyes and peered off across the pasture. "More likely a tree went down on a line."

Kate held up a finger. "There's no wind."

"Okay, then a car hit a pole or a transformer blew. They'll have it fixed pretty quick."

"On Saturday?" Kate echoed.

"They have crews on call for emergencies. Shit happens on Saturdays, too."

66

"Oooh. What you said." Way-Ray wagged a finger. "Now you gotta put money in the swear jar and carry out the trash for a week."

"Way-Ray," Evie yelled. "Bring me a flashlight and a jug of water from the storeroom."

"On it!" Way-Ray shot off, knees pumping.

"How long do you think the power will be out?" Kate asked.

"Depends on the problem. If it's a bad accident along the highway, it might be a few hours."

"Well, I don't need electricity to get the garden weeded, but we need to keep that fish frozen, and we need water for a dozen reasons. I'm going to call the power company."

"Probably a waste of a call. Somebody will have let them know."

"Unless somebody isn't home or hasn't noticed." Kate realized she sounded belligerent, forced a smile, and took a step back. "I don't want to make an assumption and find out later we could have had the lights on sooner."

"There's that." Jackson shrugged. "Guess I'll go sand those shelves for Way-Ray's room. All I need for that is elbow grease and patience."

Kate watched him go, noting he favored his leg more than usual, walking with a hop and a hitch that made her wince and turn aside. Somehow, she had to persuade him to have surgery soon.

Without the hum of the refrigerator, the tick of the clock on the stove, and the drip of water into the sink, the kitchen seemed ominously quiet. Kate stepped out onto the porch and punched the power company's outage reporting number into her cell phone. It rang six times before a man answered with the vague voice of someone who might have been asleep.

"Our power is out," Kate said. "The account is in the name of Evie Hopkins. We're north of Castaway Beach. Is there a problem out this way—a line down, a blown transformer?"

Keys clicked and the man swallowed, burped, and swallowed again. "Nope. No lines down. No transformers out. Not a thing wrong except you haven't paid your bills for more than three months."

"What?" Kate reached behind her and gripped the doorjamb. "That can't be right. I paid those bills. I know I did."

"Sometimes checks get lost in the mail."

Kate could almost hear the quotations marks around the words "lost in the mail." "All three of them?"

"We've had customers swear that happens."

"Well, if it did, how come we never got a notice that we were behind?"

"Maybe those got lost in the mail, too." His tone implied that the possibility of that was right up there with aliens from outer space arriving to settle the global warming debate. "All I can tell you is right now your account has a balance due of more than seven-hundred dollars."

Kate stormed to her desk, jerked open the bottom drawer, and snatched out the file labeled "UTILITIES." Dumping it on the table, she found the last power bill, the check carbon stapled to it. Running her finger down the bill, she found the notation for a previous payment credited. "But last month's bill shows I was paid up at the end of May. And I sent a check for the June bill ten days ago. Two hundred and forty-seven dollars."

68

"Well, the records don't show that it was credited to your account. So it never got here."

"Hold on." Kate scrabbled for the folder that held bank statements. The most recent one showed a debit to the power company. "The bank statement shows they paid you." She glanced at the due date on the power bill. "Four days before the due date on the bill. I have proof right here in my hand. This is a mistake. Or a computer glitch. Somebody must have hit the wrong key or mixed up accounts."

"Well, there's nothing I can do, nothing anyone can do on a Saturday. Bring what you got down to the office Monday morning and see somebody in billing. If it turns out we're wrong, they'll get it straightened out."

He stressed the words "if it turns out we're wrong," making it clear that, in his mind, such had never been the case in the past and never would be in the future.

"Monday morning!"

"They don't work weekends." His tone implied that was not only unfair, but an insult to everyone who did, himself in particular. "Bring your paperwork and come in Monday."

Monday morning was forty-eight hours away. Who knew how long it would take "somebody in billing" to set things straight then? And how long after that to get the power back on?

"What are we supposed to do until then? We have no water. This is a wildlife rehabilitation center. We have sick birds and animals. Can't you turn the power back on just for a couple of days? I promise I'll be there the minute you open on Monday to straighten this out. I'll bring a check right now. I'll bring cash."

69

"I don't have the authority to take money or override shut-offs."

"Well who does? Who turned it off?"

"You'll have to come in Monday." The man disconnected.

"Damn it!" Kate tossed the phone on top of the open files. "Damn bureaucracy."

"I caught you swearing," Way-Ray chanted from the doorway. "Twice. You have to carry out the trash for two weeks and put extra money in the jar."

"From the look on her face, it doesn't appear this is a good time to bring that up, young man." Evie pushed past him into the kitchen. "What's going on?"

"The electric company turned off our power. They claim we're three months behind."

"Well I don't believe that for a single minute." Evie patted Kate's arm. "If I was still in charge of the money we might be that far in the hole and worse, but you'd sooner chew on a rock than pay even one day late."

"Chew on a rock," Way-Ray echoed. "Ugh. Who'd want to do that?"

"Nobody." Evie glanced at the open files on the table and her eyes narrowed. "Way-Ray, go find Jackson. Tell him we need to have a meeting right now and lay out some strategy."

"Meeting. Strategy. Right now." Way-Ray dashed out.

"There's nothing we can do until Monday. Then I'll have to take all the records to the billing department and they'll probably have to call the bank and it will take hours to get it straight." Kate dropped into a chair and pinched the bridge of her nose, trying to halt the headache blooming inside her skull. "All because a computer program messed up or somebody accidentally hit the wrong combination of keys."

"If it *was* an accident."

Kate's frustration gave way to surprise, then anger. "You don't think Paul—?"

"Of course I do." Evie got a carton of orange juice from the refrigerator and poured herself a glass. "Got to drink this before it goes bad."

"But how could he?"

"Money. A few hundred dollars would make a big difference to a lot of folks around here. And there are some who'd help him out just for the pleasure of making my life difficult."

"Or mine." Jackson took the carton from her hand, raised it to his lips, and drained it. "Remember Arlene?"

Kate flashed on an image of a woman with cat's eyes wearing a tight yellow jumpsuit. "From the treasurer's office?"

"Where I helped you write that big check last summer to pay the taxes," Way-Ray volunteered.

"Right." Jackson tossed the carton into the recycling tub and sat. "Her sister Phyllis works for the power company. She's the head of the billing department."

Kate dug her nails into her palms. This was revenge delayed, a delicious cold dish for the woman who believed herself scorned. "Great. It could be a week before we get the lights on. A month."

"I knew we should have replaced that blown generator when I saw that sale in the spring," Jackson said. "No matter how far it bent the budget, we should have done it."

"We should have done a lot of things," Evie told him. "While we're sitting around in the dark tonight you can recite your rosary of regrets to your heart's content."

"When it gets dark, can I have a candle up in my room?" Way-Ray asked.

"No," Kate and Evie said at the same time.

Way-Ray gave Jackson a hopeful look.

"Ditto. If it falls over and starts a fire, there's no water to put it out. Old as this house is, it will be a pile of ash when the fire department gets here."

"Awwwww, come on. I'll be careful. I'll put the fire extinguisher right next to it, honest. And I'll get a bucket of sand, too."

"No." Evie paced to the doorway and stared out across the pasture, hands on hips.

"You're no fun." Way-Ray opened the freezer. "If I can't have a candle, I'm having an ice cream on a stick. They're gonna melt anyway."

"All right," Kate said. "But stand over the sink so you don't drip on everything."

"We're stuck like this for a few days. Nothing we can do right now but roll with the punch." Evie paced from the doorway to the stove. "Kate, get a sheet of paper. Let's make a list of what needs to be done and who needs to do it."

CHAPTER 7

"Number one," Evie said when Kate had a yellow pad and pen ready, "no one mentions that we think someone might have done this on purpose. Way-Ray, that means you, too. Don't say a word, not even to Sean or Rhea."

"But they'll figure it out," Way-Ray said between licks at his chocolate-covered treat. "Because on account of Kate always pays everything on time. Everybody knows that. And on account of Paul wants your property. Everybody knows that too."

Evie gave him a look that could freeze molten lava. "If they figure it out for themselves, then fine, but they don't get it from you."

He blinked. "Okay. What you said."

"We can't let Paul or whoever is behind this know how tough they're making things for us and we can't let them know we think they did it on purpose." Kate gathered power bills and bank statements back into their file folders. "We have to pretend this power outage was caused by a computer glitch or human error. We have to pretend it's no big deal. Maybe you

73

can even pretend it's kind of fun to be without power."

"It would be fun if I had a candle in my room," Way-Ray muttered into the sink.

"Not negotiable." Jackson slapped the flat of his hand on the table. "Look me in the eyes."

Kate put a restraining hand on Jackson's shoulder while Evie gave him a nod of approval. Way-Ray turned, inch by inch, careful to keep the dripping ice cream bar over the sink. "I was kidding about the candle."

"I know. But this isn't the time for kidding. We have to focus and think ahead or Paul will win," Jackson said in a tone that was both firm and gentle. "It's like playing checkers or chess, only way more serious. Paul's first move was the rumor that we had rabid animals here. When Kate called the TV stations, that was like jumping his piece."

"And taking it off the board." Way-Ray stuffed the ice cream bar into the corner of his mouth, took a huge bite, and mumbled around it. "So he couldn't use it again."

"Right. But now he made another move and got our power turned off."

"So we jump again! Maybe we can turn off Paul's power." Way-Ray grinned. "Or punch holes in his tires. Or bake him some brownies filled with the stuff that makes you poop."

"No," Jackson said. "This time we'll pretend it's no big deal. We'll make him wonder why we're so calm and what we're going to do next."

Way-Ray poked his index finger against his forehead. "Mess with his head?"

74

"Yes," Kate agreed. "But we can't do that unless we concentrate, agree on our strategy, and play as a team."

"If we lose, the critters lose most of all," Evie added. "I know you don't want that."

Way-Ray shook his head. "No, but I don't wanta wait, I wanta do something back to him right now."

"I know you do," Jackson said. "It's hard to hold anger inside. But that's what we have to do."

Way-Ray puffed out his lips and scowled.

"We have to be sure about our next move. It's like some of those games you play. If you take your shot too soon and you miss, or you barely hit the bad guy, then what?"

"Then they come after you harder and faster."

"Right, so we have to get him to come out in the open."

"Then we blow him to pieces!" Way-Ray yelled and punched with his fists, sending the last blob of ice cream sailing across the kitchen, shedding droplets on the table and floor. "Ooops."

Kate tore paper towels from the roll and handed them to him. "Could we talk about this in less violent terms? Without referring to shooting and blowing people up?"

"Hard to do with boys his age," Evie said. "And you let him play those games."

Kate sighed. She'd caved on video games because Jackson pointed out that all Way-Ray's friends had them and if he didn't, he'd feel like she had as a child—denied both fun and a chance to be with friends because of her parents' philosophy, a philosophy she couldn't understand and saw as a wall between herself and happiness.

Jackson squeezed her hand. "In this game, Way-Ray, we get more points if we can get the bad guys to fall into a trap."

"Awwww." Way-Ray sucked the last of the ice cream from the stick. "What fun is that?"

"Trust me." Jackson bracketed his mouth with his hands and whispered. "Was I wrong about the rubber snake?"

Way-Ray grinned. "Heck, no. Rhea jumped a mile and screamed for five whole minutes. It was way funnier than the time we threw it at her."

"You two better not even think ab—"

"That's settled then," Evie interrupted. "We all keep our lips zipped. Now, job number two. The fish freezer will be fine for a day if we don't open it, but we need to take our frozen food down to Rhea's and buy a mess of flashlight batteries."

"Way-Ray, run out to the storage room and bring in those three coolers stashed under the bottom shelf. Then put everything from the freezer into them." Kate stood and rummaged in the kitchen junk drawer. "I'll handle the food and the flashlight batteries—we're down to just two in here and they look like they've been around for years. I'll pick up a few more flashlights, too."

"Big ones." Way-Ray tossed the stick and paper towels into the trash on the way to the door. "Like the one Curtis has in his patrol car."

"Cheap ones," Evie said when Way-Ray was gone. "Certain people keep dropping them so there's no point in buying the best." She pointed to the yellow pad. "Number three, we'll need water for the birds and to flush the toilets.

"I'll take care of the water," Jackson said. "I've been meaning to buy some barrels to catch

76

rainwater for the garden. I can fill them at Rhea's. As for flushing the toilets, instead of hauling water in to fill the tanks, why don't I just borrow that portable can Jim uses when he's got a big crew working a project?"

Evie wrinkled her nose. "Those things reek."

Kate laughed. "Says the woman who puts up with pelican puke."

"Well, I'm used to that."

"If you can get used to that, you can get used to anything," Jackson said. "Or you can clip a clothespin on your nose. What else do we need to do?"

"I'll fill the coolers with ice in town so we can save what's in the refrigerator—the milk and mayonnaise and sandwich meat." Kate added ice to the list. "And I'll pick up paper plates and get a full tank of propane for the grill so we can cook and make coffee."

"Can't get by without coffee," Jackson agreed.

"And Way-Ray and I can stop by the library and pick up books to keep him entertained." Kate made another note and tugged at her earlobe. "Unless he'd rather stay with Sean for a few days."

"My money's on choice number two. The TV works there and it's a ten-minute walk to the ice cream shop." Evie fanned herself with the edge of her hand. "One good thing, we won't need to worry about keeping the critters warm."

"Or ourselves. And we don't have air conditioning, so we won't miss it." Kate blotted her forehead with her shirtsleeve. "The forecast says it's going to cool down tonight when the marine air moves in."

"Got any more lemons you want to toss into that lemonade," Jackson joked. "How about that our

77

power bill this month will be lower than usual? Or that Way-Ray won't expect you to bake cookies? Or that this would be the ideal time to call up everyone we know and invite them out for a star party?"

Kate looked up from the note pad. "That's a great idea."

"A party?" Evie raised her hands in protest. "With no power and one portable pooper we don't know for sure we can borrow?"

"No, calling up everyone we know. Getting the word out that we're without power. Asking for someone to loan us a generator—a small one, not for the house but for the hospital trailer and the big freezer." Kate tapped the pen against the pad. "We'll make it clear we're willing to be uncomfortable, but we're concerned we might lose some of our patients without enough lighting to feed and clean them and without fans to cool them down."

"I'll bet someone's got one to loan us for a bit," Evie mused. "Most folks have a generator on hand for the winter—like we did until it went south."

"It's a good idea." Jackson looked at the computer's dark monitor and the silent phone. "But it sounds like a lot of hours of calling around."

"I have an idea about that, too." Kate stood, snatched up her cell phone, and pulled a file folder from the bottom drawer of the desk. "I think Melinda Cummings will be eager to help."

Evie gaped. Jackson slapped the table. "That rumormonger?"

"Exactly. She's been eating a lot of crow since the phony rabies scare. She even called me to apologize."

"Never thought I'd see *that* day," Evie muttered.

78

"Me neither. And I don't think it was an idea she came to on her own. I suspect Lois leaned on her long and hard."

"Gotta love Lois." Jackson stood and rubbed his bad leg. "All right, I vote you call Melinda and wind her up. I'll—"

With a crash and a tumble of coolers, Way-Ray burst through the door and sprawled on the floor.

Evie shook her head. "Tried to carry them all at once, did you?"

Way-Ray sat up and glared at the doorway. "I had 'em balanced all the way to right there. If I hadn't'a tripped . . ."

"It's a guy thing, right?" Jackson stepped around a blue and white cooler and stretched out a hand to pull Way-Ray to his feet. "Fill them up from the freezer—without breaking anything. I'll bring the truck around and we'll load them from the porch."

Kate opened the file folder. "I'll be with you as soon as I call Melinda."

By nightfall, a borrowed generator was chugging outside the hospital trailer and another, bought at a bargain price from a man who wanted a bigger one, was alternately powering the pump and the freezer that held fish for the birds. Way-Ray and Sean ran across the pasture, playing hide and seek by turning their flashlights on and off. The adults sat in lawn chairs upwind from the portable toilet that Jim would soon truck back to town, sipping iced drinks, swatting mosquitoes and, by the light of a guttering lantern, performing an autopsy on the day's events.

"I guess this round ended in another draw," Rhea said, "but I sure hope we find a way to knock Paul out of the ring soon. Everybody knows he was behind this."

"But we have no proof unless one of his flunkies turns on him and points a finger," Kate said.

Evie snorted. "It'll be a cold day in hell before that happens."

"The devil will be wearing striped leg warmers," Jim Whitaker added.

Kate giggled at the image. A man of few words—no surprise given that he was in conversational competition with Rhea, his sons, and his mother—Jim used those words to craft interesting images.

"You can bet if Phyllis is responsible she covered her ass by using another computer terminal. And you can bet she's got a plan for how to shove the blame on someone else," Jackson said. "But it had to be her. She's as spiteful as her sister. And Arlene wrote the book on backbiting and retribution. If I'd been sober I would have seen that long before I did."

Kate squeezed his hand. That was all water under a distant bridge.

"Plus they both lie like a politician who thinks the public's too dumb to catch him fibbing," Evie said.

"Politicians," Rhea mused. "There's an election for at least one of the county commissioners this year, isn't there?"

"If there isn't," Evie said, "there ought to be."

"We should vote them out and start over," Jackson grumbled. "Every one. If we started from scratch, we might get a few who didn't owe so many political debts. Or at least a few who didn't owe the usual suspects."

"Like Paul and his buddies," Kate said. "What we need is someone who would put the brakes on that golf course development plan."

"Someone who thinks this place is worth more to the community as it is," Evie said.

"Someone," Rhea said, "like me."

Jim groaned.

"Don't." She swatted his arm. "You sound like a moose with hemorrhoids."

"I feel like a moose that's been hit by a meteor. If you're on the county commission, who'll run the store and take care of the kids? And my mother?"

"Being commissioner isn't a full-time job. Now that I have things organized in that store, there's a lot of downtime. When winter closes in, if we get three customers a day and one of them isn't Kate it will be grounds for celebration."

"Hey," Kate protested, "I don't come *every* day."

"Yeah," Jackson said. "You missed one day the week before last. I marked it on the calendar."

"As for the kids," Rhea continued, "Kyle's been pulling more than his weight helping both of us. He makes a better breakfast than I do and needs about as much taking care of as one of those elite military commandos."

"But Sean—"

"Needs to get started down the path to self-sufficiency. As for your mother, the less she has to do, the more time she spends dreaming up ailments." Rhea leaned forward, her eyes sparkling in the lantern light. "I could do the job, I could be a commissioner. You know I could."

"Sure you could," Kate said. "You're sharp, you're a quick study, and you're willing to admit what you don't know and learn it."

81

"And if you took a vow of silence," Jim added, "you might have a chance of getting elected."

Rhea swatted him again. "You're the one who better take a vow of silence or you won't be getting lucky for the rest of your life."

"It's the painting season." Jim laughed. "I'm too exhausted to get lucky. Between now and October I'd need a blood transfusion to get my equipment in a condition where lucky was even a distant possibility."

"More than I needed to know," Evie said. "But Jim's got a point, Rhea. You and I have the same habit of telling it like it is."

"Well, maybe people are finally sick and tired of pie-in-the-sky promises that get broken in no time flat. Maybe they're ready to *hear* it like it is. Besides, even if I don't win, it might scare the crap out of some of those old boys."

Kate shivered. It was one thing to scare Paul and those in the county's political hierarchy. But the sharks Jackson had told her about were different. They didn't scare easily.

Maybe they didn't scare at all.

Maybe they attacked.

CHAPTER 8

Late Sunday afternoon, Kate packed soft drinks, hot dogs, rolls, mustard, containers of salad and chips, utensils, paper plates, napkins, and matches into an insulated knapsack.

Under the threat of having to help Sean clean his room, Way-Ray had returned home and circled the kitchen table, watching her. "Don't forget the marshmallows. They're the most important part."

"And don't you forget flowers for your mother. That rose bush along the pasture fence has some nice blooms."

"I'll get 'em and catch up." Way-Ray raced out calling over his shoulder. "I gotta get a shovel, too. 'Cause the tide is going way, way out today."

"The perpetual search for pirate treasure." Evie raised her feet to a vacant chair and rubbed at one swollen knee. "Wish I had half his energy."

"I'd settle for a quarter," Jackson said. "Or even ten percent with no pain."

Kate stuffed a bag of marshmallows into the knapsack and turned to study him. Dark skin sagged beneath his eyes and the whites were bloodshot. "Is your leg worse today?"

"Worse than what?" He flashed a smile. "Evie's cooking?"

"Worse than yesterday," Kate said in a sharp voice. "Worse than last week."

"I heard you up walking around half the night," Evie added. "Expected to hear you howl every time you took a step. It's not getting better, Jackson. When are you going to give in and have that surgery?"

"When the work is finished here."

"The work will *never* be finished here. There's always something breaking down or falling apart." She stopped rubbing her knee and slapped the table. "I got along without you for a lot of years, Jackson Scovell, so don't pride yourself thinking we can't survive while you get up to scratch after they slice you open and put in some screws. We can get by for six weeks."

"More like six months," Jackson said.

"Six months, six years," Evie waved that aside. "Kate and I are strong and determined women. We'll manage."

"And you're not supposed to be doing half the things you're doing now," Kate said. "Especially lifting. You're making things worse."

"Worse is the new normal," Jackson said with a hoarse laugh. "I'll have surgery in the fall. The late fall."

"See that you do." Evie swung her feet to the floor. "If not, I'll fire your ass."

Jackson put a hand over his heart. "You'd fire a man with a disability?"

"I'll fire a pigheaded man without a lick of sense. You bet I will." She stomped off across the kitchen. "Now I'm going to catch forty winks before I check on that owl again. Don't wake me up trying not to wince."

"Toughest boss I ever had outside of the military," Jackson said when she was gone.

"And she's right. The longer you put off surgery, the harder it will be for the surgeon to piece you together. If you wait too long . . ."

They let than hang between them. After his last visit to his doctor, Jackson said only that the man was blowing things out of proportion in order to panic him into surgery and make a few bucks. Kate suspected more and, when Jackson wasn't around, searched the internet for information about spinal discs and the prognosis for those who didn't seek help in time. The word "paralysis" came up again and again.

For Kate, the choice was simple—have surgery and have it now. But she didn't bear a web of scars from previous journeys under the knife.

"We'll manage while you heal." She zipped the knapsack. "And what we can't manage, we'll put off until you recover."

"I know you will." He stood and dug his fists into his lower back, then limped over and closed the door to the living room and Evie's bedroom beyond. "I'm not worried so much about the chores and the projects as about Paul's next move. He knows what I could do to him without breaking a sweat, and he knows you can't hold me back if he goes beyond rumors and inconvenience. If I'm laid up . . ."

Kate gripped his shoulders. Was it her imagination, or was there less flesh on the bone and

85

muscle she felt through his faded black T-shirt. "It's not all on you, Jackson. You're not the only one standing between us and Armageddon. There's Chief Lowell and Curtis and, heck, even Rhea and Jim and Lois Reibach. And you said yourself that Paul's a coward."

"I also said it was his friends I'm worried about. If they get tired of waiting for him to deliver and take matters into their own hands . . ."

Kate slid her hands down his arms and tightened her grip. Definitely less flesh. How much weight had he lost? "Evie has a shotgun on the top shelf of her bedroom closet. If someone threatens her birds—or one of us—I have no doubt she'll use it. And I'll get one of your guns if I have to."

His lips twitched again and he pulled her against his chest. She felt him swallow and swallow again. "Think about it," she said. "It's not like you'll be an invalid for months. You'll be out of bed and walking some by the second day."

"Walking like an arthritic crab. And on so much painkiller my mind will be scrambled."

Kate tipped her chin and looked up at him, smiling to soften her words. "Those pain pills you're taking now have you half scrambled already."

His eyes sparked, but Kate didn't back down.

"It's true. You used to sleep like a cat. The least anomaly, a sound or current of air, and you'd be up and alert. Now, when you take those pills, you go so deep it's a struggle to get to the surface."

The skin around his lips turned white with anger. "Then I won't take the pills. Problem solved."

"Problem *not* solved. As Evie pointed out a minute ago, if you don't take the pills you can't sleep at all." Kate stood on tiptoe and pressed her lips against his, holding them there until he relaxed and kissed her—a peck, but still a kiss.

"Enough for now. Let's get to the beach." She shrugged the knapsack straps across her shoulders. "I'll take this if you carry that quilt, the towels, and the binoculars."

Jackson narrowed his eyes, then nodded and picked up the faded quilt and the worn towels, one brown and one striped pink and orange, both thin in the middle and frayed at the edges. They set off down the road and, not far from the barn, turned onto a narrow path carved through a head-high wall of blackberry bushes heavy with green fruit.

"I always feel like I'm entering a fortress when I pass through here," Kate said. "Or touring a battlefield where soldiers dug in and mounded up the earth in front of them."

"Redoubts," Jackson said.

"Yes, redoubts." She turned the word over as they walked, breaking it apart. Doubt. Redoubt. If she didn't know what it meant, she'd think it was "to doubt again." "I suppose it's from Latin."

Jackson grunted but said nothing.

The trail emerged from the blackberries into what once was a broad pasture where the dairy herd had grazed in summer. Now the pasture was waist-high with salal and Oregon grape and saplings shouldering shrubs aside to get more sunlight. Kate slid her sunglasses from her pocket and put them on. "You don't know? You're not going to spout off its provenance and its meanings though the ages?"

"No, but I'll look it up when we get home."

"Hey." Feet pounded down the trail behind them. "Wait up. I'm dropping my flowers."

87

Kate turned to see a bouquet of roses bobbing along, the top of Way-Ray's head just visible beneath the swaying blooms. In a few seconds he caught up, panting, his blue T-shirt dark with sweat across his chest and along his spine. "I want to go first. I want to go point."

"*Walk* point," Jackson corrected.

"What you said." Dragging the shovel behind him, he squeezed past, releasing a cloud of pollen and tumbling a bee the size of Kate's thumb from a blossom. It buzzed past her ear, circled, and came straight at her eyes, bouncing off the left lens of her sunglasses.

Kate yelped, dropped to a crouch, and covered her head.

"Scaredy cat." Way-Ray laughed. "It's just a bee."

"A bee the size of a beagle," Kate said.

"He's gone now." Jackson tugged at her hair.

Kate stood. "How come he didn't go after you, Way-Ray? How come he went for the innocent bystander?"

"'Cause bees are bee-ad," Way-Ray said.

"More likely they're bee-fuddled," Jackson said. "Or bee-wildered."

"Well, I'm bee-yond the edge of my patience with puns," Kate said. "You two walk ahead. I'll bee right bee-hind."

Giggling, Way-Ray trotted off and Kate inched to the edge of the path and waved Jackson past. She hung back, watching him walk. His scarred left leg, as always, swung wide, the knee bending only a few degrees. And his back curved a little, bulging to the right. How could he stand it? How had he convinced himself that pain was a price he had to pay for— For what? For love?

She remembered when Way-Ray lay in a coma and Jackson told her he was done with drinking, that he recognized pain made things real and he wanted that, wanted her.

Was she part of the problem? Did he interpret her strength and independence as a challenge to him, a bar set higher? Did he feel he might lose her if he displayed weakness, might alienate her when he had to depend on her while he recovered?

And if he did feel that way, was he aware of the reasons? Could he change them? Or were his beliefs so strong or so fundamental that nothing would alter his perception?

She knew him well enough after a year to recognize that he would refuse counseling for the same reasons she would. There were places inside that they each guarded. She could never take one of his secret spots by storm. He would have to invite her in. Would his pain hasten that invitation or cancel it?

The field sloped to a stand of young firs. Beyond their shade lay another field, long and narrow because the headland, a flow of basalt that had spilled westward during what Kate thought of as a time before time, constricted to a blunted point. On the south side of the headland the brush had been beaten back and grass scythed around the weather-blasted split-rail fence that enclosed the Hopkins' family cemetery.

What would happen to it if developers got this land? Would Evie be able to specify that the cemetery be undisturbed? Or would the graves be dug up and the coffins moved, the ground graded over and sculpted, a cup set into turf, a flag planted? How would Way-Ray react?

Don't go there.

Stay with today.

Kate halted beside Jackson where the trail forked to the cemetery, and slipped her hand into his. "It's such a beautiful spot. Peaceful."

"Yet fierce." He nodded to the west where the headland fell away to the ocean. Whitecaps topped the waves and the faint booming of breakers crashing against rocks was a backbeat for the pulsing whisper of the onshore breeze.

Way-Ray dropped the shovel, slipped through the sagging cemetery gate and knelt at a white marble headstone carved with a hummingbird. He'd picked that image himself, saying that when she cooked or cleaned his mother moved as fast as one of the tiny birds.

"Hummingbirds are fierce." Kate had watched them fight over a feeder, diving at each other, colliding in midair and falling to the ground only to rise and go at it again. "Amanda was fierce."

Jackson settled his arm across her shoulders. "So are you."

Kate heard pride in his voice and smiled, then wondered again if he believed she put too much stock in strength—both physical and mental—and showed distain for weakness. She kissed the edge of his jaw, more prominent than a few weeks ago.

How much weight had he lost? Was he making a conscious effort to try to reduce stress on his back and leg, or had pain eroded his appetite? She tried to recall what he'd had for breakfast and lunch and could think of nothing except coffee, a handful of Way-Ray's sugary cereal, and a chunk of cheese. But then, at mealtimes she focused on Way-Ray, coaxing him to do more than nibble at foods that were nutritious, checking to be sure he didn't scrape green beans or coleslaw into a napkin to haul out to the geese.

"I wonder what he tells her," Jackson said.

Lips moving, head nodding, Way-Ray fanned the roses and laid them on Amanda's grave, then pointed across the headland, south toward Castaway Beach.

"Secrets." Kate felt a stab of jealousy and abandonment. Did Way-Ray share things with his dead mother than he couldn't tell her? Was she to blame for that? Was she too inaccessible, too distant, too intent on her job and the thousand chores around the rehab center? Or was she simply, as she had feared, inept at the task of raising a child?

"Kids love secrets. It's a way to have control in a world full of adults." Jackson pulled her close and whispered. "Didn't you have secrets?"

Kate thought for a moment. "I suppose you could call them secrets. There were certainly things I didn't want my parents—or anyone—to know."

Because telling about them would reveal my soft spots and make me weaker in their eyes. And weakness was a flaw. It proved I wasn't a perfect child, so they would love me less.

She froze at that flash of insight. In order to allow Jackson to be weak she, like a puppy rolling over to display its tender belly, might need to reveal weakness by sharing more of the painful memories she held close.

Way-Ray stood, dusted off his knees, picked up the shovel, and ran to them, leaving the gate to swing closed on its own. "Want me to carry something?"

91

Why not start to show weakness right now?

"Sure." Kate shrugged off the pack. "I'll take the shovel if you take this. My back's sore from all that hoeing in the garden and this weighs a ton."

"I can lift a ton without even sweating." Way-Ray threaded his arms through the loops and snugged them across his shoulders. "I'm super strong. When I get bigger, I'll be as strong as Jackson."

"As strong as Jackson, huh?" Kate ruffled Way-Ray's hair.

"Yeah. That's as strong as anybody can be."

Kate winced. What good would it do for her to encourage Jackson to reveal weakness if Way-Ray expected superhuman strength? "I didn't know that."

"Well, it's true." Way-Ray started off along the trail that skirted the north edge of the headland.

Jackson shook his head. "I don't know where he got that idea."

"Hero worship," Kate said. "You're the man in his life."

"Well, he ought to worship the woman in his life, too." Jackson cupped his hands and called after Way-Ray. "Strong isn't all there is. What about being smart? As smart as Kate?"

Way-Ray halted, turned, and tapped his head. "It's summer. Kids don't get smart in the summer. That's for school time."

Kate feigned amazement. "I didn't know *that* either."

"Well, it's true. I'm gonna get all A's when school starts. You'll see." He gazed at the cemetery. "My mom would be proud of me, huh?"

"Super proud." Kate swallowed tears and remembered the day when she stopped at Amanda's trailer in Grassy Ridge and faced a grim choice—take Way-Ray with her or leave him with a wounded mother who believed she couldn't love him because of the man who fathered him.

She squeezed Jackson's hand. "I think she would be proud of us all."

CHAPTER 9

A long wooden stake driven into the ground and topped with a storm-battered duck decoy marked the top of a trail that zigzagged down the splintered face of the headland. The first few feet of that trail were almost vertical and, after Way-Ray was clear, Kate threw the shovel ahead, crouched, hung onto the gnarled roots of a long-dead tree, and swung about, her toes seeking a level landing gouged into the slope.

"Gotta drive some rods in here and build a set of steps," Jackson said.

"How many times has one of us said that?" Kate asked.

"A million," Way-Ray ventured.

"Not that many," Kate corrected. "But at least a hundred."

"Definitely this fall," Jackson promised. "It will be easier to drive in stakes when the rains come back and the ground is soft."

"I'll help. I like to hammer," Way-Ray called over his shoulder as he darted off to the first switchback.

When she reached it, the trail cast to the south, and Kate got a view of the tidal marsh that she and a few dozen volunteers had worked on in late winter and early spring. Rushing to beat the northward migration and nesting season, they dragged driftwood and brush to fill ditches dug decades earlier when the land was drained for pasture. With pickaxes and hoes they gouged channels through dikes thrown up to keep a tiny stream—nameless as far as Kate knew—within its banks. As if assuring her that the work had paid off, a blue heron stabbed its bill into the shallow water and came up with a fish, a wiggle of silver in the afternoon sun. Kate drew in a deep breath of salty air and felt for a moment as if she could spread her arms and sail across the marsh.

The trail switched north and led her to a view of a tiny cove, deeper than it was wide, a crooked finger of water poking between this headland and the one to the north, hooking at the tip. A scrap of beach, most of it not visible until the trail reached the end of its final jog, rimmed the tiny cove. A tangle of driftwood—some deposited by the tide and some hauled from the surf to dry out and fuel bonfires—marked the edge of the sand and the beginning of a tumble of grapefruit-sized stones. Beyond that, among larger rocks, tenacious shrubs clung to clumps of earth sloughed from the cliff looming a hundred feet and more above the cove.

A pair of peregrine falcons nested in a scrape on the face of the cliff. On stormy spring nights Kate thought of them sheltering their eggs from buffeting wind and rain. She didn't have a capacity for on-going sacrifice at their level. And she didn't have Evie's ability to revel in each success and not dwell

95

on lost causes—birds so battered or starved they died as she attempted to save them.

Peering down the sinuous trail at Way-Ray, Kate considered all she longed to protect him from—and all he'd already suffered. She thought of his only remaining relative, a grandmother locked in prison after plea bargaining a sentence for what would surely be the rest of her life, convicted as an accessory in the murder of Way-Ray's mother and her son's attempt to kidnap the boy.

Despite her rage and the pain in her leg, Kate felt sparks of compassion for Justine, an abused woman turned abuser. Once, awake before dawn and inhaling the warming spring wind, she almost rose from bed and wrote a letter seeking— What? A connection? Justine, after all, was the only blood family Way-Ray had, and there were things he might wish to learn about her or his father.

"For example?" Jackson asked when she told him.

"Like . . . I don't know . . . anything that would make Wayne Jessop seem like something more than a man who tried to kill the mother of his child."

"Leave it alone," Jackson advised. "Unless we need medical history we can't get any other way, or Way-Ray insists he wants to make contact with Justine, leave it alone."

"What if she reaches out to him?"

"She has no right to do that. Not as far as I'm concerned."

"But she has different ideas about what's right. We saw that last summer. What if she does?"

"We'll head it off."

"You mean open his mail? Not let him answer the phone?"

"Maybe. But we'll get him mentally set, make him aware that she's doing it for her, not for him. If he wants a relationship, we'll monitor it. We won't allow her to manipulate him and we'll show him how to fact-check every damn thing she says and make sure he doesn't get his hopes up that she'll change. She won't."

Kate recognized that he was right, but still had a nagging feeling that there must be something she could do to prompt Justine to examine her actions, ask for forgiveness, and seek redemption.

"Don't hold your breath," Evie told her. "That woman's bad to the bone. Rotten. Rot can't be cured. I end every day hoping she never tries to get in touch with that boy and he never wants anything to do with her."

"Don't poke that hornet's nest," Jackson added. "Leave it alone and you won't get stung."

Kate took their advice. She never wrote the letter. But regret stayed with her, like a deep bruise, sore and slow to heal.

The trail narrowed and she stumbled over a root, skidded, and then paused, ordering herself not to think about Justine, gazing at the inlet Way-Ray named Treasure Chest Cove. He and Sean were undeterred by Jackson's observations about underwater rocks that could tear the bottom out of a boat at low tide and the shape of the cove that funneled and amplified thrashing waves when the tide was high. Panting and grunting, the boys dug for iron-bound chests they were certain must be buried on the beach.

So far they'd uncovered only plastic bottles, running shoes lost from a container ship bound from Asia a decade before, bits of shell, the skeleton of a gull, and a rusted bucket. Theorizing that pirates used it to haul water, their hopes soared and for days they dug like desperate moles. Holes and piles of sand dotted the beach. Evie began calling the spot Swiss Cheese Cove while Jackson referred to it as The Minefield. Finally, Evie ordered them to fill in the holes instead of leaving that to tide, wind, and rain. Double work ate away at their enthusiasm for digging and now they seldom brought shovels along.

Kate started off again, sometimes leaning on the shovel, careful to plant each foot as the trail grew even steeper, ridged with roots and littered with stones. Two switchbacks ahead Way-Ray descended with the speed, agility, and immortality of youth.

"Be careful," Kate called after him.

"Word's not in his vocabulary," Jackson said.

"Well, it's the most-used word in mine. For all the good it does."

Before they'd gone a dozen yards, Kate slid twice and Jackson lost his footing once, his bad leg giving way, pitching him sideways against the rocky slope with a thud that made her ribs ache.

Kate scrambled close and stretched out a hand, then drew it back and glanced away, watching a pair of ducks lift off from the tidal marsh, letting Jackson struggle upright alone. He brushed off his army-green cargo pants and gathered up the quilt and towels as if they were shreds of his pride. For a few seconds he eyed the shovel, but didn't ask to use it as a crutch. And Kate didn't offer.

The trail veered right, following the northern flank of the headland toward the tip of the cove, snaking among stubby evergreens twisted by the wind, bent parallel with the slope. Some had half their roots

98

exposed and Kate used those as a railing where jutting rocks turned the trail into a steep, slanting staircase. "I'd hate to come down this trail in a hurry or on a dark night."

Jackson grunted and slung the quilt and towels over his shoulder so he could use both hands.

"Maybe I should see if any of the volunteers would be interested in working on it," Kate mused.

"It's not like there aren't a hundred other projects for them to tackle," Jackson said. "Besides, we're about the only ones who come here."

"Extending that bit of logic means it will be one of us who hurtles to the rocks below."

"Be hard to hurtle unless you took a running start and jumped far enough to set a world record. Otherwise you'd hang up in the bushes or land on a ledge. Probably never even hit the rocks."

Kate gazed at the mass of vegetation sprouting from crevices, a dense snarl of branches and vines, thorns and thistles, moss and ferns. "Thanks for clearing that up. I feel safer already."

"I'm gonna get driftwood for the fire," Way-Ray called from below. "Hurry up so I can light it."

"We're hurrying." Kate reached the end of the trail and the jumble of boulders she always crossed like a crab, afraid of sliding off and falling or catching a foot in a crevice and snapping her ankle.

When Evie first brought them to the cove last summer, Jackson leaped from rock to rock, but today he dropped to all fours, his bad leg straight to the side as if he was stretching before a run. Kate kept silent and didn't acknowledge the change for fear he'd abandon this new caution.

It was a six-foot drop from the top of the final boulder to the basalt slab that paved the way to the sand at the tip of the cove. She'd jumped once, favoring her wounded right leg, and paid for it with a throbbing pain in the arch of the opposite foot that lasted a week.

"Toss the shovel and go on," Jackson said. "I'll throw this stuff to you when you're down."

Kate flung the shovel like a javelin; metal rang on rock when it struck. Then, facing the boulder, she grasped the lip and lowered herself until her toes touched. Except for fist-sized depressions filled with water, sand, and tiny barnacles, the slab at the bottom was dry. Kate caught the bundled quilt and turned her back, leaving Jackson to make his way without a witness to his pain.

The tide was ebbing, falling back to a minus mark later that evening. At its lowest point, it would reveal the only other path in or out of the cove—a path they'd taken just once to see if it could be done. A thread of rocky beach started beyond the basalt slab she stood on. That beach was just wide enough for them to skirt the headland—walking single file—and reach the tidal marsh. A lengthy slog through that led to a trail that wound along the stream, into the forest on the far side of Evie's property, and then to the far edge of the pasture behind the new owl enclosure.

Not every low tide revealed the rocky beach and few left it clear for long. When waves surged back, they drowned the narrow beach in moments and then swelled into the cove and swallowed the basalt slab.

To teach Way-Ray and Sean about the strength and speed of the incoming tide, Kate and Jackson had brought them down the trail just before a storm to watch water as deep as they were tall wash over the basalt. After that, they set visits to the cove by the tide tables Kate printed out each month and never allowed the boys to come alone.

When she reached their picnic spot, Way-Ray was hard at work, lugging chunks of driftwood to the fire pit in the lee of an enormous log ferried to the far edge of the beach and abandoned there by a monster storm years before. Several times over the winter they found the log shifted—once even lying perpendicular to the water. Jackson used those shifts as an opportunity to teach Way-Ray about the power of the ocean and warn him against standing on or playing around logs even in surf only a few inches deep. It didn't take much to float a log, roll it, and crush a child who hadn't noticed the danger or wasn't able to jump clear.

"I dragged a whole bunch of stuff up to the get-dry pile. There's lots more driftwood than last time," Way-Ray said.

Kate leaned the shovel against the log and pulled a folded newspaper from the knapsack he'd set by the fire pit. "I guess the ocean thinks we should have the biggest bonfires ever this summer."

"The ocean doesn't think." Way-Ray laughed and dropped his finds. "This one looks like a snake and the other looks like an octopus if I squint, but it's really just a little old stump."

"Old stumps burn a long time, even little ones. Now we need some chips to get the fire going." She pointed to the strip of sand above a dark line of debris deposited by the tide. "Dry ones. From up there."

"On it!" Way-Ray darted off, shoes digging at the sand, spraying it up behind him.

101

"Don't go poking in the bushes," Kate reminded him.

"I won't. 'Cause if I disturbed a bird or somethin' Evie would skin me."

"Right." That reason worked, but it wasn't hers. One late autumn day when Way-Ray was in school, she and Jackson had come to the cove and discovered a young buck, splayed out on the stones above the high tide line, its neck and legs horribly twisted.

"Must have been running from something," Jackson speculated. "Running hard. Momentum carried him out a long way."

Kate stared at the buck's sunken eyes and swollen tongue, at the flies settling into a deep gouge in its flank. She thought of Amanda, killed and dumped in a ravine by the man she'd tried to lead away from her son. "We can't let Way-Ray see this."

"He sees worse on some of those video games. Guys blown to bits, heads chopped off."

"But that's not real."

Jackson had raised an eyebrow, but didn't argue further. Together they hauled the carcass almost to the base of the cliff, covered it with a mound of stones, driftwood, and sand, then topped the pile with a few hardy shrubs shorn from the top of the cliff by a recent slide. By now the carcass might be little more than bone and hair and antlers.

Kate crumpled the newspaper and glanced around, expecting to see Jackson swinging toward her.

He was nowhere in sight.

102

She stood, shading her eyes against the lowering sun, and studied the jumble of rocks she'd crossed and the flat slab below them. Not a trace of Jackson.

Shivering, she jogged down the sloping beach. Wavelets pushed by the breeze lapped at the side of the slab. Slack water. No current to carry Jackson out of the cove if he fell in. Besides, he was a strong swimmer, even with his bad leg, so unless he was injured in the fall—

"Jackson!"

She scanned the cove but saw nothing except a green plastic bottle bobbing a few yards from shore.

"Jackson!"

She peered into the water, but saw only a scattering of barnacles and a solitary starfish.

What had Jackson been wearing? Running shoes that had once been white and were now the color of dirt. Worn green pants. A black T-shirt with a logo so faded it might have been anything from a tractor to a buffalo to Mount Rushmore.

She ran along the tongue of lava to where the headland curled above and it narrowed to a point that splintered away into that rocky beach. Her feet tangled in a snarl of kelp and she went down on one knee, thrusting her hands out, rock scraping her palms. "Jackson. Jackson. Where are you?"

Nothing.

She ran back, spotted his shoes at the base of the rock with the binoculars stuffed into one of them. So he'd climbed down the final boulder. He'd taken off his shoes. And then?

"Jackson!"

"Up here." His voice was a rasp of sound, almost lost in the swish and wash of water on rock.

103

"You scared the hell out of me." Kate peered at the slope but saw nothing. "Up here where?"

"About twenty feet and a little to your left. Didn't intend to frighten you. I saw the opportunity and took it."

She swept her gaze back and forth. "I don't see you. Opportunity to do what?"

He laughed. "To take Way-Ray up on that bet about camouflage. Go get him and see if he can spot me."

"In a minute." Kate squinted at the slope once more, determined that she would pick Jackson out. There were no rocks large enough to hide behind, nothing but a few scrawny trees and a low, dense growth of shrubs and vines. If he'd burrowed into that, surely she'd see broken branches and crushed leaves. "How do I know you're where you say you are? How do I know you're not throwing your voice from somewhere else?"

He chuckled. "If I could do that I'd be up at the house in the hammock instead of lying here contorted like a soggy pretzel. Get Way-Ray before I'm so stiff you need a pry bar to get me up."

Smiling, Kate retrieved the binoculars and found Way-Ray building a pyramid of sticks and chips around the crumpled paper. She handed him the binoculars. "Jackson's taking you up on that bet you made about camouflage before all the reporters came looking for the imaginary rabid animals. He's up on the hillside playing hide-and-seek."

"Where?" Way-Ray leaped to his feet. "Give me a clue."

"I don't have a clue. I can't see him."

"I will. I have super-power eyeballs."

He took off down the beach and she bent and wove a few more sticks into the pyramid, then braced larger pieces of driftwood against each other and across the top. When she was done, she shook out the quilt. The pink and orange towel fluttered loose and fell to one side. Kate shook the quilt again, but the brown towel didn't appear. Jackson must have dropped it on the trail. She spread the quilt a few feet from the fire pit and anchored the corners with more wood.

When she turned to check on Way-Ray, he was inching out along the tongue of lava, his gaze riveted on the crevices above. "Not that far," she yelled and pointed. "He's above the rocks where we climb down."

Way-Ray jogged back and positioned himself with the sun at his back, scanning the hillside through the binoculars. Kate strolled over and joined him, squinting, drawing her gaze left to right, up and down.

"He's not there," Way-Ray said after a minute.

"He is," Kate said.

"Did you see him?"

"No, but I heard him."

Scowling, Way-Ray turned to face her. "Maybe he snuck off while you came to get me."

"Are you calling me a sneak?" Jackson asked.

Way-Ray jumped and let out a yip. "Where are you?"

Jackson was silent.

"I'm gonna find you." Way-Ray clambered up the rocks to the trail and scanned once more.

Kate hunted for a shape that didn't belong. But the settling sun cast long shadows from each rock and shrub, and the strengthening breeze set those

105

shadows swaying and twitching. "I give up," she called after a few moments.

"I don't," Way-Ray said. "I'm gonna find him."

"What about hunting for treasure?"

"I'll do that next time."

"What about dinner?"

"I'm not hungry yet."

Kate thought of Jackson knotted among the rocks on that slope. By now the pain in his leg must have a life of its own. "Well, I'm starving. I'll go light the fire."

"Hey." Way-Ray stamped a foot on the trail, setting free a trickle of pebbles. "That's my job."

"But you're busy."

He took the binoculars from his eyes and turned to look at her. "Just a few minutes, okay? I gotta find Jackson. I think he's right—"

"Here?" Jackson asked.

Way-Ray swung around. A bush shuddered and the ground beside it trembled and rose up.

"Huh?" Way-Ray rubbed his eyes. "How'd you do that?"

"Camouflage." Jackson lurched to his feet and flapped the brown towel he'd used to cover his head and arms. Leaves and twigs were crammed into rips in the cloth and he'd stuffed grass and branches in the pockets of his cargo pants. "Come up here, youngster, and see how I fooled you, then prepare to fork over your money."

Grumbling about the sun making too many shadows and the wind blowing leaves around and the binoculars being all messed up because Sean used them last, Way-Ray climbed up to inspect Jackson's hide, then raced ahead to light the fire. While he devoured two hot dogs and half a bag of

106

chips, Jackson told him about the history of camouflage, how ghillie suits were developed by Scottish gamekeepers, and how the suits broke up the outline of the person in hiding. He talked about how to pick a spot where you could blend in, and how to keep your mind and your body still, whether you were the hunter or the hunted.

"How long do you have to stay still?"

"As long as you need to."

Way-Ray shoved three marshmallows onto the end of a stick. "How long is that?"

"Depends on the situation. A few minutes. A few hours. Maybe all day."

"All day?" Way-Ray thrust the stick into the flames. "What if your nose itches or you have to, uh, you know?"

"You don't scratch. You hold it."

"What if you can't?"

"Then somebody spots you," Kate said. "And you get caught."

"And your mission is a failure," Jackson said.

Way-Ray pointed at Jackson with his marshmallows, the browned outside crust sagging from the melting interior. "How long can you be still?"

"Hours."

"How many hours?"

"I don't know." Jackson snatched the top marshmallow from the stick. "As long as it takes."

"Hey, those were mine." Way-Ray gobbled the remaining toasted treats. "I'm gonna practice tomorrow. Real hard. After dinner you can time me. I bet I can stay still for an hour."

Jackson chuckled. "I bet you can't."

"Can so!"

"How much more money do you have to lose?"

"Ten dollars. I get my allowance on Friday."

"Ten dollars is a lot of money," Kate cautioned. "If you lose, you won't have enough money to go to the movies with Sean."

"I'm not gonna lose, Kate." Way-Ray snapped the marshmallow stick in half. "Stop saying I am."

Kate raised her hands, warding off his burst of anger.

"She said 'if,' Way-Ray." Jackson snatched the pieces of the broken stick and leaned forward, his face inches from the boy's. "Listening is as important as keeping still. If you can't listen, you won't know when it's safe to move."

Way-Ray scowled and clenched his fists, but in a moment ducked his head. "I don't wanna bet with you anyway. It's all stupid. Hiding in the bushes is dumb."

Jackson shrugged and leaned back against the log. "Then let's hope the day doesn't come when you have to do it."

Kate felt a chill and held her hands over the embers. What had Jackson imagined that made him say that?

Chapter 10

Late Monday afternoon, feeling like she'd been mangled in an industrial-size blender, Kate dragged herself into the ice cream shop.

"Did you get the power company straightened out?" Rhea called.

Kate peered at her friend over the heads of a gaggle of preteens leaving sticky fingerprints on the thick plastic panel that kept them from plunging their hands into the tubs of ice cream arrayed in the freezer case. As Rhea bent to scoop some for Kate, Kyle towered beside her, a scoop in one hand and a cone in the other. With a bored expression, he gazed at the first child in the ragged line, a girl with sandy blond pigtails who seemed more interested in him than the three dozen flavors lined up in the case. He waggled the scoop at Kate but didn't speak. Like his father, Kyle was a man of few words.

Kate waved back and trudged to the end of the counter where Rhea met her with a cone mounded with cashew and caramel ice cream buried under a

109

mass of chocolate sprinkles. "Can't serve liquor in here, so you'll have to make do with this. Now, what's the story?"

"Well, the short version is that the power will be back on sometime this week. Sometime. Not tomorrow or the day after. Just some vague time out there in the future." Kate bit off a huge mouthful of ice cream, hoping a brain freeze would chill her seething mind.

Rhea patted the pocket of her smock, pulled out a mint, then stuck it back. "And the long version?"

An icy spike drove through her head. Kate gasped, her eyes watered, and she stomped her feet. "Ooohh. That smarts." She snatched up a napkin and wiped her eyes. "The long version, from the lips of Phyllis, who finally condescended to make herself available after a lengthy lunch that began just as I arrived, is that there was an unfortunate series of errors."

"Not just one error," Rhea marveled, "but an entire unfortunate series."

"Broadens the scope of deniability." Kate sucked ice cream and sprinkles from the rim of the cone. "Phyllis is certain the errors originated with an employee who conveniently left her job late last week to move to Vermont where she's now living in a back-to-nature commune in a remote location. No phone. No forwarding address."

"Ah, a series of errors and the off-the-grid excuse." Rhea pulled out the mint again, popped it in her mouth, and crunched the candy to bits.

"Not to mention the holiday-tomorrow excuse and the ever-popular we're-so-short-handed-you'll-have-to-be-patient-until-we-can-rectify-the-situation stance."

110

"Oh for the love of macaroni and cheese." Rhea dug for a second mint. "It's not like they have to string a new set of lines. I'll bet all she has to do is tap a few computer keys."

Kate followed a ribbon of caramel with the tip of her tongue, savoring the slick texture. "If she breaks a nail, our power could be out for a month."

Rhea stuffed the second mint back in her pocket and fiddled with a butterfly clip, shoring up her leaning topknot. "I'm glad you can joke about it. I would have strangled her on the spot."

"Then I'd really be in the dark—in a jail cell. We decided to go at this problem like it was no big deal, so I did—or at least managed the best I could given that I knew every word out of her mouth was a lie." She found a cashew, nibbled it free. "What did you learn about running for office?"

"That I've got two weeks of butt-busting labor to fill these with signatures so I can get my name on the ballot." Rhea reached for a heap of documents lying beside the cash register, pulled several from the top, and slapped them against the ice cream case.

The pigtailed girl squeaked and blurted, "Chocolate chip."

The girl behind her giggled and two boys at the rear of the line groaned. Kyle cocked his head, but made no move to fill the cone. "I'm sure," the pigtailed girl said. "Really."

Kyle leaned over to scoop, a curl of black hair escaping from his painter's cap and trailing across his forehead. "He's so cute." The second girl in line hugged herself and sighed deeply enough to empty her lungs. The boys groaned again, mimicked her words and actions, then punched each other in glee.

Kyle flushed and Rhea rolled her eyes. "My son, the teen idol," she whispered. "Remember how clumsy he used to be?"

Kate nodded, recalling the day they met when he tripped over his own feet and smashed a wastebasket. Last summer Rhea called him a one-man demolition team, but over the winter, thanks to a basketball coach who prodded his players to enroll in ballet classes, Kyle developed balance, control, and a sense of how much space he inhabited.

"Doesn't so much as crack a cone now." Rhea smiled with pride and passed over the papers.

One-handed, Kate shuffled through the lined pages with headings for printed names, signatures, and addresses. "That's a lot of lines to fill."

"Yeah, but there's no place busier than an ice cream shop in a heat wave. After that little cool-off we had yesterday it's heating up again. Fast. They're saying it's gonna hit 90 tomorrow and who knows what the day after. That means I can fill most of those spaces without leaving this building."

Rhea snatched the papers back and fanned herself with them. "And there's more good news. Lois is running for the other seat."

"Can she do that?" Kate caught a drip of ice cream before it reached her knuckles. "I mean, doesn't the county pay part of her salary? Isn't that a conflict of interest?"

"She's taking leave to run—hasn't used a vacation day in a dozen years so she's got plenty coming. If she's elected she'll dump her relationship with the Dewey Decimal System in a heartbeat."

"But I thought she loved running the library."

"She does, but she says if we don't change the way we set priorities, pretty soon there won't be a

112

library to run. Plus, after what happened this morning she's two miles beyond furious."

Rhea paused. Kate gnawed at the edge of her cone, then took the bait. "What happened this morning?"

Rhea gave her a made-you-ask smile. "Well, when I went in to see about running, they told me that I couldn't because I missed a deadline. I was embarrassed and majorly unhappy, but I should have done my homework, you know?"

Kate nodded and munched another nut.

"I stopped by the library to drop off some books—Jim's mother goes through a romance a day—and mentioned to Lois that my political career never got off the ground. The next thing I know she was locking the door and dragging me back to the elections office and citing some obscure county regulations that say I can toss my hat into the ring if I get a whole bunch of signatures by a certain date."

The mint came out. Rhea studied it and jammed it back. "Then the clerk—she's another pal of Paul's—made the mistake of telling Lois she was wrong."

Kate whistled. "Major miscalculation."

"You bet. Lois got up a head of steam the way she does and called for the boss and the boss's boss and when they finally agreed she was right and got the forms for me she told them to get two sets because she was running for the second seat that's up."

Kate laughed. "I bet she got an apology then."

"Oh, yeah, from the whole chain of command. But Lois didn't take time to listen, she grabbed her papers, got out a pen, and headed for the pizza place and the noon rush. She'll probably have all the names she needs by dark."

"Dark. Yikes." Kate chomped down the last of the cone. "Gotta run. If I don't get to the store and buy something to make a decent dinner we'll be eating chips and dip and using a flashlight to find them."

"What's wrong with that," a boy at the back of the line asked.

Rhea shot him a scathing look and Kate hustled for the door.

Back home, she found Evie on a lounge chair on the porch, a washcloth on her forehead, her cheeks flushed. Way-Ray sat on the floor by her side, fanning her with a cookie tin. "Jackson said she looked like she was going to stroke out and told her to sit here and cool off until you got back."

Stroke out?

Heatstroke?

Or something else?

Something worse.

"I'm only sitting here because I deserve a little rest now and then," Evie groused. "Not because a man who doesn't have sense enough to come in out of the sun himself ordered me to."

Kate set her sack of groceries on a chair, stepped to Evie's side, and laid a hand on her cheek. "You're hot as a griddle. Did you take some aspirin?"

"Of course I did. How stupid do you think I am?"

Kate knew enough not to take a stab at answering that. She slid her fingers to the pulse point on Evie's neck and felt her heartbeat. Rapid, but strong. "Did you faint?"

"Of course not." Evie batted Kate's hand aside and pushed herself to a more upright position. "Felt kind of woozy. That's all."

Kate assessed Evie's condition. Her voice was strong, she'd used both of her hands, her facial muscles were all working, and her speech wasn't slurred. No obvious signs of a stroke that might paralyze or kill her.

"It's hotter than the hinges of hell out there." Evie turned the washcloth over and ran it across her cheeks and down her neck.

Kate glanced at the thermometer by the door. Barely eighty.

"This happens at the start of every summer," Evie said. "Once I get used to the heat I'm fine. No need to make a federal case of it."

Kate thought back, but couldn't remember Evie having similar problems last summer. But then, she hadn't been here every day. "How much water have you had to drink since you felt dizzy?"

"Two big glasses," Way-Ray answered. "Jackson told me to watch and make sure she drank all of it, but slow. She didn't spill even a drop."

"I told Jackson I'd drink it," Evie snapped. "Don't know why he thinks he needs a spy keeping watch on me."

Way-Ray fanned faster, his eyes sparkling. A smile twitched Kate's lips and she covered by turning toward the kitchen. "I'll get you some iced tea and then make something light for dinner. How does tuna salad sound?"

"Like my mom used to make?" Way-Ray piped up.

"Exactly like that," Kate said. "I'll put all the pickles and onions and stuff on a plate for the rest of us."

115

"But how are we gonna make toast for the sandwiches?"

"We'll put the bread on the grill."

"It will burn fast if you're not careful," Evie warned. "You can't run off and leave it like you do with the toaster."

"I'll watch it every second 'cause I had practice spying on you." Way-Ray set the cookie sheet down, curled his fingers into mock goggles, and peered through them. "And can we have potato chips? The barbecue ones?"

"Lots of them," Kate said. "I just bought a big bag."

Salt might help Evie hydrate. But if her blood pressure was high, then salt could be a bad thing. Kate wished she had the equipment to check, wished she could log onto the Internet and search out symptoms and advice.

"When's the power coming back?" Evie asked.

"Soon." Kate attempted a casual tone.

"When's soon?" Way-Ray asked. "Before I wanna watch TV tonight?"

"Um, well, tomorrow's a holiday so—"

"That rat." Evie tossed the washcloth aside, swung her legs off the lounger, and struggled to her feet. "I'm going to call him and—"

"Let him know he's getting to you?"

Evie ground her teeth, then dropped to the lounge chair again. "Freshen up my wash rag, Way-Ray. Let the water run for a minute so it's good and cold."

Way-Ray plucked the washcloth from the floor, jumped up, and darted into the kitchen.

"When?" Evie asked in a voice as hard as granite.

"Maybe a few days. It's complicated."

"It's criminal is what it is."

116

"Possibly. Probably. But I doubt we can prove that."

Evie's lips crimped but before she could speak Way-Ray charged back with a dripping washcloth. "Thank you. Just let me cool off another few minutes and then we'll go check on the gulls."

"Jackson said he'd do that."

"He has too many other things to do and we all know he doesn't have much of a way with birds. They don't need to be scared any worse than they are."

Way-Ray handed Evie the cloth and looked up at Kate, his eyes dark with anger. "Somebody ran over a bunch of gulls on a beach. A lot of 'em died."

"Got two survivors with broken wings. Banged up pretty good." Evie folded the cloth and laid it across her forehead. "Don't know if they'll make it."

Kate shook her head in anger and disgust. "Why would someone do that?"

"Probably they were driving too fast and weren't paying attention." Way-Ray told her. "Or maybe they like to hurt things."

Like your father and uncle.

Kate turned the conversation away from that. "Well, lucky for the birds, what you like to do is help them get better."

"I helped Evie wrap up their wings because the volunteer who brought them had to go off someplace and there was nobody else except Jackson."

"I wouldn't have thought it because of the way he and Sean flit around here like bats with a coffee habit, but he's got a real knack for working with critters." Evie patted his arm. "He talked to those gulls and they calmed right down."

117

"That's 'cause I've been practicing holding still." Way-Ray raised his chin. "I'm gonna be stiller than Jackson could ever be. You'll see." He grinned. "I mean, you won't see. I'll be so still I'll be practically invisible."

"That will be amazing. But right now why don't you be fast instead of still. Go check on the gulls and report back. Don't try to handle them, just see how they're doing. We'll feed them after dinner." Kate laid a hand on Evie's shoulder. "You're not getting out of this chair unless there's an emergency."

"Seems like lately," Evie grumbled, "emergency is where we start from."

Chapter 11

Thursday morning, as they were eating cold cereal, a fan on the counter groaned to life. "Power's on." Kate leaped to turn on the refrigerator and plug in her computer.

"Yay." Way-Ray beat his spoon against the table. "Television tonight. And toast right now." He bounced from his chair and fed two slices of bread into the toaster.

"And hot coffee. Real coffee." Jackson pushed his mug of warm instant coffee aside and shot to the sink to fill the coffeemaker.

"It's 83 degrees out there already," Kate said. "I'd rather have a cola. Or iced coffee."

"My body doesn't know it's caffeine unless it goes down hot." Jackson measured beans into the coffee grinder and fired it up with a rattling whine. "Besides, real men don't drink iced coffee."

Evie snorted. "Another reason to be glad I'm not a man. I'm having my coffee with cubes until this heat breaks. If it ever breaks."

119

"Paper says Sunday." Jackson fitted the filter into the basket, dumped in ground coffee, and poured water into the well.

Evie snorted again. "The only thing the paper gets right is the date in the top corner. And that doesn't always hold up to close scrutiny."

Twisting the lid off a jar of peanut butter, Way-Ray staked out the toaster while the aroma of brewing coffee filled the kitchen. Kate sucked in the rich scent. "You know, I think I'll have a cup of that after all. It smells so good."

"Want a piece of toast?" Way-Ray asked.

"Sure."

He opened the red cooler beside the refrigerator. "With lots of melty butter?"

"Melty butter." Saliva pooled under Kate's tongue. "Yum."

"Funny how much you miss little things when you don't have them," Evie mused. "You can suck it up and deal with the big stuff, but it's the little things that pile up and wear you down."

"Like not having the dishwasher and toast and TV." Way-Ray got out a tub of butter. "Except not having TV was a *big* thing."

"For you," Kate pointed out. "Not for the rest of us."

"That's 'cause you don't 'preciate it like you should." Way-Ray spread his arms. "TV is the greatest invention ever. And video games are number two."

"Greater inventions than cars and trains and planes?" Jackson asked.

"Sure. 'Cause if you have TV you don't need any of those because you don't have to go anyplace. You can just stay home." He plucked a piece of toast from the toaster and put it on a plate for Kate. "Especially if you're luckier than me and you get all the channels and have the best new games."

"Guess I'll go check on my critters." Evie stood and headed for the door. "I hear a full-fledged wheedle coming on."

"What's a wheedle?" Way-Ray plunged a knife into the center of the jar of peanut butter. "And what's a full-fledged one?"

"When you try to coax or persuade someone to do something you want and you don't stop when they say no, then you're wheedling." Jackson poured coffee, added milk, and passed a cup to Kate. "And when something is full-fledged, it has all its feathers and it's ready to fly."

"Huh?"

"Did Mr. Dictionary confuse you?" Kate asked with a laugh.

"I guess." Way-Ray spread peanut butter a quarter-inch thick on his toast.

"Well, you just implied that you're not as fortunate as other kids and hinted—without any attempt at being subtle—that we should sign up for more TV channels and buy more video games."

Way-Ray concentrated on getting peanut butter to the extreme edges of the crust. "I guess."

"And you know that I believe we already have plenty of channel choices and you know that we agreed you get a new game only when you save up to buy one or on your birthday or Christmas. Right?"

Way-Ray tongued a glob of peanut butter from the knife. "Uh gueff."

"Then I guess you were starting to wheedle, weren't you?"

121

He worked the glob from cheek to cheek, then nodded.

"And if Evie hadn't mentioned it," Jackson said, "you might have wheedled a little more and then even more until it was a full-fledged wheedle."

"But I might not have." Way-Ray stuck the knife in the dishwasher and screwed the lid on the peanut butter. "I might have stopped all on my own."

"Always a possibility," Kate agreed.

"But a remote one," Jackson said.

Way-Ray rolled his eyes. "Okay, maybe I wouldn't have stopped on my own. But what if I do something special, can we get more channels then? And can I get a new game without spending my own money?"

Kate sipped coffee. "I suppose that would depend on what you did and how special it was."

"How about if the house caught on fire—not 'cause I had a candle or anything—and I saved Evie?"

"If you did that, I'd buy you a new game."

"What if big scary monsters attacked and I saved you and Jackson?"

"Monsters, huh? That's worth two games."

Jackson clinked his cup against hers. "And a premium channel."

"Cool." Way-Ray bit into his toast. "I'm gonna write that down so you don't forget."

An hour later, Jackson and Way-Ray set out to return the borrowed generator. Since there were no volunteers scheduled that day, Kate got busy washing the dozens of dirty towels that piled up while the power was out. Between loads, she caught up with the spreadsheets that kept track of birds and animals taken in and treated.

She was about to enter the gulls—both doing surprisingly well—when she heard the chug of an exhausted engine and looked out to see a rusty van pull up behind Evie's truck. A man of about twenty vaulted out, sun-streaked hair brushing against his naked shoulders. Heedless of the hissing geese and the sharp gravel in the parking area, he jogged barefooted to the house, the metal rings on his ratty cargo shorts clattering. A girl of about the same age, dressed in a lime-green tank top, crisp white shorts that set off her coffee-with-cream skin, and a pair of designer sandals with two-inch heels followed, wobbling through deep patches of gravel and giving the geese a wide berth.

Kate met them at the porch steps. "Can I help you?"

"We came to see Eve Hopkins," the boy said.

"She's tied up right now."

Almost literally. Evie was clipping a tangle of fishing line from a starving pelican brought in half an hour ago.

"I'm Kate Dalton. I work with Evie. Did you bring an injured bird or animal?"

"No, but that's what we came about." The girl's voice was low and breathy. "The dead birds on the beach."

"The ones that were hit a few days ago?"

The boy frowned. "No. Last night or maybe this morning."

Kate drew in a sharp breath. "How many? Where?"

"At least a dozen. On the beach at the south end of town. Some were squashed flat and had tire

123

tracks on them. Others were just busted up. One was still alive but it couldn't fly."

"We tried to catch it, but it went into the ocean." The girl fished a tissue from her pocket and blotted the edges of her eyes, taking care not to smudge her mascara. "And then it got pulled under by a wave. When we were walking back to our motel we saw a guy driving right next to the water and we yelled at him to get off the beach because he was scaring the birds."

"He said he didn't give a shit about birds," the boy said.

"And he said he had a right to drive there." With a vicious tug, the girl ripped the tissue in two and wadded the pieces in her fists.

The boy put his arm around her. "So we went to the visitors' booth by the market and told them about the birds and a woman there told us about this place and we came to find out what we can do to stop people from driving on the beach and killing birds."

Helping Way-Ray feed the rescued gulls, Kate had the same desire. These visitors wouldn't like what she had to tell them. "Well, the short answer to that is, 'Not much.' Vehicles are allowed on some beaches at some times of the year. Unless someone doesn't have a license, is driving in a restricted area, or driving over the posted speed limit, or endangering others, or deliberately swerving into flocks of birds with the intent to hurt them, then that person has a right to drive on the beach."

"That's stupid." The girl's tone was petulant, like Way-Ray's when he argued for a later bedtime.

"If that's the law, then we should change it." The boy spoke with confidence, as if he'd confronted

124

things he wanted changed before and managed to do just that.

"Change what?" Evie came along the path from the hospital trailer lugging a laundry basket mounded high with more soiled towels.

"The law about driving on the beach," the boy told her.

"There was another incident this morning," Kate said. "Or maybe during the night. At least a dozen birds."

"Damn it." Evie dropped the basket. "Any survive?"

"One, but they couldn't catch it and it may have drowned."

"Double damn it." Evie kicked the basket, scattering towels.

"It's murder. That's what it is." The boy drew in a breath, puffing out his meager chest. "We've got to make the beach off-limits to vehicles."

"Good luck with that." Evie massaged the small of her back with her fists. "Driving on the beach is a tourist draw. And tourists bring money."

"It's always about money." The girl freed her mane of glossy black hair from a ponytail, combed it with her fingers, and secured it again. The diamonds in her earlobes flashed in the sunlight. "Money, money, money."

"Fact of life in our age and this economy," Evie said.

"You sound like you don't care," the boy challenged.

"I care." Evie wheeled on him, a wine-dark flush sweeping up her cheeks. "Don't think for one single second that I don't."

He's in for it now, Kate thought. He'll get a lecture that will pin his ears back. And Evie will get worked up and I'll have to tie her in the lounge chair for the rest of the afternoon.

But Evie's shoulders slumped and her voice dropped. "I care. You bet I care. I'm the one who patches up the birds that survive. But after falling off my high horse one too many times, I learned to stop tilting at windmills."

The two young people exchanged puzzled glances. "Windmills?" the boy asked.

"It's a figure of speech," Kate said, feeling like she was channeling Jackson and his dictionary. "It's a reference to Don Quixote who attacked windmills thinking they were giants. The expression means fighting a battle you can't win."

The girl stamped her foot, raising a spurt of dust that marred the sparkly red polish on perfectly shaped toenails. "Have you *tried* to fight this law?"

"You bet," Evie said. "The first time I saw the carnage a joyrider left behind I was beside myself. Birds have hollow bones that shatter like glass. When a car or truck plows into them, they kind of explode. Out of two dozen birds that jerk hit, only one pulled through. One!" She kicked the scattered towels into a heap. "As soon as I got that bird's wings wrapped, I was on the horn to everybody who held office or had any influence in this state. I gave them all a piece of my mind."

"And what happened?"

"Nothing." Evie hunched as if she'd suffered that defeat just a moment ago. "Nothing happened." She gathered the towels into the basket. "Come on in out of the heat and I'll explain the lay of the land."

126

Kate backed up to make way. "I'll get some lemonade."

"Thank you," the girl said. "We didn't think it would be this hot in Oregon."

Evie dropped onto the lounge chair. "Where you from?"

"Santa Fe," the boy answered. "I'm Abel Moorhouse and this is Cassie Castillo."

Evie nodded. "What brings you up this way?"

"Just traveling around the country. Going places we've never been." Abel unfolded an aging aluminum lawn chair, dusted off the woven seat with the edge of his hand, and placed it for the girl. Cassie sat without acknowledging his effort, as if being waited on was something to be expected, a trivial and ordinary part of their relationship.

Chivalrous.

And entitled.

A complementary pair.

It could work, Kate thought as she opened the freezer. Until chivalry wore thin and/or was crushed by relentless entitlement. Until Abel decided that chivalry might be a form of servitude.

While she mixed up a pitcher of lemonade and got out tall glasses, Kate wondered how they met, why they connected, and what held them together. Santa Fe was an eclectic city, rich in history, heritage, arts, and culture. It had many wealthy residents— newcomers and those with roots deep in the past. From her bearing, it appeared Cassie might come from a family like that, a family with money to match its pedigree. Perhaps the boy came from the upper crust as well. Maybe the rusty van was a prop and his frayed clothing more costume than

127

commitment to a simple life or a statement against consumerism.

"I started this place," Evie said, "because a year to the day after my husband died, I found a cormorant with a broken wing on the beach below here. Somebody shot him."

"Why?" the boy asked.

Kate stopped stirring lemonade to listen. She'd never heard this story, never thought to ask why Evie started taking in wounded creatures.

"Who the hell knows why? Idiots shoot at birds all the time just because they can—songbirds, eagles, owls, even hummingbirds."

There was silence for a moment, then the girl asked in a near whisper, "What happened to the cormorant?"

"He pulled through, no thanks to me. I did just about everything wrong catching him. He was so stressed by the time I got him to a vet I thought his little heart would explode. Well, I was mad at myself, and mad at the fool who shot him, and mad that my husband died and left me with nothing but this tired farm and an aging dairy herd . . . but I wasn't mad at that bird. No matter how exhausted and miserable I get, I'll never be mad at a critter that's just doing what it was put here to do. And whenever I get so tired I can hardly move, I close my eyes and remember how it feels to open a cage and watch an eagle fly free again because I helped it heal."

Evie's voice trailed off and Kate squashed the last remaining bit of frozen concentrate against the side of the pitcher and stirred again, the spoon ringing off the glass.

"I can be shrill about what I think is right," Evie said. "And I hate to back down or back away from what I believe in. I could browbeat lawmakers and bureaucrats seven days a week if they let me corner them."

Kate lined up glasses, filled them with ice, and set them on a tray. When they teamed up after Kate recovered, she advised Evie to work on persuading lawmakers with facts rather than pummeling them with opinions. Evie had complained at first, saying she'd be damned if she'd suck up to a politician, but lately she toned down her rhetoric a few degrees.

Kate returned to the porch, set the tray on a low table, and poured lemonade. As if she knew what Kate was thinking, Evie shot her a wry smile and went on talking to their visitors. "I enjoyed every minute of that browbeating, but it didn't get me anyplace. In fact, it probably knocked me back a few steps. And it sure as hell wore me out."

Kate handed Evie a tall glass, studying her. Was she suffering from some physical ailment that was sapping her strength?

"Why are you staring at me like that?" Evie snatched the glass from Kate's hand. "You'd think I had two heads."

"Thank goodness you don't." Kate handed drinks to their visitors, giving them a wink. "I couldn't take two mouths spewing sarcastic comments."

"That's what I get for giving you a home," Evie muttered, a twinkle in her eyes. "This is the payback for allowing you to work 24/7 at a thankless job for low pay."

Kate raised her glass as if toasting that remark. "Don't forget the second-rate accommodations and the complete lack of vacation time."

"So there's nothing we can do?" the boy asked after a moment. "Jerks will keep on plowing into flocks of birds."

"They'll do that even if there's a law that bans driving on the beach." Kate sat on the end of Evie's lounge chair. "They'll show off or get drunk or say they're just birds and who cares or—worst of all—they'll think they're doing the world a favor because they heard birds carry diseases."

The girl's face crumpled. "That sounds like you think it's pointless to try to do anything at all."

"No, but I think it's pointless to try to change things from the top down. We have to lobby to keep the restrictions that are already in place, we have to report violators, and we have to push to have them prosecuted. But the most important thing we can do is to educate people—lawmakers, local businesspeople, schoolchildren, tourists—everyone."

"And it's an uphill battle, but we have to get the community involved or at least aware." Evie set her glass on the floor. "Most of the motels and rentals post our fliers about the dos and don'ts of interacting with critters on the beach, but plenty of business folks can't relate to what we do—I mean, this is a money-losing operation and I don't run it like a zoo. Except for educational groups now and then, we don't encourage visitors and we don't sell snacks or let them pet the deer. Now, I don't necessarily need every business on the coast to support me, although that would be icing on the cake, but I *do* need them to tolerate me."

She leaned forward and patted Kate's arm. "And little by little we're winning them over."

Except Paul. Kate held the cool glass to her forehead. And the sharks, and the barracudas, and

130

the sardines and minnows who wanted tiny bites of the big profit to be made from a golf course, a hotel, condos, and a set of high-end shops and restaurants.

"But that's all *process*," the girl spat out the word as if it was bitter, rotten. "And long-range. Besides, education won't stop the jerks mowing down birds today."

Abel put a hand on her arm to calm her.

"No, it won't," Evie agreed. "The sad fact is you can't reach people who don't want to be reached and you can't teach people who don't want to be taught."

"Well, thank you for the lemonade at least." Abel stood, set his empty glass on the table, and retrieved the one the girl held out to him.

"Where are you headed next?" Evie asked.

They exchanged a long glance, then the girl stood and stretched, displaying a gold ring in her navel. "We might stay here for a while."

The boy nodded and held the door for her. "Maybe we'll find a way to speed up the educational process."

"Increase awareness," the girl said over her shoulder. "And involvement."

"What do you suppose he meant by that?" Evie asked when they were gone. "Speeding up the process?"

Kate rubbed her temples. "I don't even want to think about it."

CHAPTER 12

"So you're trying to put out a fire before it starts."

Police Chief Sam Lowell scratched the gray whiskers on the blade of his jaw. The whisk of sound, like insects in dry grass, made Kate glance at her bare toes to make sure nothing was crawling toward them.

"Exactly. Or at least contain it. And make it clear up front that when they came to see her yesterday, Evie didn't provide the matches to set that fire."

Kate tapped the piece of paper she'd set in the center of Lowell's desk—a desk piled high with folders and loose papers shedding a rainbow of sticky notes. "I wrote down their names and a description of their van. I didn't think to get the license number." She held up a hand. "And Jackson already gave me a lecture about being out to lunch on that, so you can save your breath."

Lowell smiled and squinted at the paper. His eyebrows advanced on each other like warring wooly caterpillars until he pulled his half-glasses from the holster clipped to his belt and slid them on. "You don't know where they'll set this fire or when?"

Kate remembered the kids saying they'd confronted a man driving on the sand after they discovered the dead birds. "Maybe on the beach at the south end of town. But I have no idea what that something will be, although I doubt it will involve an overuse of 'please' and 'thank you'."

"Not shy and retiring types, huh?"

"They're polite, but angry. They're young. Idealistic."

She sighed and leaned back as far as the narrow, straight-backed chair would allow. Lowell's office was as short on frills as it was on space. "Evie and I did our best to explain how things are and what we're doing to educate people, but they didn't want to hear that we can't rope off the beaches."

"I'll let Curtis know to keep an eye out." Lowell slid his glasses back into their holster. "I hope to hell their fire doesn't start on a Sunday."

Kate smiled. Lowell's Sunday afternoons spent casting lines into rivers and bays were what enabled him to come back to work on Monday with a high degree of calm control. "If they mess with your fishing day, they'll be in doo doo so deep the only way out will be down."

"I like that. Might use it some time." Lowell stood and hitched at his belt. "You get the power back on out there?"

Kate wasn't surprised he knew they'd been cut off. He'd have to be living under a rock not to. "Yesterday morning." She got to her feet and picked up her purse. "From now on I'm paying the bills in person and I'm not walking away until they hand over a receipt. In front of witnesses."

133

Lowell leaned forward and rested his hands on his desk. "So far this piddly shit has been annoying and inconvenient, but smart money says it could get worse before long. You keep your eyes peeled, Kate, and tell Jackson to do the same. Paul's got a big streak of yellow down his spine and he doesn't have much in the way of imagination, but some of the folks he runs with . . ."

The sharks.

She didn't ask how Lowell knew about them. Knowing was his business. "Jackson's aware of them. And his permanent address is at the high end of orange alert."

"Not a bad place to pick up your mail in this day and time. But his back's got him in a world of hurt whether he'll admit it or not. You call if you need me, even if that dings his pride."

"Count on it."

Kate shook the meaty hand he held out, then crossed the lobby in two steps, let herself out through a door warping under the constant assault of salt-laden air, and walked down the street to the ice cream shop. Young girls were three-deep at the counter and Kyle, looking a shade less bored and a shade more full of himself, was juggling ice cream scoops to a chorus of oohs and ahhs. A few boys stood at the back of the group making vain attempts to disguise their jealousy with claims about their own abilities—all superior to Kyle's. The shop smelled of vanilla and strawberry, hair gel and perfume, deodorant and hormones.

Rolling her eyes and snapping a hair clip onto her topknot, Rhea met Kate at the end of the counter. "Wants me to pay him an extra fifty cents an hour for drawing a crowd and for making a video he put up on the Internet. I told him he'll get me to pay when he gets his audience to spend enough to make it worth my while to have them underfoot."

She dug a scoop of hot pink ice cream from a tub and plunked it into a sugar cone. "This looks like bubble gum, but it's cherry-brandy with dark chocolate chunks. Trust me."

Wary of the color that screamed preteen, Kate took the napkin-wrapped cone and tasted the ice cream with the tip of her tongue. Flavor swelled in her mouth, sweet and rich and warm. She licked again. "Yum. Are you allowed to sell this to minors?"

Rhea put her finger to her lips and winked, "Only until someone rats me out and Chief Lowell shuts me down."

"You won't have to worry about that any time soon. I have a feeling he's about to be busier than he likes."

Rhea frowned and patted the pocket of her smock. "Paul making more trouble?"

"Probably, but we haven't seen it yet." Kate swallowed a huge bite of ice cream, shivered, and told her about Abel and Cassie.

"Probably just popping off the way kids do." Rhea shot a glance at Kyle who had abandoned the scoops and now had four apples in the air. His movements seemed effortless, almost graceful. "You wouldn't believe the stuff that comes out of his mouth during those rare moments he bothers to pry his foot from between his lips."

Kate grinned at the image of Kyle's size-14 foot in his mouth, then nibbled at her cone and thought back to Abel's parting words. "It sounded pretty serious to me. More a promise than a threat."

135

"Well, you've got to factor in hormones. A girl and a boy of that age, out on their own, they're probably a hundred miles from here by now sitting in a hot tub, scrubbing each other's backs and all manner of other things."

A boy at the edge of the crowd gawked at her. "What other things?"

Rhea flushed, pivoted, and yelled, "If you've got so much time and energy, Kyle Whitaker, go mop the back room."

Two apples thudded to the floor. The crowd let out a collective gasp.

"As for the rest of you," Rhea said. "This isn't a theater and we're not putting on talent shows. This is an ice cream store, a place where—get this—we sell ice cream. But the problem is that we can't sell it unless somebody buys it."

She scanned the array of open-mouthed faces. "Anybody want to do that? Anyone got any money? If not, clear the deck for paying customers."

With a rumble of muttering, the kids filed out. Kyle scooped up the apples, slammed them into the trash can, and stomped into the back room.

"Our slow time's from 4:30 to 5:30," Rhea yelled after him. "You can perform then and I'll fork over an extra two bucks for the whole show and run your video camera to boot. But tell your fan club if a real customer appears they better make way and they better be polite. If not, I'll tell their parents that—"

Kyle peeked around the doorway. Kate saw only his eyes, but the crinkles at the corners indicated he was grinning. "Tell them what?"

"Don't you worry, Mister, I'll think of something."

136

"You always do." He dodged into the back and in a few seconds Kate heard the splash of water and caught the scent of lemon cleaner.

"Nice compromise."

"Just shooting from the hip as usual." Rhea blew on the tip of her index finger as if it was a gun barrel in need of cooling.

Kate felt a pang of jealousy. Being a mother seemed to come so easily to Rhea and to some of the women she met at school activities. Yes, she had days when she felt almost comfortable caring for and guiding Way-Ray. But then there were darker days when he challenged every idea, refused to consider compromise, played his you're-not-my-real-mother trump card, and brought her to the brink of responding in toxic ways.

"Hey," Rhea said. "I got almost all the signatures I need."

"Already?"

"Thanks to Lois. She's a wild woman. She called all her friends and they called their friends, bought wine and cheese, and organized sip-and-sign parties. She's got her forms ready to turn in any minute now. I should fill mine by tomorrow night and squeak in on the Monday deadline. I need nine more names and then another two dozen for insurance."

"Insurance?"

"In case someone who signs isn't a registered voter or there's another reason a name can't be counted. Lois says we need a lot of insurance because the incumbents will lean on the elections folks to nitpick every signature and try to keep us out of the race."

Rhea dug a mint from her pocket and crunched it to bits. "That's their job anyway—they're required to check the signatures—and I don't fault them for doing a thorough job, but I'll be biting my nails down to the knuckles until I get word that we're in the clear."

"And if you're not?"

"We'll run as write-in candidates." Rhea popped another mint into her mouth.

Kate thought back over her voting experience. Never had she written in the spaces for write-ins except once when, frustrated by candidates she felt lacked experience, intelligence, or any shred of common sense, she wrote in the name of a neighbor's dog. It had been an act of uncharacteristic spontaneity and pointlessness that later sparked conflicting feelings of remorse and liberation. "Do write-in candidates ever win?"

"They're long shots, but with Lois in the race, that's where I'd put my money."

"Me too." Kate gobbled the last bite of her cone. "The two of you will give a whole new meaning to 'business as usual' in this county. You'll rock Paul's little world."

CHAPTER 13

Late Sunday night the shrill of a phone yanked Kate from sleep. She sat up in a spill of moonlight, heart thudding, fingers clawing at the edges of the triangles forming a pattern of stars on the quilt.

"It's the rehab center phone," Jackson said. "Evie will get it in her room."

Kate fell back, her mind churning over midnight calls from months past. A deer hit along the highway. A young owl tangled in a volleyball net.

The ringing stopped. In a moment something clattered downstairs and Evie cursed, clumped up the stairs, and called out in a tense whisper, "Somebody broke into Rhea's house. She wants you over there."

Jackson switched on his lamp and hurled himself from bed. Snatching his jeans from a hook on the back of the door and scooping his running shoes from the floor, he pelted down the stairs behind Evie. Kate pulled on a T-shirt and a pair of shorts and went after him, snatching up a pair of flip-flops and detouring to the end of the hall to peer in at

139

Way-Ray. He was splayed out across the sheet, snuffling like a puppy. Until he was slept out, it was difficult to wake him. Tonight she was grateful for that.

Downstairs she found Evie standing by her desk, gripping the phone as if she might heave it at someone. "They're all okay. Except Mutant. He got his jaws into one of them and took a beating for it."

"One of them?" Kate asked.

"Rhea said there were two. They got in through the laundry room."

Jackson grunted. "Just a slide bolt on that door. And the doorjamb was cracked."

Kate wasn't surprised that he'd noticed and could recall details. Even when he seemed relaxed, Jackson was hyper-aware of his surroundings. It was as if he was always anticipating an attack—or at least the possibility of one.

"I'll stay with Way-Ray," Evie said. "I need my sleep. And he'll only be in the way."

"The same goes for us." Kate said when they were roaring toward Castaway Beach in Jackson's beat-up truck. "There's nothing we can do after the fact."

"Rhea wants us there for a reason," Jackson said. "Otherwise she would have let it go until morning. She's not the panicking kind. Neither is Jim."

True. Rhea was the poster child for level-headedness. So there could be more to this than hand-holding and commiseration over what had been stolen. Not that Rhea and Jim had much worth taking. Their TVs were several years old, the computer was a dinosaur, and her jewelry and her mother-in-law's together wouldn't bring more than a few hundred at the most generous pawn shop.

They pulled up in front of Rhea's place and parked behind one of the two police cars owned by the town of Castaway Beach. Light spilled from every window, defining the haphazard shape of the house. Kate thought it looked like it had been built by a dysfunctional committee or a child with a set of giant building blocks and instructions to use every one of them. The original house, a square two-story, sat on an acre at the south end of town. There was plenty of room to add on and Jim had done just that, building a garage and a carport, a deck, an office, a laundry/sewing/mud room, a master bedroom, an apartment for his mother, and an area for the boys with a spiral staircase winding up past bedrooms to a third-story hangout with windows on all sides.

The front door was open wide and Rhea hustled out wearing a pair of lime-green pajamas and bright blue bunny slippers with black button eyes and flopping ears. Her wiry hair, freed from its usual topknot, stuck out on one side like a pirate's black flag.

Kate ran to hug her. "How's Mutant?"

"Looks like he'll lose a couple of teeth at the least. Jim and the boys took him down to the vet's to get an X-ray." Rhea twisted a strand of hair and chewed on the end. "Poor guy. I'm kicking myself for bad-mouthing that stubborn mutt every day since we got him from the pound."

"No one can blame you for that," Kate said. "A dachshund-Labrador mix with jaws like a crocodile and an appetite like a black hole."

"Dog was a walking ad for spay and neuter," Jackson added.

141

"Yeah, he was all that, and as obedient as a tsunami, but he earned his keep tonight. He got a piece of one of them and ran them out before they got past the kitchen."

"What did they take?" Kate asked.

"I won't know for sure until Jim gets back and checks his office." Rhea peered over her shoulder and lowered her voice. "But I'm pretty sure all they took was the clipboard with my signature forms."

"Oh, no." Kate clutched her arm. "You were so close."

"I was more than close. I had all I needed, plus twice the insurance names I planned on. Got the last one about nine tonight."

"This is Paul's work," Jackson growled. "Gotta be."

"But as usual he lacked the balls to do it himself," Rhea said. "Kyle got to the window in time to recognize a couple of young thugs who didn't accumulate enough credits to make the trek across the stage when their class graduated in June."

Jackson's eyes narrowed. "They wouldn't be the same two who hang around the parking lot at that new motel begging for spare change?"

"That's them. But lately they've moved up from scrounging for coins to bullying for bills. I didn't tell Curtis that Kyle recognized them. Didn't tell him about the forms, either."

"Why not?" Kate asked.

"Because if he decides he's got enough evidence to go after them, odds are they'll see him coming and destroy the forms." Rhea laid a hand on Jackson's shoulder. "I want those pages back."

Jackson nodded as if the task was not only possible but easily accomplished.

Kate frowned. "What if they destroyed the forms already?"

"Then Lois and I scramble around and try to recreate the wheel before the office closes tomorrow afternoon. But I have a feeling that if Paul's the one behind this, he and his pals will want to see those pages—to see who signed for me."

So they can seek retribution.

Kate shivered and Jackson pulled her against his side, his muscles taut beneath the bare skin of his chest. "Paul will want deniability in case those kids are caught."

"Deniability?" Kate asked.

"Probably hired them over the phone using a phony name and arranged a drop. Left part of the money up front. Set a place for them to leave the forms."

He flexed his shoulders. "Does Kyle know where they live?"

Rhea shook her head. "He's got the good sense to keep a decent distance. But he heard they commandeered a tearer-downer behind that boarded-up antique store out south beyond the city limits sign."

Kate knew the place, one of many small houses without a decent foundation, its walls and roof sagging with rot courtesy of winter rains and lack of upkeep from a landlord waiting for property values to rise once again so he could sell the lot or bulldoze and rebuild. Inside, it would reek of mouse droppings and mildew, cat piss and dry rot.

"That's less than half a mile from here," Jackson said. "Did Kyle see a car?"

Rhea shook her head. "He didn't say."

"You hear one?"

143

"With Mutant yelping and the boys yelling and Jim cursing and his mother screaming herself hoarse? I'm lucky my eardrums aren't ruptured in so many places I could use them for tea strainers."

Kate grinned. Rhea's sense of humor was alive and well. Somehow that made her feel this would all work out.

"Has Curtis checked the yard?" Jackson asked.

"I doubt it. He's got his hands full trying to keep Jim's mother from cleaning up the kitchen before he photographs the blood spatter and gets fingerprints."

Jackson limped to the truck, pulled a flashlight from behind the seat, and went around the house. He returned in a few minutes with a wolfish smile, eyes shining. "Unless they parked a good distance away—and from what I've heard they don't have enough brain cells between them to do something that smart—they're on foot and one of them won't be moving too fast. Does Kyle have a ski mask?"

Kate blinked, but Rhea gave no sign that she found the question unusual. "The sports stuff's in the garage."

Jackson limped off once more and returned with a pair of bright yellow bib pants, a puffy pink jacket, and an orange ski mask. "Jim's not here, Kate, so you're it."

"It? What does that mean?"

He tossed his keys to her. "You drive the getaway truck."

"Don't break the speed limit or run any stop signs," Rhea said with a chuckle. "If you're pulled over, the fashion police will take him straight to jail."

144

Jackson scowled, jerked open the passenger door, and shoved the gear into the footwell. "You want your signature forms or not?"

"Who knew he was so sensitive?" Rhea gripped Kate's shoulder. "You be careful. Do what he says."

"*Exactly* what I say," Jackson added. "Without arguing."

Rolling her eyes, Kate climbed behind the wheel of the disreputable orange truck, slammed the door, clicked her seatbelt, and jammed the key into the ignition. The engine coughed and shuddered. No surprise. The truck was more eccentric than a mad scientist and as user-friendly as nuclear fallout.

Slick fabric swished as Jackson rammed his legs into the ski pants. "Stomp on the gas."

Kate pumped the pedal and twisted the key again. The engine roared, coughed, and roared again. She jammed the stick shift into reverse, crimped the wheels for the turn, and let out the clutch. The truck shuddered, jerked backward a full length, and stalled.

"Treat it like you're the boss." Jackson hunched into the pants and pulled the suspenders across his shoulders.

"It knows I'm not. It's a one-man truck and any grain of respect or loyalty it has is to you." Kate shifted into first, tromped the gas again, and twisted the key. The starter ground and then the engine caught. They lurched over the edge of the lawn and onto the road that led to the highway. "What's the plan? Drive up to the shack and ask them for the forms?"

"Nope." Jackson pulled on the pink jacket but couldn't zip it more than a few inches at the bottom. "Drive *into* the shack and fight them for the forms."

145

"You're kidding." Kate braked as they approached the highway. Nothing coming in either direction. Fearing the engine would die on her once again she skipped the legal full stop and pulled onto the blacktop. "Besides the fact that we'll be destroying someone's property, this truck's liable to disintegrate on impact. And besides *that*, everyone knows this mobile scrap heap belongs to you. So you might as well forget that mask and the rest of your ski-bunny disguise. Chief Lowell will be waiting at the house to arrest us when we get home."

"Only if these kids call him." Jackson rolled his shoulders and stretched his arms. The cuffs slid halfway to his elbows. "Which they won't, because that leads to questions about what they did to piss me off. These aren't winners of the Castaway Beach citizens-of-the-year awards."

Kate thought about that for a moment. "Okay. What's the plan?"

"Unless we spot them before we get there, you coast up to the old antique place and let me out, then count to twenty, come on down the road past the shack, then turn and hit it from the back. Brake just before you make contact so you have some control and don't go through the wall."

"Control. Sure thing. No problem."

"You'll manage." He pulled the ski mask down to his eyebrows. "Just don't start worrying about what-ifs and legalities. You can bet they didn't before they broke into Rhea's. Hit that shack square in the center of the rear wall."

"And you'll be . . . ?"

"Waiting for them at the front door. In this bad-taste disguise." He slid the ski mask over his face

146

and reached beneath the seat for a tire iron. "Carrying a little extra persuasion."

"What if they have guns?"

"If they had guns, Mutant would have more holes in him than a golf course."

"Maybe they have guns but they didn't take them to Rhea's," Kate argued. "Maybe Paul warned them not to."

"These aren't kids who take advice—not good advice, anyway." Jackson pointed through the windshield. "There's the antique store. Kill the lights. The moon's up. That's all you need."

Kate let off the gas and coasted to a stop. Her fingers felt like chunks of frozen metal and her heart fluttered without rhythm. She wondered if Jackson had ever felt fear or if, even before his military training, he had more nerve than she'd ever possess.

Jackson gripped her arm, turned her so her gaze met his in the gauzy light. "After you hit the wall, get loose as fast as you can, and get back to the highway. Put the truck across the road so they see it and think twice about running that way. Then give me a minute or two. No more than three. If you don't see me coming by then, get back to Rhea's."

"Without you?"

"Yes."

"But—"

"Don't argue. Follow the plan." Jackson leaned in, his lips brushing hers, the mask tickling her nose. "I'll get back. I always do."

Then he was out, stooping low, moving faster than she thought possible.

147

CHAPTER 14

Kate locked the doors and began to count. As she reached three, he disappeared into the shadows beside the former antique shop. From four to nineteen, she interspersed numbers with short whispered statements. "Jackson's right. This isn't legal, but it's justice."

At twenty, she fed gas and turned onto the dirt road that ran past the antique shop and shack before it continued across a field toward a tiny lake and a string of cottages at the foot of low hills climbing to the Coast Range. A barbed wire fence supporting a mass of blackberry canes leaned in on her left and the store hulked on her right. She passed it and then cruised by the shack. Light glimmered through cracks and knotholes in the walls, making it look like a huge rustic candle holder. She spotted a pale car with darker fenders parked in front of the door and reminded herself to block the highway.

Fifty feet farther on, well before the lake, she turned. The front wheels thudded into a shallow ditch and she pitched forward, the seatbelt biting into her breast. The rear wheels spun, then caught; the truck nosed up, and she was in the field arcing toward the shack, jolting over furrows, tires sliding on hummocks of grass, dry and slick.

Jackson hadn't said how fast she should be going when she hit the wall, but Kate figured ten miles an hour would be enough to shake the structure without crumpling the hood and shoving the engine into her lap. The truck was ancient and laced with rust, but it was huge, heavy.

She lined up with the center of the wall, gunned the engine, got the truck up to twenty, then braced her hands on the wheel, mashed the brake pedal, and rode the skid to her target.

The truck hit with a shriek of metal and a groan of rotting wood.

The wall shuddered, splintered, and caved inward.

Someone shouted.

The front wheels thudded against something hard—maybe a support beam.

The rear end bounced and slammed to earth again.

Another shout.

A scream.

Kate saw shifting beams of light and darting movement.

Then the engine convulsed.

She slapped the shift into reverse and hit the gas. "I'm in charge," she said through clenched teeth. "You *will not* die and leave me here."

The engine snarled and the truck jittered, tires spinning. Kate choked on acrid exhaust and dust. Then the bumper broke loose, dragging chunks of

149

broken board into the field. She backed up, jouncing across the furrows, realizing just before she hit the ditch that she should turn the truck around and come at it front on. She shifted into first and spun a doughnut and a half before rocketing across the shallow trench.

Moonlight glazed the dirt road and she caught a flicker of movement from the corner of her eye but didn't turn, didn't want to see Jackson beating or being beaten. Whichever it was, he would have a grim but satisfied smile. He was somehow more alive in kill-or-be-killed moments, filled with an emotion akin to joy.

Driven by the need to know he was still standing, she peered over her shoulder. Saw nothing.

At the highway she veered left and then swung hard to the right and braked, blocking the road beside the derelict store. She slipped the shift into neutral and waited, counting again. A hundred. A hundred and eighty.

Her right foot slid to the edge of the brake pedal, closer to the gas. Her left hovered above the clutch. Her fingers gripped the shift.

Jackson said three minutes. No more. He and Rhea told her to do what he said, exactly what he said.

That meant leaving now, leaving him.

But he would never abandon her.

She knew that in the same way she knew how to breathe. She knew that with the same certainty that she could find the North Star on a clear night. Jackson would never leave her.

And she hadn't *agreed* to follow his instructions. In fact, she rolled her eyes. That was like crossing her fingers behind her back.

In the sea of life where Jackson was a shark, she was a barnacle, stuck to the spot she claimed, difficult to dislodge.

Metal clattered in the bed of the truck.

Startled, Kate peered through the rear window of the cab, saw only the usual litter—bits of rope and wire, a frayed tarp, two bricks.

Something tapped the half-open window of the driver's door.

She yelped and twisted about.

A hand smacked the glass, leaving a dark smear.

Kate yelped again and trod on the gas. The engine shrieked. The truck didn't move.

"It's in neutral," Jackson said.

Kate unsnapped her seatbelt and opened the door with trembling hands. Dizzy, she slid over to the passenger side and put her head between her knees.

"I told you to leave after three minutes."

Jackson slammed the door, tossed the ski mask onto the floor, and slapped the shift into first. "I told you to follow the plan. I told you not to argue."

"I didn't argue." Kate raised her head and glared at him. "I just didn't leave."

Jackson growled and the truck churned gravel and roared onto the highway. They drove in silence, Kate watching him from the edges of her eyes. He should be glad she waited. The walk would have been torture on his bad leg and people might have seen him, seen the blood on that ridiculous puffy pink jacket and those screaming-yellow pants.

She rolled down her window the few inches it would go and sucked at the stream of cool night air, ignoring his anger.

When they made the turn onto the road to Rhea's house, Jackson chuckled. By the time they reached

151

her driveway he was howling with laughter, choking out words between each howl. "You didn't argue. You just didn't leave."

He stopped the truck behind Curtis's patrol car, killed the engine, and pounded on the wheel with the heels of his hands. "You didn't argue. You just didn't leave."

Kate folded her arms across her chest and glared.

Jackson blotted his eyes on the collar of the puffy jacket. "I'm glad you're on my team, Kate."

"Are we a team?" Kate asked, speaking low and fast. "Are we two people working together? Or are we a captain and a crew or a boss and an employee?"

He turned to face her, pulling off the pink jacket. "Yes, we're a team. But there are times when you need to—"

Rhea tapped on Kate's window. "Did you get them?"

"Like taking candy from a baby." Jackson slid a hand beneath the bib of the ski pants, pulled out a sheaf of papers, and passed it over.

Rhea riffled through the pages. "Yessss!" She did a little dance, the ears on her bunny slippers flopping to expose their pink undersides.

Kate unlocked her door and slid out as Curtis emerged from the house with a camera and what looked like an oversized tackle box. "Hey, Jackson. Hey, Kate. I heard Rhea call you. Thought you'd be here sooner."

Rhea stuffed the signature forms under her pajama top. "They had a flat tire."

"Probably a piece of metal from that wreck by the post office." Curtis came closer and squinted at the truck. "You ought to get some new tires. And that bumper's pushed out of shape. Looks like you might have hit something not long ago."

Kate swallowed, closed the door so Curtis wouldn't see the pink jacket or yellow pants, and bit her tongue. Jackson cleared his throat and opened his mouth. But it was Rhea who spoke. "More like he got hit *by* something," she said with a laugh. "Way-Ray and Sean were jumping on the bumper the other day to make the suspension rock."

"Kids." Curtis shook his head. "Well, if you back that truck up a little, Jackson, I'll head to the office and process the evidence and get started on my report. Rhea, your mother-in-law went to bed. She said to tell you she got the house back in order."

"Thanks for everything, Curtis." Rhea drew Kate toward the house. "Back in order, my foot. That's code for she did all the work. My idea of getting the house back in order would be moving her out of it."

Kate giggled, a manic sound, too high pitched, screechy. She slapped a hand over her mouth.

"Sounds like you're a little shell-shocked," Rhea said. "Let's have a cup of tea and something filled with fat and sugar. I want to hear everything."

"I can tell my part in ten seconds. I drove the truck into the back wall of the shack and then I drove it to the road and waited."

"That explains the condition of the bumper. You're lucky those tires didn't blow out and strand you. I've seen more tread on a snail's belly."

Rhea led Kate through a living room filled with soft chairs sporting wide wooden arms, a sofa long enough to nap on, a fireplace with a broad stone hearth, and a couple of lamps that said they were in the business of throwing light not winning the approval of a decorator.

In the kitchen, Rhea hooked a spindleback chair with her foot and swung it away from the table. "Sit."

Kate sat and watched while Rhea filled a kettle and pulled a box of chocolate covered cookies from the closet. She shook the box and shrugged. "Down to just crumbs. But never fear."

Finger to her lips, she opened the drawer beneath the oven, lifted the lid from a cast-iron frying pan stored there, and came up with a sack of malted milk balls and another of caramel-pecan rolls. When Jackson limped through the door a few minutes later, Kate's teeth were gummed with caramel and Rhea was pouring steaming water onto teabags in a trio of mugs.

"Ski gear's out back under the deck," Jackson said. "You'll need to wash it soon."

"In cold water, I presume. After pre-treating for stains."

Jackson pulled out a chair and dropped into it. "Couldn't be helped."

"I didn't expect any different." Rhea set the mugs on the table. "I was thinkin' while you were out there, what if Paul—and I bet my sagging butt he's the man behind this—refuses to give them the rest of the money he promised because they didn't hang onto the forms?"

"Same thought I had." Jackson dunked his teabag.

Kate poured milk into her mug. "That would set up a second act to this drama."

"Exactly." Rhea grinned and popped a malt ball into her mouth, then leveled a finger at Jackson. "I hope you left them able to walk and talk and throw a punch."

154

"Mutant probably hurt them worse than I did. They might have a few loose teeth and there will be at least one black eye between them, but most of what I damaged was their pride."

He shot them his wolfish grin. "And there's nothing like the ache of injured pride to make a man try to even a score."

CHAPTER 15

Two days later, Rhea called, her voice filled with excitement and delight. "I asked Maureen over at the hospital to keep her eyes and ears open and, sure enough, Paul's in the emergency room right now being treated for abrasions, contusions, lacerations and a host of other injuries ending in I-O-N-S."

Kate wanted to shout the news to Jackson, but Way-Ray was still at the breakfast table, smacking floating bits of cereal into a lake of milk with his spoon, fighting an imaginary battle complete with explosive mouth sounds and an occasional evil laugh or a "Take that, you."

Touching Jackson's arm, she mouthed, "Rhea."

Jackson set his coffee mug down and ambled around behind Way-Ray to the sink. As she joined him, Kate tilted the phone and asked, "What happened?"

"He said the paperboy missed the porch. When he tried to fish the newspaper out of the rock garden, he lost his balance and tumbled down the slope."

"But the—"

"I know! The paper doesn't come out until tomorrow. And Maureen says Paul's pajamas were covered with prints from two different types of shoes. And he had thumb and finger bruises on his arms."

"Those punks found him," Jackson said.

"Gotta be them," Rhea cackled. "Because if Paul fell reaching for the paper, you can bet he would have stopped off to see his attorney about suing the paperboy before he went to the hospital."

Kate chuckled, felt a spike of guilt, and asked, "How serious is it?"

"Well, he's in a lot of pain and he's got a concussion. They'll probably keep him overnight."

"Smart move," Jackson said, "given that tendency to sue you mentioned."

"Yeah. Well, I'll leave it to you to tell Evie. And, hey, I turned in my signatures with three witnesses watching and another making a video recording in case some of those pages wander off and someone claims I never had them in the first place. Looks like I'm on the ballot."

Jackson did a fist-pump.

"Congratulations," Kate said. "We'll give Evie the news."

"The news about what?" Way-Ray turned from his cereal-bowl battle.

"Rhea has enough signatures to be on the ballot." Kate returned the phone to its cradle. "If you're not going to eat the rest of that, put it out for the geese."

"Aye aye, Admiral." Way-Ray snapped off a salute, picked up his bowl and dashed off.

"Admiral?" Kate stuffed his spoon and glass in the dishwasher. "Yesterday I was a captain."

"Looks like he gave you a promotion."

"If I'm an admiral now, what are you?"

"Well, I was a major. But it looks like we've switched to naval ranks so I'm probably the fleet admiral."

Kate grabbed a sponge and wiped down the counter. "So you still outrank me?"

Jackson closed Way-Ray's cereal box and returned it to the pantry. "Yeah, but a lot of good that does since you never follow orders."

"I don't like that word—orders." She turned to face him, the sponge clutched so tight water dripped on her sandals. "And I don't like the idea of someone giving me orders just because that person is a man or thinks he outranks me. But that doesn't mean that I won't follow orders when—"

"When you want to?"

"No!" Kate threw the sponge in the sink. "When they make sense!"

"To you." Jackson rolled his eyes.

"Yes. I'm not going to blindly follow a command. You know as well as I do that history is littered with tragic incidents where people did just that."

"Yes, but . . . Ah, the hell with it." Jackson closed the pantry door. "We're never going to resolve this. We'll be white-haired and toothless and—"

"You'll still be ordering me to go off and leave you to limp home—if you can get that far before your spine snaps and you have to pull yourself along on your belly."

She turned and put the lid on the sugar bowl, hating herself for being a nag, hating him for not taking better care of his wounded body. "Never mind. Just never mind."

158

He slid his arms around her, pulled her against his chest, and nuzzled her neck. "I'm glad you didn't drive off and leave me. But next time you decide to ignore my . . . plan, I want you to remember that if I'm worried because you're in danger, I can't focus like I need to. Can you do that much?"

Kate relaxed against him, wanting to agree. Then she pulled away, needing to make clear what she was agreeing to. She was a ranking officer on this team, not a raw recruit. "I promise to consider that if *you* promise to consider that if I'm worried about you or Way-Ray, then I might put fear for my own safety aside."

She turned to face him, rubbing her nose against the point of his chin, inhaling the sweet and sharp scent of shaving lotion. "Maybe instead of telling me to leave in three minutes, you could have told me to wait three minutes and then move a little farther up the highway. Or you could have told me to cruise back and forth so I'd be a moving target if they tried to get me but in the neighborhood if you needed me."

He chuckled and kissed the tip of her nose. "Hindsight is great, isn't it? Think of all the things that would be different, all the time you wouldn't waste crying over spilled milk, if we could rewind and edit the past."

Kate cupped his face in her hands. "I would never edit out the part where I met you."

"I seem to remember you thought I was a tramp at first. And when you found out I worked for you, you wanted to fire me."

"But I learned the futility of that." She drew his head down and kissed him. "So I took a more creative approach to motivating you."

159

"A vast improvement over unemployment." Jackson ran his hands down her back and kissed her eyelids. "Too bad we can't do this all day, but someone has to tell Evie about Paul. Want to flip a coin?"

"No, I'll do it. You and Way-Ray need to pick up Sean and then go get a load of fish before there's a rebellion in the pelican enclosure."

"There's just a short list of what I'm frightened of, Admiral, but plotting pelicans is right at the top." He pivoted on his good leg. "I'll round up the young seaman and we'll take my battleship into town."

Kate stood for a moment on the porch watching the geese scatter ahead of him as he swung his bad leg in a rocking gait, then walked out to the hospital trailer. Dawdling, she paused to watch a squirrel nibble a bud and again to listen to two crows complain to each other from the tops of neighboring trees.

She'd volunteered to tell Evie not because Jackson had chores to do, but because she felt guilty—a continuous state of being fostered by parents who somehow transformed gratitude for what they had into penitent self-condemnation for the same thing. When she took biology in high school, Kate decided that accepting blame and feeling shame were like other attributes passed down from her parents—the shape of her face, the color of her eyes, the length of her fingers and toes. Being aware of it reduced the symptoms of this "inherited disorder," but didn't cure the disease. By being aware of guilt, however, she could work to contain its emotional impact and try to factor it—or most of it—out of her decision-making process.

160

She wasn't glad that Paul had been beaten and was in pain, but the assault erased any doubt he was behind the theft of Rhea's election forms. And it balanced the scales of justice. After all, he intended that Rhea suffer an enormous setback. And, in selecting the punks who carried out his plan, he had to realize there might be violence.

Mutant, who bore the brunt of the initial violence, would recover from his cracked ribs and get by without the three teeth he lost. And in all probability Paul would recover from his physical injuries, too.

But what about the blows to his ego? Would the beating he received tip the scales toward more violent efforts to thwart Evie's plans?

And what about the sharks? How would the men with big money react to Paul's failure?

Kate paused at the concrete blocks that served as steps to the hospital trailer. What if the sharks were behind the beating and the young punks merely the muscle? Perhaps the assault was both retribution and warning—notice that Paul needed to get smarter and tougher if he intended to swim in the same waters.

And what if Paul decided to back away? Could he? Or was their hook set too deep?

Kate reached for the door handle. Jackson, more cynical and more accustomed to strike-and-counter-strike strategy, must have thought of this already, perhaps realized it even as Rhea passed along the news about Paul's injuries. Was that why he'd raised the issue of following orders again?

She opened the "new" door to the trailer—a door Jackson had scavenged from the throwaway pile at a construction site. It wasn't warped like the previous one, didn't stick in the frame or screech

161

out a complaint when she opened it. In a strange way, Kate missed that, although she had to admit the silent door didn't goad Evie's patients into frenzy like the old one had.

A sandpiper with a single eye peered through the bars of a cage as she crossed what she referred to as "the ward," and a Greater Scaup retreated to the rear of its cage. Evie stood beside a metal table holding a bird that to Kate's untrained eye looked like a gull.

"Northern Fulmar," Evie said. "Don't see them often near shore. They can fight like wildcats when they're healthy, but this one's weak as a newborn chick."

The bird watched Evie with dull eyes as she offered a sliver of fish. "Do you think he knows that you're trying to help?" Kate asked.

"Sure. And he's hoping I put him in a five-star cage and give him sparkling French water and sushi." Evie's prickly tone implied Kate's question was ludicrous.

Despite a year of working with her, Kate sometimes felt off balance with Evie, still felt the need to defend or explain herself. She chewed at her lower lip and kept silent.

"I hope he *doesn't* know I'm trying to help," Evie said after a moment. "Because there's not a damn thing I can do if he's stuffed with plastic."

Kate closed her eyes, holding back tears for this tiny life fading away because of the dross of progress. Each month they saw more and more birds starving because they scooped up plastic scraps in the search for food. Not only did plastic bits clog digestive systems, but they delivered a concentrated dose of toxins absorbed from the

162

ocean. Way-Ray, researching a project for school, read her a report about a bird with more than 450 pieces of plastic in its belly.

Evie opened a cage and set the bird on a folded towel inside. It tottered to the back of the cage and Evie closed the door and turned to face Kate. "If you walked all the way out here with good news you would have blurted it out by now, so I assume it's the opposite."

Starting with Rhea's success in an attempt to soft-pedal Paul's situation was pointless, so Kate left that for later. "Paul's in the hospital. He's got a concussion and cuts and bruises."

Evie went white around the eyes. "Will he be okay?"

"Maureen thinks so, but they'll keep him for observation."

Evie glanced upward, then closed her eyes for a second. "What happened?"

Careful to keep her tone neutral and without inflection, Kate said, "He told the nurse he went out to get his paper, fell into his rock garden, and tumbled down the slope."

"Paper doesn't come out until tomorrow."

Kate said nothing.

"This has to do with those boys who took Rhea's election forms, doesn't it?"

"That's possible."

"Hmmph. Probable is more likely." Snatching up a bottle of disinfectant solution, Evie sprayed the table and wiped furiously with a handful of paper towels. "He stepped in a hornets' nest. Never mind that he's acquainted with those hornets and should have steered clear."

163

She threw the towels at a wastebasket, missed, cursed, and kicked the basket. "He's my son. And he's hurt. I have to go."

She pointed at Kate as if she held a gun, her hand shaking. "He's my son. No matter what he did, he's hurt. I have to go."

"I know."

"You don't know anything." Evie pushed past her and out the door. "You don't have children."

"I have Way-Ray," Kate whispered when Evie was gone. "I'm raising an orphaned boy because I killed his father. Don't tell me I don't know about pain and guilt and regret."

Evie returned a few hours later, slumping into the kitchen, her feet dragging. Watching from the edges of her eyes, Kate shuffled papers at her desk and cast about for something to say that didn't convey assumption or judgment, didn't contain even a milligram of pity, and wasn't an obvious effort to snag information. She settled on an observation about the weather. "They say there's marine air coming in tomorrow afternoon."

"Can't be soon enough for me."

Evie poured lemonade, sat at the table, and kicked off a pair of woven leather sandals worn thin at the heels. She drank down half the lemonade and fanned herself with a newspaper Jackson had folded to display the crossword puzzle. "If I hit the lottery, I'll get air conditioning in my truck and this house. There's only two or three weeks in the year we need it, but when we do . . ."

Kate let that hang, hoping Evie would fill the silence.

Evie fanned faster, finished her lemonade, and tapped the glass on the table. "Where's Jackson?"

"Sharpening the post-hole digger. Hopefully in the shade."

"And where's Way-Ray?"

"He and Sean are out at the edge of the woods working on their camouflage and practicing keeping still for more than a minute at a time."

"That'll be the day."

Kate shuffled more paper, waiting. Evie didn't hang onto her dark moods for long. She got past them in a few hours and got on with life, sometimes with an announcement or apology, but usually without. That was fine. What Kate needed was a clue about where things stood between them.

Evie trudged to the refrigerator and filled her glass with ice. "I can be a touchy old woman, can't I?"

Kate felt herself slump with relief. The storm had passed. "That's a loaded question if I ever heard one. If I say 'no,' you'll call me a liar and if I say 'yes' you might call me worse."

Evie laughed. "I've done both, haven't I?"

Kate raised her eyebrows and in a moment Evie laughed again. "How did I get along without you?" She gestured at the stacks of paper on the desk. "And I don't mean that crap. I mean, how did I survive living out here by myself getting as crusty as week-old bread?"

"Yet another loaded question," Kate said with a smile.

"That's just what I mean. You keep me honest about myself." Evie went back to her chair. "Although most of the time that's not an enjoyable

165

experience. It's like having surgery without anesthetic."

She sipped lemonade, her gaze sliding away from Kate's. "Speaking of surgery, the doctors say Paul won't need any. There's no bleeding on his brain."

"That's good news. How's he feeling?"

Evie dropped her head and ran a finger around the rim of her glass. "He wouldn't talk to me except to say what happened was my fault for standing in the way of progress."

The words lit a fuse in Kate's brain, but she gripped the edge of the chair and kept her expression bland. To side against Paul right now might lead to words that couldn't be laughed about later.

"He said if I had the sense God gave a grapefruit I'd sell this place and stop wasting my time cleaning up bird shit."

Kate decided to go with the conversational flow and try to gauge Evie's emotions and intentions. "Well, that *is* about the worst part of the job."

"But it's not the *whole* job." Evie tapped her glass on the table. "And what the hell would I do if I wasn't doing this? Sit and rock on the porch of a home for old ladies?"

"You'd last about ten minutes."

"That's five more than the old ladies rocking with me would. I'm not known far and wide as good company—for human beings that is." She glanced around the kitchen. "That's probably reason number one to keep this place going, don't you think?"

"I think it's your place, Evie," Kate said in a quiet voice. "You shouldn't consider anybody but yourself when you make a decision about what to do with it."

166

"Paul's scared." Evie peered into her glass, rattled ice cubes, sipped, rattled again. "He's got his tail deep in a crack, doesn't he?"

CHAPTER 16

"What did you say when Evie said that?" Rhea asked later that afternoon.

Kate leaned in her usual place at the end of the display case. Kyle, using a broom to herd sand tracked in from the beach and bits of paper peeled from cones, kept peering at her from beneath a thick tumble of hair. At his insistence, she was nibbling on his latest experiment, a concoction of chocolate chunks, roasted hazelnuts, and toffee brickle mixed into rich vanilla ice cream and stuffed in a waffle cone. She shot him a thumbs-up, took a larger bite, and mumbled around it. "I told her I didn't know."

"Pwah." Rhea blew air between her lips. "Paul's tail is so far down in the crack he can't see daylight. He made promises he can't keep and pissed off some heavy hitters with less sense of humor than scorpions."

"Or so we assume. Maybe the theft scheme was all his idea."

"And maybe I'm going to cook a nutritious dinner tonight instead of hauling home another pizza." Rhea rolled her eyes. "Paul's no dummy. He figures all the angles before he makes a move and he hates taking risks like I hate finding gray hairs." She patted her topknot. "I'll bet my last pack of mints he did it to prove himself to the big-money men."

"Maybe. But given the way Evie's been blowing hot and cold about him, I'm not about to tell her anything that isn't objective fact—with annotated footnotes. And even then—"

The door banged open and two preteen boys charged in waving their arms. "Kyle! You gotta see what's going on down at the beach. There's people wearing bird suits and jumping in front of cars and yelling!"

Kyle dropped the broom. "Cool." He pulled a video recorder from the pocket of his cargo shorts and started after the boys. "Watch the store, Mom. I gotta make a video."

"Don't get run over," Rhea called after him. "And if Curtis shows up, stay out of his way. And if he tells you to get back, you jump to it before he's done speaking and don't give him any lip."

Kyle's voice floated back to them. "Yeah, yeah, blah, blah, blah."

"Don't blah-blah me, young man, or you'll be paying rent."

The door banged closed, scattering the pile of debris beside Kyle's fallen broom. "You can't get good helpers anymore, even when you give birth to them." Rhea nodded toward the beach. "You think it's those kids who came out to Evie's place?"

"Abel and Cassie? I can't imagine who else." Kate glanced at her watch, then plucked an extra napkin from the dispenser on top of the display case. "I'll check it out."

"The same advice I gave Kyle goes for you." Rhea dug a mint from her pocket. "It's almost low tide and the only breeze to be had is down by the water. That beach will be crawling with kids and cars."

"I'll be careful." Kate wrapped the napkin around the base of her cone and, nibbling as she went, followed a chipped and pitted concrete sidewalk to a narrow street that led to a public parking lot and access to the beach. The lot was packed with cars and trucks and travel trailers festooned with lawn chairs and bicycles. A thin layer of sand covered the lot, obscuring the white lines painted on the black surface. That sand did little to insulate against the heat and she could almost feel her flip-flops melting. Picking up the pace, she ran the last few yards across the dune on a tongue of asphalt that stretched to meet the slope of the beach and a rough road of rock and gravel packed into soft sand.

A horn blasted off to her left and a deep voice shouted words Kate hoped Way-Ray never learned. She shaded her eyes with her hand and peered along the beach. A truck with oversized tires crept toward five people wearing rubber beaks and masks and flapping the enormous sleeves of shirts painted with feathers. The protesters held picket signs and were spread out with a yard or so between them, forming a barrier in the packed sand between lapping waves and the tumbled heaps of kelp and broken crab shells that marked the ocean's retreat from high tide.

Kyle, camera to his eye, stood knee-deep in the surf between the truck and the protesters. A pack of kids cavorted behind the protesters, cawing and cackling and hooting.

A siren whooped behind her and Kate leaped from the road and spun to see Curtis behind the wheel of his cruiser. His eyes were narrowed, but his lips turned up in a smile.

No surprise there. A protest might bring the media and Curtis loved seeing his name in print or his image on the TV news.

Kate chewed the last bit of her cone, tucked the napkin in her pocket, and hustled along in the wake of the cruiser as the shouts of protesters grew more distinct. Shading her eyes again, she made out the words on their signs. "Birds die when fools drive! Ban beach driving! Wild birds not wild parties."

The truck's brake lights flared, then went out. Driver and passenger leaped from the vehicle and advanced on the protesters. They were burly young men dressed in jeans and T-shirts with ball caps pulled low over their eyes. Arms out at their sides, fists clenched, they strode to within two yards of a protester wearing a broad yellow bill and shirt with feathers painted brown and gray and teal. The protester didn't give ground, but turned his picket sign so the stick pointed at the men like a lance.

Curtis whooped his siren and pulled up beside the truck.

The cavorting kids went into a huddle for a few seconds and broke out of it with a chant: "Curtis, Curtis, he's our man. If he can't arrest them no one can."

The strip of Curtis' neck between his collar and his crew cut glowed cherry red as he walked toward the confrontation. How much of that, Kate wondered, was due to self-conscious embarrassment and how much to pride or his awareness of Kyle and the camera. He halted and hitched at his broad belt. "What's going on here?"

The truck's passenger spoke over his shoulder. "These fools are blocking our way. We were just about to move them aside."

"Well, I'm here now and I'll take care of that," Curtis said. "You can get back in your truck."

"I'm staying right here until they give way," the driver said.

Curtis hitched his belt again. "Sir, you need—"

"Get back in your truck, bird killer," a protester dressed like a gull snarled.

The kids behind him took up the cry. "Bird killer. Bird killer!"

Curtis said something but it was lost in a cacophony of sound. The truck driver raised a fist. The duck-billed protester held the picket sign like a shield. Curtis hustled to get between them, but not fast enough. The driver threw a punch. The protester parried with his sign. The driver punched again, trying to work around Curtis, his fist glancing off the picket.

Meanwhile, the truck's passenger lowered his head, stretched his arms out, and ran at two smaller protesters, carrying them with him into the surf. The two remaining protesters plunged into the water to help their friends. The chanting kids screamed and scampered up the beach to safety.

The duck-billed protester took a step to the side. The driver did the same and threw a third punch, spinning with it.

His fist slammed into Curtis' neck.

Curtis staggered backward, mouth gaping, eyes flaring.

"Oh shit." The driver's eyes widened.

"You're going to jail," the duck-billed protester yelled.

"And you're going to the morgue." The driver leaped at him and bore him to the sand.

Hands clawing at his collar, Curtis dropped to his knees, his lips moving like those of a fish jerked from the water.

Kate darted to his side. "Lie on your back and tip your head."

She pointed at Kyle. "Call 911. Tell them we need an ambulance. Then call for Chief Lowell. Now!"

Kyle dug for his phone and Kate knelt beside Curtis, unbuttoning his collar, then sliding one hand under the back of his neck and lifting gently to open his windpipe. "Don't try to talk. Blink your eyes if you can breathe even a little."

Curtis' eyelids fluttered, then closed and opened again. Kate bent close and heard a wheeze of air through his lips. "You'll be okay. Try to stay calm."

Curtis cut his gaze toward his right and Kate saw the driver and the duck-billed protester locked together, rolling along the beach. Beyond them, a jumble of arms and legs and heads eddied in the surf.

"The ambulance is on the way." Kyle raised the camera and moved in for a closer shot of the fight on the sand. "So's Chief Lowell."

The driver landed a final punch, got to his feet, kicked the protester in the ribs twice, and ran for his truck.

"License plate," Curtis wheezed.

"Got it." Kate wrote the letters and numbers in the damp sand beside Curtis. "Feeling better?"

Curtis squeezed her hand. "Feeling stupid."

173

Kate smiled. "Don't beat up on yourself. You were just in the wrong place at the wrong time. That's what I'll tell the chief."

CHAPTER 17

"Wow." Way-Ray gaped, a brown smush of hamburger and bun thick on his tongue and teeth. "We shoulda gone to town with you. We missed all the fun stuff."

"Fun stuff?" Evie stabbed at her salad with her fork. "A punch to the throat can close off your windpipe. Curtis could have died."

"But he didn't." Sean stuffed a trio of French fries into his mouth. "Kate saved him."

Kate shook her head. "He didn't need a lot of saving. All I did was get him to relax and breathe."

"And those kids in the surf." Evie waved off Kate's protest and glowered at the boys. "That wasn't fun stuff either. They could have drowned."

"Kate would have saved them, too," Sean said with the certainty only kids possess.

"You're a legend in your own time," Jackson told her with a grin. "Now what you need is a cape and a pair of thigh-high boots. And tight shorts and a tank top cut down to . . ."

"To where?" Way-Ray asked.

175

"To none of your business." Evie turned her glower on Jackson and dropped her voice to a whisper. "Save that for upstairs and later."

"My idea exactly." Jackson chuckled and winked at Kate. "So the chief sorted things out?"

Aware her cheeks were bright with embarrassment, Kate focused on stabbing her fork into a spear of broccoli and dipping it in a puddle of blue cheese dressing in the center of her plate. "He did, thanks to the help of a couple of firefighters who came along behind the ambulance. He arrested Abel and the truck passenger and he's out looking for the driver."

"I bet Curtis puts him in jail for a hundred years," Sean said.

"A thousand," Way-Ray agreed.

"And he has to eat liver every day."

"And beets."

"And cereal without any sugar."

"That's the ultimate punishment, all right," Jackson agreed. "But what happens to him won't be up to Curtis."

"Why not?" Way-Ray asked. "Curtis is the one who got punched."

"Right. And he's hurt and mad and embarrassed and he wants to get even and then some. That's why he doesn't get to decide on the punishment."

"That's stupid." Way-Ray bit off another mouthful of burger and mumbled around it. "Who does?"

"Someone who's impartial," Kate said.

"Im-what-chal?"

"Impartial," Jackson said. "It comes from Latin. It means somebody who wasn't involved and doesn't have an interest in how things turn out."

Way-Ray and Sean looked at each other, shrugged, and rolled their eyes.

"Oh for the love of a limping loon," Evie said. "A judge, you goofy boys. A judge will decide what happens to him."

Sean picked up a spoon and pounded it on the table. "Like those guys on TV with the black bathrobes and the wooden hammers?"

"Gavels," Kate said. "They're called gavels."

"No way." Sean shook his head. "Everybody knows gravels are rocks."

"Rocks!" Way-Ray exploded with laughter, blowing burger bits at Sean who retaliated by spewing French fry shrapnel back at him.

Evie scraped back her chair, snatched her plate, and carried it to the counter. "For the life of me I don't understand why every conversation has to disintegrate into a second-rate comedy show or a food fight."

When Sean and Way-Ray laughed harder, she glowered at Jackson and Kate. "Sometimes I wish I was living here by myself again." She stomped out to the porch, calling over her shoulder. "Sometimes I think I should check into that home for old ladies where I could have some peace and quiet and eat a meal without a circus going on around me."

The screen door slapped shut behind her and in a moment the glider swing out under the trees set up a steady pulsing squeak.

Way-Ray and Sean gawked, their eyes wide. "She's pissed," Sean whispered. "At us."

"Nuh-uh," Way-Ray said. "She didn't hardly eat any of her dinner. She's acting like she's pissed at everybody. At the whole world."

177

Jackson shot Kate a "you handle it" look and took a huge bite of his burger. She'd told him about Evie's visit to Paul in the hospital, but Way-Ray and Sean wouldn't understand the complexities of that relationship.

"Evie's hot and tired," Kate said. "She's had a long day and she's worn out. She'll feel better after the weather cools down."

"She shoulda ate her dinner," Sean said. "Mom says food makes you feel better. So does taking a nap."

"That's true. But sometimes people are too upset to eat. Or sleep."

"Yeah," Way-Ray said. "And if you eat when you're mad you might puke."

"Hurl big time," Sean agreed, starting to giggle.

"Or call Ralph." Way-Ray demonstrated, bending forward and cupping his hands around his mouth. "Rrraaalllppphhh."

"Or barf," Sean contributed. "Woof your cookies."

"Blow chunks."

"Enough." Kate thumped her fist on the table.

The boys went silent, gawking again.

"This is exactly what Evie means. This is why she lost her appetite and left the table."

Way-Ray jabbed the remains of his burger with his forefinger. "But we're funny."

"Funny to yourselves," Jackson agreed. "To the rest of us, not so much."

"And there's a time and a place for funny," Kate said. "As a matter of fact, didn't your teacher mention that you needed to work on figuring that out over the summer? Wasn't she concerned that other teachers might not be as understanding and tolerant when you disrupt their classes next year?"

"I guess." Way-Ray ducked his head and turned his attention to the pile of French fries on his plate, using his forefinger like a jackhammer to break them into bits.

"Well, maybe this would be a good time for you to work on that." Kate speared a slice of cucumber and dipped it in her dressing. "You and Sean can make a list of times and places when it's okay to be funny and another list of times and places when you should be a little more . . . contained."

"Contained? Like in a cage?"

"Or a jar?" Sean piped up. "Like those bugs we caught."

Kate aimed the cucumber slice at Jackson. "You take it from here. And don't tell us that contained comes from Latin."

"Well, it prob—"

Kate slapped her free hand on the table. "I don't care if it comes from Swahili or Icelandic or Navajo or from whatever language they speak on Mars."

"Got it." Jackson snapped off a salute and turned to Way-Ray and Sean. "If you contain something you hold it in. That's what Kate wants you to learn to do. It's just like learning about camouflage and being still. You don't have to do it all the time, just when it's necessary."

Sean crossed his arms and pouted, but Way-Ray stopped poking his fries and wrinkled his nose. "When is it necessary? When Kate or you or Evie or my teacher says so?"

"Yes, and other times too."

Sean's pouting lower lip protruded farther. He picked up his fork and balanced it there, crossing his eyes. Way-Ray started to giggle.

179

"Times like right now," Jackson said in a steely voice. "Times when you're supposed to be listening and thinking instead of acting like a couple of mindless fools."

He edged his chair around so he was facing Kate and lowered his voice. "Between you and me, those two better hope they make it as comedians because they'd never cut as firefighters or in law enforcement or the military. They'll last about two minutes in boot camp before they're on their knees cleaning latrines with toothbrushes while a sergeant calls them maggots and screams at them to scrub harder."

Sean and Way-Ray peered at each other from the edges of their eyes. "What're latrines?" Sean whispered. Way-Ray shrugged.

"That's a shame." Kate pretended to ignore the boys and forked up the last cherry tomato. "I know how hard they've been working on their camouflage skills. Way-Ray's even making a ghillie suit. But you're right, not everyone has the ability to concentrate and focus."

"What're latrines?" Sean whispered again.

Kate put her napkin to her lips, smothering a giggle. Jackson's eyes sparkled and his shoulders twitched as if he had hiccups.

"Probably something Latin," Way-Ray whispered back. "But I don't wanta ask 'cause Jackson might tell us and then Kate might have a cow." He pushed back his chair and tiptoed toward the living room. "There's a dictionary on the bookshelf. We better look it up."

Sean followed on his heels. "Then maybe we better clean up your room. At least the dirty dishes so you don't get ants."

"Good thinkin'. Then we can practice containing ourselves."

When they were out of sight, Kate released her laughter, muffling it with the napkin. Jackson rocked in his chair and pounded a fist on the table. "That's the hardest part of trying to discipline a child," he said after a moment, "keeping a straight face."

"Not that we do a good job of that." Kate wiped her eyes.

"Well, we're new at it."

"Not that new. It's been a year."

"Best year of my life." He ran his fingertips down her arm.

Kate shivered. "Mine, too."

Jackson leaned in to kiss her. Wheels crunched on gravel and a horn let out three quick blasts, touching off a frenzied honking from the geese.

Kate checked the clock on the wall. "Rhea's early."

"If that's Rhea, she got a new muffler and brake pads *and* changed her mind about leaving Sean with us tonight." Jackson brushed his lips against hers. "Let's take this up again later. I'll leave it to you to remember where we were."

"If I forget, will you start from the beginning?"

"I've never known you to forget anything. But starting from the beginning works for me."

Two car doors slammed and a deep voice boomed, "Evening, Evie. Hot enough for you?"

Jackson snorted and stood. "Bert Connors, bank manager, head of the chamber of commerce, and cliché king. He's a buddy of Paul's and I'll give you just one guess which side of the golf course development plan he's on."

181

"Evening, Bert," Evie said. "Evening, Sandi. Grab a seat in the shade."

Kate got to her feet, looking to Jackson for context.

"Sandi Evans. Sandi with an "i." Probably drew a little heart over it when she was in high school. She owns the beauty salon stuck in between those two antique shops down from the ice cream parlor. Pink door. Christmas lights in the window."

"Ah." Kate ran her fingers through her shoulder-length chestnut hair. The last time she got a trim was when she took Way-Ray to the barbershop at the end of May; she hadn't been to a salon for years.

Jackson smiled and tucked a strand behind her ear. "Don't let Sandi get her hands on your hair. I like it just the way it is—not teased and tortured and sprayed with some substance the EPA should have banned decades ago, not dyed or curled or primped or—"

"You better quit before you say washed or combed."

Jackson put a hand over his heart. "Do you think I'm that crass and insensitive?"

"Can I get back to you on that?"

Outside a lawn chair gave a metallic groan and another creaked. "What brings you two out this way?" Evie asked. "Come to make a donation? Or do a little volunteer work?"

"I'd love to lend you a hand, Evie," Bert said. "But the bank keeps me hopping and there are only so many hours in a day."

"Bert likes to spend most of those hours in a cushioned chair in an air-conditioned room." Jackson headed for the door. "Let's see why they're so far from civilization as they know it."

182

Kate hung back, gathering plates from the table. "It sounds like they came to see Evie. We shouldn't get in her space—not right now."

Jackson paused in the doorway.

"Well, Evie." Bert cleared his throat, a sound that reminded Kate of a lovesick bullfrog. "No point in beating around the bush or sitting out here sweating through a lot of small talk. We came about those kids protesting on the beach."

Kate set the stack of dishes on the counter and joined Jackson who was staring across the porch in the opposite direction from the lawn chairs clustered beneath the trees. He pointed to a huge polished brass flowerpot on a stand in the corner. Kate squinted and, between the cascading blooms of a red geranium, spotted a miniature convex reflection of Evie and her visitors. Feeling a fleeting guilt about eavesdropping, she told herself Evie knew they'd heard the car horn and didn't expect they'd plug their ears and close their eyes.

"We want you to talk with those kids," Sandi added. "They might listen to you. Explain that it's legal to drive on the sand. Tell them it's a tourist draw and most drivers are responsible."

"Already did," Evie snapped. "They didn't want to hear a bit of it. Told me the law was crap and they intended to speed up the process of change."

Jackson leaned against the doorjamb, putting his weight on his good leg.

"Of course you told them you were opposed to any rash action," Bert said, his sarcasm as heavy as the day's humidity.

"Didn't get a chance." The tiny reflection of Evie shifted, got to its feet. "And if you're implying that I drew up the operations manual for their protest,

183

Bert, then grow some balls and come right out and accuse me."

"Now, Evie," Sandi said, "Bert didn't say—"

"I know damn well what he *didn't* say. Bert Connors has been talking around subjects since he first put words together. He's an expert at *not* saying all kinds of things—unless he's telling someone they won't get a loan from his bank and even then he doesn't *say* it. No, he puts it in writing and lays the blame on his board of directors."

Sandi's reflection leaned forward. "Now, Evie, let's put personalities aside. Old business, too. We want to know we can count on you to work with us and with the community, to make sure Chief Lowell is proactive, and that the courts follow through with prosecution. We want everyone to take this threat seriously."

"Threat?" Evie's voice rose and she reeled backward. "This isn't a terrorist plot. It's a few kids in bird costumes."

Bert's raised his hands, his chair groaning again. "Listen, Evie, I know we haven't always seen eye to eye in the past, but this protest *is* a threat. It's a threat to the integrity and safety of our community. Protesters aren't good for Castaway Beach. They attract an unstable element."

Jackson raised his eyebrows.

"Right," Sandi said. "The next thing you know there will be more of them than that private campground can hold. The town will be filled with people who have no regard for private property, public health, or sanitation. They'll be sleeping in their cars and on the beach, washing at the spigot in the park, clogging the town toilets, and then doing their business who knows where."

184

"They'll bring drugs," Bert warned. "And sell them to our kids."

"Ah," Evie said. "I see."

"Good." Bert rubbed his hands together. "I'm glad we're on the same page about this."

"I believe in private property, I'm concerned about public health, *and* I'm opposed to drug-dealing," Evie said. "But for the rest of it, the enormous threat to the integrity and safety of the community, I think we're not only *not* on the same page, but we've got different books."

"Different books?" Sandi asked.

"Right. Your book is all about economics. It has protesters attracting hordes of wild-eyed idealists with long hair who won't want it cut or styled, activists who won't spend money on motels and meals and souvenirs and won't buy cocktails at the taverns or beer at the market because they brought their own drugs. Oh, and they certainly won't be making offers on real estate and coming to the bank for loans."

Silence stretched to a ten-count, then Bert's chair squealed as he levered himself upright. "I'm not surprised that you're mocking us," he said in a tight voice. "You pride yourself on opposing progress, so this is about what I expected. But I'm deeply disturbed that you're making light of such a serious problem."

"It's not Armageddon, Bert. It's kids in bird costumes trying to get a little attention for something they believe in. The less fuss you make, the less attention they'll get, and the sooner they'll leave."

"But they're breaking the law," Sandi said. "Creating a public nuisance. We have to get tough."

185

"Well, you'll have to get tough without me." Evie leveled a finger at Bert. "And I'm telling you right now that if tough is the way you go, your 'threat to the community' will get bigger. You had five kids on the beach today. If you bring the hammer down, you could have twenty tomorrow and two hundred by the end of next week."

Kate nodded. She'd seen that happen, protests swelling because those in power tried to put them down. In college, she'd joined in, caught up in the chanting of the crowd, the intense welling of emotion, her belief in the cause, and the feeling that change was possible, that their voices might be heard, that they might make a difference.

A shadow swept across Jackson's eyes and she wondered if he was remembering being on the other side of a protest, tasked with containing it. Or was he thinking about those drawn to protests not because of their belief in a cause but because of the scent of potential violence and their yearning for a fight? Kate had seen people like that, heard their taunts, struggled not to respond.

"Thanks for your opinion, but the hammer's coming down." Bert stormed to his car, Sandi in his wake. "You better tell those kids to move along if they don't want to be under it when it hits."

CHAPTER 18

Car doors slammed, the engine roared to life, wheels spun, and gravel machine-gunned against tree trunks. Kate tugged at the sleeve of Jackson's T-shirt and they retreated to the kitchen and got busy with the dishes. In a moment, the screen door hinges creaked and Evie's halting footsteps came across the porch. "I assume you heard that," she panted.

"Hard not to," Jackson scrubbed at a dried glob of catsup on the rim of a plate. "Bert never makes a point without raising his voice."

Evie dragged herself to her chair and slumped into it, fingers on the pulse point in her neck. Despite her tan, her skin was gray, the pouches of flesh beneath her eyes were purple-black, and her white hair, usually standing in tufts, lay flat against her head, yellowed and soaked with sweat.

Kate bent to look into her eyes. "Are you okay?"

"Worked myself up talking to those fools." Evie's gaze slid away. "It's hot as a blast furnace out there. I could use a little cold lemonade."

187

"Lemonade. Coming right up." Kate got a clean glass from the cabinet and dug ice from the freezer, her gaze fixed on the older woman as she worked. Evie removed her fingers from her neck and rubbed at her left arm, then massaged her shoulder.

Heart problems?

Muscle strain?

Stress?

Kate filled the glass and carried it to the table. "You sure you're okay?"

"Of course I'm sure," Evie snapped. "Hot and tired. And my arm aches from carrying a bucket of fish. That's all."

Kate wet down a dish towel. "Let me put this on the back of your neck."

Evie didn't argue. Her breathing had slowed and whatever pain she had in her arm and shoulder wasn't evident as tension in the rest of her body or fear in her eyes. Still, Kate longed to count off the beats of her heart, take her temperature, interrogate her about other symptoms.

Jackson slid the last plate into the dishwasher, turned, and leaned against the counter. "If that's all and you're not bullshitting us, then tell us what we can do to help so you can get some rest and stay out of the sun."

Evie waved that aside. "You do enough around here. I can—"

"But if that's *not* all that's wearing you down," Jackson went on, his voice flinty, "then you'd better be honest with us. If you go down, you take this whole place with you."

Scowling, Evie rocked back in her chair. "Where do you get off talking to me like that? You work for me."

188

"Wrong. I work for myself. And I always will."

Kate fought a smile, remembering her weeks as manager of the Wade in the Waves Motel and her failed attempts to manage Jackson.

Evie's scowl deepened. "Well you're doing your work on my property and I'm paying you for it."

"We both know the pay is a joke, Evie, and we both know I'd be here with Kate and Way-Ray if you didn't give me a single dime. I'd be here if I had to pay you to let me stay."

With a grimace, he shifted to his good leg. "You and I have the same attitude about money. And commitment. That's why you set up this place and why you bust your ass to keep it going."

Evie picked at a loose thread on the pocket of her T-shirt. "Seems I'm just running in place anyway, patching up birds and setting them free so they can get shot or hit or starve all over again. I've been thinking there's not much point. I might not keep this going much longer."

Kate swallowed hard, but Jackson only shrugged. "That's your decision to make, but it's a decision that affects all of us. Play fair and let's get what you're thinking out on the table."

Evie worried the thread, but said nothing. Kate took a step toward her, but Jackson held up a hand. "Evie, if that pain in your arm is a heart attack on the way, then you have a choice—ignore it and face the consequences, or get help and head it off. If that pain is stress, then you've got the same kind of choices—you can let it wear you down until it makes you sick and maybe kills you, or you can deal with it."

He paused and rubbed the stubble on his chin. The dry whisper of sound filled the room and Kate

189

realized she'd been holding her breath. Evie snapped off the loose thread but didn't look up.

"Now, there are only four or five ways I know of to deal with stress. You can eliminate the source, you can try to ignore it, you can push it off onto someone else, you can drink or drug it to a dull throb, or you can face it, talk about it, and wrestle it down."

He moved to the table, pulled out the chair beside Evie's and sat. "From my experience, ignoring it isn't possible, and pushing it off doesn't work unless there's somebody to push to who doesn't push back. Drinking and drugging create their own problems and their own stress. I'm living proof of that."

Evie rolled the lemonade glass back and forth between her palms. "So you're telling me I have a whole bunch of choices but no damn choice at all."

"Pretty much."

Kate slipped into the chair on the other side of Evie. "We're also telling you we'll support your decision."

"How you gonna do that if I decide to shut this place down and turn the land over to Paul?"

"With great difficulty," Jackson said with a chuckle. "Biting my tongue every minute."

"We love this place," Kate told her. "And it will break Way-Ray's heart if we have to leave. But you can't let how someone else will feel hold you hostage to something you want to walk away from. The bottom line is that this place is yours. What happens to it is up to you."

"I just wish I knew whether I . . ." Evie took a long drink. "I got so many people telling me I'm old and crazy and out of step with the rest of the community

190

and standing in the way of progress that I'm starting to think they're right."

She raised her head, pain a dense shadow deep in her eyes. "I feel like I can't trust anyone. The worst part is I'm starting to feel like I can't trust myself."

Kate put a hand on Evie's shoulder, a tight knot of bone and muscle. "I know what you mean. Last year, when I came to Castaway Beach with Way-Ray, I felt like I was wading through a swamp, going in circles. Every decision I made was the wrong one and every decision made things worse."

"I've been there, too," Jackson said. "Sometimes cold sober, and sometimes . . ."

Evie gripped his arm. "You're past that now."

"Maybe." He shrugged. "No way to know for sure until I die."

"Well, that's a comforting thought. Is that when I'll know whether I'm crazy or not? When I kick off?"

"Crazy's different from drunk. You can't measure your blood-insanity level by blowing into a machine. It's a matter of definition and perception."

"Another comforting thought."

"You're not crazy," Kate assured her. "But there's a contingent in this town that wants you to think you are."

"And if you're second-guessing yourself to the point of causing physical pain," Jackson touched her left arm, "then their plan is working."

Evie drew in a long breath and nodded. "Just like always, I'm my own worst enemy."

"Aren't we all?" Jackson laughed. "But you've got to admit skirmishes with ourselves make life interesting."

"I could do with a little less 'interesting' and a lot more of whatever the alternative might be." Evie drained the rest of her lemonade, leaned back in her chair, and scraped her fingers through her hair, plowing it into damp furrows. "How do I know? How the hell do I know for sure if I'm going around the bend or if somebody is changing the highway signs to make me think that?"

Kate jumped up, hustled to her desk, and snatched up a yellow pad and a pen. "Write things down."

Evie gawked at the pad as if it was an exotic bird discovered thousands of miles from its home range. "What things?"

"Start with what you know is true." Kate laid the pad and pen on the table.

"Well, there's the first problem." Evie released a bitter laugh. "I'm not sure."

"Then make a bunch of lists," Jackson suggested.

"I hate lists. Never seem to get to the end of them."

"Tough. Make some. What you're sure is true, what you think might be true, what you wonder about. What you're sure is sane and what's dubious. Like that." Jackson stood and nodded to Kate. "We'll do the evening rounds for you."

"I can—"

"No you can't. Not today."

"Write this in the positively true column." Kate followed Jackson to the door. "You have a hard time allowing *anyone* to do *anything* for you."

"That's not—"

"And you thrive on arguments." Jackson swung down the steps to the yard, calling over his shoulder. "Write that down in the true column."

Kate trotted to keep up. "Do you think she will?"

192

"I don't know. But maybe we got her thinking. That's all we can do short of strapping her into the bed of her truck and hauling her off to the hospital for a physical."

Kate laughed at the image. "Or hauling her off on a long vacation."

"I doubt she's ever taken one of those. You can't just drive off and leave a dairy herd to look after itself." He pointed at the eagle enclosure. "Or these birds. And in the long run, they'll tip the balance. She hasn't walked away from them in the past and she won't do it now."

"But now she's older. Tired. In pain."

Jackson wrapped his arms around her. "All the more reason for her to stay in the place she knows best."

When they returned after lingering to watch the stars blink on over the pasture, Way-Ray and Sean were at the table eating ice cream.

Jackson pointed at a thick sludge topping the mound in Way-Ray's bowl. It was an odd brownish red with curved chunks. "What is that?"

"We were almost outta chocolate sauce and other things, so we had to do what Kate did when we didn't have any noodles for the tuna casserole," Way-Ray said.

Jackson bent to examine the bowl. "You used tortilla chips?"

"No, we imp . . . improvised." He ducked his head and mumbled, "I bet that comes from Latin."

Sean punched his arm.

193

Way-Ray winced, glanced at Kate, and increased the speed of his words. "Or some other old language or one that's not so old. But it doesn't matter and we don't have to talk about that right now so nobody has to get mad at anybody, okay?"

"Fine with me." Kate grinned at Jackson. "What did you improvise with?"

Sean dug a spoon into the chocolate sauce jar and brought up more of the odd topping. "We mixed the chocolate with the rest of the caramel and some peanut butter we nuked to make it soft."

"Then we mixed in that gooey marshmallow stuff and blackberry jam and those nuts Kate hides at the back of the freezer," Way-Ray added.

"You found Kate's secret stash of cashews?"

"She should hide them better if we're not supposed to have them," Sean said. "Beside, we only took a few. Kyle says plain ice cream is too smooth and needs texture."

"Texture," Kate echoed. "Who knew?"

"If Kyle says you need texture, that must be right. He's the expert." Jackson got the tub of chocolate ice cream from the freezer. "Mind if I try some?"

"Nah. We got lots now that we mixed it all together." Sean stuffed the spoon back in the jar and pushed it across the table.

"You want some, Kate?" Way-Ray asked.

"I'll pass. You had me up to the blackberry jam."

"That's what Evie said before she stopped writing on that big pad of paper and went to bed."

Jackson arched his brows. "Did she say anything else?"

Way-Ray thought for a moment. "Don't make a lot of noise, don't leave a big mess for Kate, and uh . . ."

194

Sean squirmed and flushed. "She said she's glad we're here and um, that she loves us."

"Hmmm." Kate glanced at Jackson.

"Yeah. Seems a little extreme for Evie." He scooped ice cream into his bowl. "She definitely said that?"

"Yeah." Way-Ray swirled melted ice cream and topping together. "She said she loves us even though sometimes we drive her to dis . . . dis. . ."

"Distraction?" Kate asked.

"That's it, distraction." Way-Ray scratched his head with a grubby finger. "And that's weird because me and Sean don't drive and we don't even know where distraction is."

"Right here." Jackson laughed and pointed to the center of the table. "This very spot is the center of the capital of the great state of perpetual distraction."

Wide-eyed, Way-Ray and Sean gazed at the salt and pepper shakers, the sugar bowl, and the napkin holder. "The capital," Sean breathed. "Wow."

"If this is the capital, we need a flag." Way-Ray raised his spoon and waved it, sending drops of melted ice cream flying across the table.

"What you need is a napkin," Kate said. "Or sponge. Or a mop."

Sean reached for the napkin holder. "Maybe we should make a flag out of napkins and put a picture of a mop on it."

"Yeah. Except napkins will fall apart in the rain."

"It's not raining now," Sean pointed out. "It won't hardly rain at all until after we go back to school."

"Ewww." Way-Ray made the gag-me motion. "What you said."

Sean clapped his hands over his mouth.

195

Chuckling, Kate tossed a damp sponge to Jackson. "I'm going to bed. You're in charge here at the capital."

As she climbed the stairs she heard Way-Ray ask, "How big is the state of distraction? Is this whole house in it? And the barn? And the cemetery where my mom is?"

"It's a big capital," Jackson answered. "And the boundaries are flexible. If a person is anywhere within a mile of you and Sean, then that person is in the state of distraction."

And if she had all the money in the world, Kate thought, she wouldn't live anywhere else.

CHAPTER 19

"Paul's out of the hospital but word is he's moving like a sloth. Got someone showing property for him." Rhea passed over a cone mounded with pale yellow ice cream laced with red ripples. "That's my take on those drinks they have out in Hawaii—lava flows—only without the liquor."

Kate wrinkled her nose, thinking of the blackberry jam mixed into the ice cream toppings, but then she took a bite. Coconut, banana, pineapple, and strawberry flavors mingled in her mouth. "Yum. This is amazing."

Rhea grinned. "Yeah. Kyle figured out how to blend it. He's got the knack." She nodded toward her son who was muscling a fresh tub of chocolate ice cream into the display case, then snapped a dangling clip back into her topknot. "Anyway, I expect Paul won't be doing much for the next week except watching his bruises change colors. Oh, and Chief Lowell says he expects they'll have the guy who punched Curtis any time now. They found his truck ditched up the coast and all the cops around are on the lookout. If he's smart, he'll turn himself in before they find him."

"If he was smart, he wouldn't have run."

"Yeah, there's that." Rhea slipped the ice cream scoop into a tub of water. "Hope nobody gets hurt before they round him up. That Abel guy got out of jail this morning. So did the passenger in the truck, the guy who put the kids in the surf."

"That didn't take long. Did they make bail?"

"Judge set them loose on their own recognizance until there's a trial—probably because there's no room in the jail unless you're more of a menace to society. Kyle heard Abel say he didn't have the money for bail and wouldn't have paid it if he did because the arrest wouldn't stand up. He said he's a pacifist and was only defending himself. He tried to stay in his cell to protest 'a corruption of justice,' but they dragged him to the door. He and his feathered friends are headed back to the beach this evening no matter what the judge told him about not courting trouble."

"That will make the folks from the chamber jump for joy." Kate turned her cone, licking drips. "Bert Connors and Sandi Evans were out at the house last night trying to convince Evie to talk the protesters into packing up before they attract an unstable element."

"You mean folks who don't use banks or beauty parlors," Rhea said with a laugh. "I bet that idea flew like a steel-belted balloon."

"Never got off the ground."

Rhea gazed toward the beach and fiddled with her topknot. "Could be those kids will draw a crowd this evening. Maybe I should show up and campaign."

Kate shook her head. "Maybe you should stay away so you don't end up in the surf."

Rhea scrunched up her mouth, then shrugged. "Good point. And I bet most of the kids who join them won't be registered voters—at least not registered around here." She plucked a mint from her pocket, turned it in her fingers, then dropped it back. "I hope they don't stir up more crap for Evie."

"Yeah, she's got so many people carping at her and saying she's nuts that she's starting to second-guess herself about keeping the place going—not after she dies, but now."

"That's not like her." Rhea frowned. "From the day she saved her first bird, that place has been her reason for living."

Kate leaned across the glass so Kyle wouldn't hear. "Yesterday, after Bert and Sandi left, she was so stressed out she said she felt like she couldn't trust herself, like her mind might be slipping."

"Lots of folks think it already has. Never bothered her before."

"She seems to be getting old. Fast. She looks smaller, grayer." Kate shook her head. "We got her making lists—things she knows are true, things she doubts, things other people say that she agrees with or doesn't. I think she'll get back on her mental game, but I'm worried about her physical condition. The heat's been bothering her a lot, and last night her left arm hurt."

"And no way will she go to a doctor. Or ask anyone to help." Rhea knuckled the edges of her eyes. "She's as stubborn as an old mule."

"Well, if there's a crisis we'll get that mule to the hospital if we have to tie her up to do it." Kate popped the last of her cone in her mouth and crunched it to bits.

"I know you will. I count on you and Jackson." Rhea leaned across the display case and touched Kate's shoulder. "And there aren't many I say that about."

Feeling tears sting her eyes, Kate blinked, nodded, and waved goodbye, not trusting herself to speak.

Outside the air felt cooler but the sidewalk was still a griddle. Kate hustled to the SUV she'd parked half a block away, outside a shop selling antiques on consignment. A black car with windows tinted cadaverous gray was angled into the next space, its wheels crimped toward the street, its rear bumper tight against hers. A faint shimmer of heat rising around the bumpers indicated the engine was running, putting out an invisible plume of exhaust. Digging her keys from her pocket, Kate strode past.

The rear window slid down, spilling chilled air and the scents of pine freshener, leather polish, and musky cologne. "Miss Dalton," a rusty voice commanded.

Kate halted, then took two steps away from the car. There was no one else on this stretch of sidewalk, but the door of the antique store was open and she heard the tinkling of a music box, a safe and soothing sound. Refusing to be lulled by it, she put her weight on her back foot, ready to pivot and run, and clutched her keys with the longest protruding from her fist so she could rake it across an assailant's face or stab at his eyes.

"Don't be afraid," the voice rasped. "I simply wish to speak with you. I have no intention of hurting you today."

200

The final word sluiced along Kate's spine like icy water. She peered into the dim interior of the car and made out a narrow nose rising like a ridge between two sunken eyes and jutting above a pair of slack lips the color of old bone.

"But tomorrow you might?" she asked, struggling to keep her voice from quavering.

The lips spasmed into a sliver of a smile. "Oh, no, Miss Dalton. *I* would never harm you . . . or anyone."

Kate bent and squinted beyond him, taking in the hulking body of the man behind the wheel and the massive shoulder of another in the passenger seat. Both had black hair and wore white shirts and black suits like their master. Both turned their heads slightly, their gazes sliding across her face, lingering on her chest. She forced herself not to back away. "But someone who works for you will hurt me if you suggest that would be to your liking?"

The man arched his brows, the action lifting heavy lids from eyes as black as his car but without its gloss or gleam. Cold, flat eyes. Shark's eyes. "On occasion," he said, dropping his voice to a grating whisper, "events can take a painful turn for those who fail to negotiate in good faith."

Faith?

In a deal with a devil like this, would faith be part of the equation?

Kate clutched her keys tighter. "I'm not aware there are negotiations underway."

"You are correct, Miss Dalton. There are, as yet, no formal negotiations. My hope is that you can soon facilitate that."

Facilitate?

201

Kate almost laughed at his choice of words and the idea of "facilitating" a shark feeding frenzy. But instinct told her this was not a man who allowed himself to be laughed at, so she kept her face still and fell back on the language of bureaucracy, and on questions instead of statements. "How do you perceive my role? And what would I be facilitating?"

The man rubbed the tip of his nose, revealing long fingernails, ridged and yellow, but shaped and polished.

Macabre.

Kate suppressed a shudder.

Sunlight flashed on the silver and turquoise ring on his third finger, on the green-blue stone mottled and veined with dark lines. "You contradict your nature by playing coy, Miss Dalton. You know very well we are discussing Mrs. Hopkins' obstruction of progress."

Kate breathed in and kept challenge out of her tone. "There are different views and interpretations of progress. How do you define it?"

"As the development of resources and potential."

"And who determines what is right when it comes to the pace and extent of that development?"

"Right is a relative term, Miss Dalton." He kept to a conversational tone as if he, too, was avoiding direct challenge. "It depends on perspective. The term has a certain . . . flexibility."

"Much like, for example, the morality of some political leaders and corporate executives?"

"It does you no good to attempt to bait me, Miss Dalton. And it makes me think less of you."

His forefinger curled into a fist that moved an inch toward Kate and then withdrew. "There are opportunities here. When the terms are on the table it would behoove you to act before it is too late, to steer Mrs. Hopkins toward a decision that would benefit many and harm no one."

"A decision to give up her land for the golf course project?"

"Exactly."

Fury blazed in Kate's brain. "And how would that benefit her? How would that not harm the creatures she rescues and heals?"

"You are being shortsighted, Miss Dalton. The work she does can be relocated. It need not cease."

His tone made it clear there were quote marks around the word "work," and that fed Kate's anger. "Evie won't want—"

"Relocation will result in more comfortable circumstances for all of you. Convince her, Miss Dalton."

The window whirred up. With a rumble of its engine and a screech of tires, the car shot onto the highway, sun glittering off its polished bumper. The caustic smells of exhaust and scorched rubber pressed against Kate's nose and mouth like a hand. Knees juddering, she gasped for breath and staggered to the doorway of the antique shop. Swallowing bile, she leaned there, listening to the tinkle of that music box slowing, stopping.

What had he meant when he said it would behoove her to steer Evie to a decision before it was too late? More to the point, what had he *not* said about the consequences of failing to do that?

"Even his ring was creepy." Kate finished her story, flopped onto her stomach, and punched her pillow. "I love turquoise, but this was a hideous shade of green. It looked like a chunk of decaying skin ripped off a dead space alien. He's the shark from New Mexico, isn't he?"

"I'd put money on that, but I'll do some checking." Jackson's voice was thick and he pulled Kate close against his side. "He never made a direct threat?"

"Not a damn thing I could take to Chief Lowell. But he *did* threaten me. He threatened all of us."

Jackson's grip tightened and Kate nuzzled the base of his throat, the wedge of soft skin between the points of his collar bones, between whiskers and chest hair. "I don't want him to know I'm scared. And I'm not going to tell Evie. She doesn't need the stress and I don't want to influence any decision she comes to about this place."

"Yeah, if Evie feels she's being pushed one way, she'll jump the other. Without looking."

"I just wish I knew what was coming and when. He said there were no negotiations yet. Then he said when the terms were on the table I should act before it was too late."

"It's a four-letter word, but you'll have to *wait* for those terms to hit the table."

"I hate waiting."

"You and Way-Ray." Jackson grinned and trailed kisses along the curve of her ear. "You have stillness issues."

Kate shivered and ran her fingernails down the center of his chest. "And sometimes you seem to like that."

CHAPTER 20

Three days passed. Three days that, by their standards, qualified as normal. Then Way-Ray shouted from the yard where he was feeding dinner scraps to the geese. "Car. A great big one."

The shark?

Kate's fingers twitched and the soapy mixing bowl slipped, clanging into the sink.

"Good thing that wasn't my good glass bowl," Evie said.

"You mean the glass bowl with more chips than a poker parlor?" Jackson asked with a chuckle.

Kate marveled at how genuine that jest sounded. If Jackson was concerned about who was in that car and what was about to unfold, he didn't show it. She, on the other hand, felt her throat constrict and her stomach knot.

"That bowl was my grandmother's. It's just a little distressed is all. Let's see what kind of shape you're in when you're over a hundred."

Evie shoved her chair back from the table. "Better go see what fresh misery is on tap. Probably a

205

delegation wanting me to hypnotize those protesters and levitate them off the beach."

"It would take a lot of hypnotizing," Jackson said. "I counted two dozen of them in that video on the news. Probably be twice as many tomorrow."

More people driving on the sand too. For every protester who joined the throng, another driver brought his vehicle to the edge of the water to make a point about what the law allowed.

"Tourism folks ought to make hay out of it." Evie clumped to the door. "Sell snacks and souvenirs. Get T-shirts made up. It's the biggest show around."

With trembling fingers Kate lifted the bowl and rinsed it with scalding water, then dried her hands and turned to face Jackson who sprawled in his chair, an oversized plaid shirt with hacked off sleeves open halfway to his waist. "You're not going out there with her?"

"Like you said, give her space."

"Not too much space." Kate surveyed potential weapons as she had on the day Paul came to dispute his mother's plan to change her will—the huge frying pan, an array of knives, the barbecue fork. "Way-Ray's out there. If it's the man who threatened me, he—"

"He's shrewd." Jackson hitched to his feet as tires crunched on the gravel of the parking area. "Odds are whatever he does won't be in broad daylight."

"It's dusk. And getting darker every minute."

"And I'm right here." Jackson caught her hands. "Breathe."

Kate hauled in a shuddering breath that made her lungs ache.

"Again." He guided her left hand to his side, to the gun in the holster beneath his shirt. "It's okay."

206

One ear cocked toward a jumble of voices from outside, Kate drew in another breath, relieved yet angry because relief sprang from tacit approval of that weapon, approval of violence. Before her encounter with Way-Ray's father and all that came after, she had different views about guns and their purpose. But now . . .

She rubbed the scar on her leg and nodded toward the door. "Let's at least go out on the porch."

"Works for me." Jackson turned and led the way, switching off the kitchen light as he passed through the doorway.

"You don't look like you're Evie's son," Way-Ray said. "And why are you all dressed up?"

Kate stepped closer to the screen and squinted into the gloom to see Way-Ray staring up at Paul Hopkins who stood behind the open door of his car as he had a month earlier. He'd parked well shy of the shadows beneath the trees and the dome light illuminated the bruise above his left eye and two others on his jaw.

"Why don't you get the geese in their pen and make sure it's shut up tight. Then go in and play a videogame or watch TV." Evie's tone made it clear that was an order. She stretched out a hand, gripped Way-Ray's shoulder, and turned him toward the house.

"But Kate said I'm not supposed to watch TV or play games until I bring my dirty laundry downstairs and sweep where I dumped out my shoes."

"Then you'd better do that." Evie tousled his hair. "Right now."

"Okaaaaay." Way-Ray flapped a hand at their visitor. "Bye, Paul. See ya later."

207

"Let's hope not," Jackson said under his breath. He lowered himself to the chaise and used both hands to lift his bad leg.

Kate frowned. He'd never done that before. Was he just tired, or had his pain reached extreme levels? Worse, were his leg muscles not responding as they should?

While she pondered whether he'd give her an honest answer to those questions, Way-Ray bounded up the steps, yanked the door open, and bolted through, letting it whap closed behind him. "Hey, why are you in the dar—?"

"Sssshhhh." Kate held a finger to her lips.

"Are you spying on Evie?" Way-Ray whispered.

"No," Jackson answered. "This is surveillance."

"Sir-Who-Ance?" Way-Ray raised his hands and shook his head, his hair swishing in the murky light. "Nah. Don't tell me. It's Latin or French or something and I bet it's kinda like being nosy 'cept you'll probably tell me you're not."

"Busted," Kate said in a low voice. "We wondered why Evie's son came to see her."

"Oh." Way-Ray nodded. "On accounta he never comes for Thanksgiving or Christmas? And on accounta he got all mad when Kate paid the taxes last year?"

Out of the mouths of babes.

"Pretty much," Kate admitted.

Way-Ray shrugged and migrated toward the kitchen. "Whatever. I'm gonna do my chores so I can watch TV."

"Are we that transparent?" Kate asked after he thumped up the stairs.

"Apparently. Let's get on with our surveillance."

Evie's voice cut across Jackson's. "We can talk out here," she said, her words so loud and distinct Kate was certain she intended that they hear.

Paul's answer was mumbled.

"There will be light enough if you get to the point."

Kate sat on the edge of the chaise and ran her hand along Jackson's scarred leg. The muscles felt tight and kinked; she kneaded them with her fingertips and heard him groan.

Paul handed a paper to Evie and she tipped it to the spill of light from the car.

"It's about ten miles on the other side of Castaway Beach," he said, his voice smooth, his words flowing like the current in a summer river, gentle but not to be denied, a current meant to carry Evie along. "There's a three-bedroom ranch-style house built about thirty years ago, a guesthouse, a detached garage, a small metal barn, and almost fifty acres and two streams."

Kate found herself visualizing it, liking what she saw in her mind.

"The house is in great shape," Paul went on. "All the appliances come with it, and the property backs up against state forest land. Zoning won't be a problem."

Evie rattled the paper. "A problem for . . . ?"

"You. For your hob— For your facility." Paul raised his voice and spoke faster, his words riding up against each other like cars in a freeway pileup. "There are no restrictions against setting up cages for birds and other creatures or even moving that old trailer out there."

"And why would I want to move it?" Evie balled up the paper and batted it to the ground. "It's fine where it is. Everything is fine where it is. Right here."

Jackson high-fived air. "Tell him, Evie."

"It appears I got the cart ahead of the horse. Let me start over," Paul said in tone more commanding than soothing.

He stepped out from behind the door, scooped up the wadded paper, and smoothed it across the fender. "I'm willing to buy this piece of property and give it to you in exchange for the farm. That piece is worth more, but we'll make it an even trade. Straight across."

The shark's words echoed in Kate's mind: *When the terms are on the table it would behoove you to act before it is too late, to steer Mrs. Hopkins toward a decision that would benefit many and harm no one.* She shivered and grasped Jackson's hand.

"That's quite a gesture from a man who loves money as much as you do," Evie mused. "But I'm sure you'll be reimbursed by your rich friends. Maybe you'll even get a bonus for clearing the way for that golf course project."

It took a moment for Paul to respond. "I won't deny that I have an interest in developing this land. These are hard economic times and that project will benefit a lot of people. There's a great deal of . . . enthusiasm for getting it underway as soon as possible."

"Before the nature of the county commission changes," Jackson muttered, "and Rhea and Lois put the brakes on."

"But the main reason I want you to consider my offer is because this property is much better for you, your volunteers, and the creatures you care for," Paul went on. "The road in to the house is paved

210

and the house itself is all one level. It has good wiring and plumbing, central heat and air conditioning, and new windows and doors. You'll be more comfortable there."

"I'm *comfortable* right here."

"I'll take care of all the details." Paul rushed on, his voice rising. "I'll hire a packing and moving company and arrange to have the utilities transferred. I'll buy new furniture—a bed, sofa, tables, chairs, dishes—whatever you want."

"Sounds almost like he's begging," Kate murmured. "Like he's scared."

"He is," Jackson agreed. "It's an attractive offer, though. I couldn't blame Evie if she took it."

If she took it, they would all be safe. The shark would veer away in search of other prey.

Kate shivered again and pressed Jackson's hand against her cheek.

"This is my home," Evie said. "What I want is to stay in my home."

"Your home is falling down around you," Paul said, his voice crackling with impatience.

"Don't exaggerate. Jackson put on a new roof and repaired the water damage in the west wall."

"Yes, but the foundation is cracked, the pipes are rusting through, the wiring is a fire hazard, and that road is a minefield." Paul paused for a few seconds and his voice grew soft and oily. "Wouldn't it be nice to live in a modern house that was warm in the winter and cool in the summer?"

Evie was silent for a long moment, then she asked in a voice as bleak as an Arctic winter, "Did you really think you could buy me? With a ranch-style house and a new mattress and central heat and

211

dishes without cracks and chips? Did you think that was my price?"

"I'm not trying to buy you," Paul said. "This swap is a win-win deal. It will be better for everyone."

"Everyone? What about your father? Are you going to hire someone to dig him up? Are you going to buy him a brand new box and bring him along? What do the zoning regulations at the new place have to say about having a cemetery in your yard?"

Paul's feet shuffled in the gravel. "I don't know. I hadn't thought ab—"

"Of course you hadn't thought. Especially not about him. Your father was dead to you long before we laid him in the ground on a day when I bet all you thought about was getting in out of the rain and scraping the mud off your shiny shoes."

"That's not— Listen to me. You have to do this."

Even in the dim light Kate could see Paul stretch out a hand and Evie dodge it, pivot, and stalk into the deep shadows beneath the trees. "I don't have to do anything, Paul, especially not save your sorry skin from a mess you helped make. Go back to your 'friends' and tell them there's no deal. Then lock your doors and get a bodyguard. Better yet, get out of town."

Kate drew in a sharp breath. "Do you think she means that?"

"Sounds like she does," Jackson answered. "At least right this minute."

Paul crumpled the paper and spiked it to the ground, then slid into the car, his skin gray-green in the harsh illumination of the dome light, his lips tight against each other. He slammed the door and in a second the engine roared and he backed away in a wide arc, wheels throwing gravel into the grass.

Kate felt queasy and bent forward, tucking her chin between her knees. "What happens now?"

"We wait."

"For what?"

"A dorsal fin in the water."

CHAPTER 21

Evie hadn't come in by 9:00 when Kate herded Way-Ray to bed. She hadn't appeared an hour later when Kate and Jackson climbed the stairs. Despite her concerns, Kate agreed when Jackson said they shouldn't hunt for Evie or mention Paul's offer when she appeared.

"She'll get more comfort from her birds than from us," he insisted. "She knows we heard the whole thing. When she wants to talk about it, she will."

Nerves stinging like nettles, Kate was awake much of the night, listening for the whap of the screen door or the creak of floorboards in the kitchen. Sometime after 3:00 she plummeted into a dark crater of sleep and was startled from it by the clatter of plates and the aroma of coffee.

Yanking on a pair of khaki shorts and a green T-shirt, she bolted for the kitchen and found Jackson at the stove frying eggs mixed with onions, peppers, and bits of sliced turkey. Way-Ray's cereal bowl, a few sodden flakes marooned in the bottom, sat in a rough circle of bluish milk droplets; Kate guessed he'd taken advantage of her absence and Jackson's

214

inattention to bomb the bowl with blueberries while making airplane noises.

With a sigh, she got a mug from the cabinet and filled it with coffee the way Jackson made it—stronger and darker than she and Evie did, but just what she needed this morning. "Where's Way-Ray?"

"Out practicing stillness." Jackson flipped his concoction, exposing browned onions in the center and a lace of egg white at the edge. "I figured he'd cramp our style if Evie turned up and wanted to talk, so I told him I always did better holding still on a full stomach."

"Mmm." Kate poured a huge dollop of milk into the mug, sipped, and trickled in a little more. "Well, leave his bowl there and don't mop up that milk."

"Wasn't planning on it." Jackson rolled back the frayed cuffs of a flannel shirt that gave new meaning to the word "grunge." "The kid knows the rules. He's old enough to do his chores without being reminded."

"Or so we'd like to believe." Kate took a longer sip and then a gulp. She could almost feel the caffeine rushing to her brain, prodding cells and synapses. "Shall we see how long it takes him to notice he left a mess and realize he needs to do something about it?"

"My money says not until lunch. And I'll make a side bet that he just shoves the bowl to the center of the table to make room for a sandwich." Jackson slid the omelet onto a plate. "You want some of this?"

Kate shook her head. "I'm not hungry." Hadn't been since the shark stopped her on the street.

"You ought to put something in your stomach." He set the plate on the table and retrieved a couple of slices of golden brown rye bread from the toaster. "It will settle your nerves."

"Food might settle your nerves, but if I ate those eggs right now they'd make a U-turn and we'd have more than Way-Ray's mess on the table."

"Suit yourself." He filled his mug, sat, and smeared butter on his toast.

Coffee mug in hand, Kate prowled the kitchen, pacing from window to door until, spotting Evie trudging along the path from the hospital trailer, she snatched up the paper she'd read yesterday and scrambled for her chair.

Jackson rolled his eyes and went back to devouring his eggs. In a moment Kate heard the soft thud of Evie's rubber boots as she kicked them off by the steps and then the creak of loose flooring as she crossed the kitchen and poured herself some coffee. "I guess you two heard what Paul had to say last night."

Kate nodded. Jackson grunted and shoveled eggs onto his toast.

"Just as well since it concerns you and it will only make me madder if I have to repeat it." Evie slumped into her chair, drank, then set the mug down and pushed it from one hand to the other. It was bright pink with white and yellow daisies on it, nothing that Evie would have bought, but something a volunteer might have given her or perhaps left behind. The circular ridge on the bottom of the cup grated against the surface of the oak table and coffee sloshed to the rim. A little cascaded over onto Evie's fingers and she jerked her right hand away and shook it.

"I'm mad at him and mad at myself because I should have thought it over." She pointed to the

216

yellow pad on the edge of the counter. "I should have written it down and weighed it out and talked with you. Most of it makes good sense and moving a few miles down the road to make way for so-called progress would settle some of the ruffled feathers in town. But it made my blood boil that he was pretending to give a hoot about my comfort when all he cares about is saving his own butt and getting his hands on—"

The phone rang and they all froze, Evie glaring at it, Kate watching her from the corner of her eyes, Jackson wedging his fork under another heap of egg. It rang again. Kate set her mug down and went to the desk.

"Those protest kids were attacked at their camp last night," Rhea squawked. "Some of them were beat up bad before Curtis got out there. One of the girls was almost raped."

Kate gasped and sat, drawing up her knees, drawing in her elbows. Rape took violence to another level. Rape was humiliation, violation. It was conquest, subjugation. And the emotional toll was dreadful, sometimes endless. "I know people are angry about the protest, but rape?"

Evie turned to look at her and Jackson laid his fork on the edge of his plate, his eyes narrowing.

"I know. I can't believe anybody around here would do that no matter how pissed off they got," Rhea went on. "Curtis says there was a bunch of them. They wore masks."

Rhea paused and drew in a breath. "That's all I know. Jim's bringing Sean out to your place. You can bet the whole mess will be on the news before too long."

217

She disconnected, but Kate kept the phone clamped to her ear, feeling as if a towering wave was about to break over her, grind her into the sand, and sweep her out to sea.

"Rape?" Jackson stood, hitched across the room to her side, took the phone from her numb fingers and rammed it into the cradle. "Who? What happened?"

"The protesters were attacked last night. Beaten up. Rhea said one of the girls was almost raped."

"Damn it!"

"It's my fault," Evie moaned. "When Bert and Sandi asked me to go talk with those kids, I shouldn't have gotten my back up. I should have gone down there and—"

"Wasted your time," Jackson said. "Their agenda was set. You couldn't have changed it."

"And how do you know that?" Evie leaped from her chair and came at him, finger poking the air.

Jackson didn't flinch. "Because from the minute they went back to the beach after the first incident, this is where it was headed."

Evie halted, her eyes glinting. "Are you saying they wanted to be beaten up? That a girl asked to be—?"

"No. But an attack of some kind was inevitable."

"Inevitable? You know that how? What are you, the supreme and mighty ruler of the universe?"

"I wouldn't take *that* job if you gave it to me. But it doesn't take a genius to see—"

"Stop it!" Kate stepped between them. "Stop it right now."

Jackson breathed through his teeth, a soft hissing. Panting, Evie poked air once more, then plodded to her chair.

218

"You're both right," Kate said. "After that first attack, those kids knew they were on a collision course with danger. But it's possible that if Evie talked with them, they might have taken another tack or at least toned down the protest."

Jackson and Evie snorted in disgust, transferring some of their anger to the peacemaker. Kate ignored them. "Arguing about it won't change what happened. And getting mad at each other because you feel powerless about that won't benefit anyone."

"I know, I know." Evie picked up her mug and glared at the daisies. "That poor girl. Those fool kids. How bad were they beat up?"

"Rhea didn't know."

"Noon news," Jackson said. "They'll have every gory detail."

Evie nodded. "That Marnie creature must be grinning like a barn cat at milking time."

"And sharpening her claws." Jackson hitched to the counter, dumped his cold coffee in the sink, and poured a refill. "She'll be out here looking for another angle, asking how you feel about the law that allows people to drive on the beach."

"Crap." Evie slammed her mug to the table and glared harder at the daisies.

"I'll write up a statement and send it to the reporters on our list." Kate turned to the desk and fired up the computer. "I'll tell them you've got some critical cases and can't spare the time to give interviews today."

Jackson scraped the remains of his breakfast into the scrap bucket and limped toward the door. "I'll talk to Chief Lowell and see if he has any leads that he might want someone without a badge to pursue.

219

Maybe the usual suspects should be questioned in an unofficial way."

Kate spun and snatched at his sleeve, felt the aging fabric rip in her grasp. "More violence isn't the sol—"

"Let him go," Evie ordered. "When they tried to rape that girl they crossed a line too far. They've got to pay and odds are that even if they're caught and there's enough clear evidence against them, the system won't set a price high enough for my liking. Hell, I'd go with Jackson and thump a few heads if I didn't think I'd break half my finger bones doing it."

Jackson raised his brows. Kate shook her head, then let the soft flannel slide from her grip and crossed her arms.

"I'll be back before dark," Jackson said. "With the town in an uproar and the media out in force, I doubt Paul or any of his associates will come around."

"I'll load my old shotgun just in case." Evie flashed him a grim smile. "Give 'em a blast of birdshot if they do."

Jackson turned a thumb up to Evie, pulled Kate close, and kissed her forehead. "See you soon."

Kate watched him clump across the porch, thinking about the thugs in the car with the shark. Would birdshot be enough to make them turn back?

"I should just shut this place down," Evie said after the rumble of Jackson's truck died away. "It's nothing but a sore spot for everybody."

Kate gave herself a minute to consider her reply and strip emotion from her voice, then she carried the yellow pad and a pen to the table and laid them in front of Evie. "Before you go any farther down that road, maybe you should define who 'everybody' is."

Evie raised her hands in despair. "Community leaders. My son."

"Okay. That's a handful of people, not 'everybody'."

"Maybe you better get your nose out of my business before I say something we'll never get over."

Evie glowered with such intensity Kate almost felt the blast-furnace heat of it. But in a few seconds the older woman bowed her head. "I'm tired, Kate. I'm so tired."

Kate patted her shoulder, feeling the knob of bone close beneath the skin. "I know."

"And it seems that every day is a fight, a damned uphill battle just to get to where I fall into bed at the end of it."

"Some days are," Kate agreed. "Especially lately. But you do good work here. You help creatures that some of the people in that 'everybody' category say don't matter."

"And maybe they're right about that." Evie hunched over, her face in her hands.

Struggling against the desire to say more, Kate retreated to her desk to prepare a statement for the media.

CHAPTER 22

Jackson returned just before dinner, his limp worse than ever, his face sun scorched and splotched with dried sweat and dust.

"You look like you were rode hard and put away wet," Evie said.

Way-Ray looked up from rubbing at spots of congealed milk with a sponge. "Somebody rode you? Like a horse?"

"Where did they put you away?" Sean flipped the broom, sending a scatter of sand toward the door. "And how come you were wet?"

"It's an expression." Kate set a bowl of fruit salad on the clean side of the table. "A figure of speech. It means someone is hot and tired and sweaty."

Way-Ray crinkled his nose and pooched out his lips. "So nobody rode you like a horse?"

Jackson sighed and dropped into his chair.

"Of course nobody rode him," Evie snapped. Snatching the pitcher from the refrigerator, she poured him a tall glass of lemonade.

"Well he looks like they did," Sean insisted.

"With spurs and everything," Way-Ray added. "He's got more holes in his shirt than this morning."

Jackson sighed again and drained the lemonade in three long gulps.

"It's an expression," Kate repeated. "Horses need to cool down after they run. Good riders walk and brush them before they put them in their stalls for the night."

"An expression." Way-Ray crinkled his nose again and slid his gaze toward Jackson. "Is it Latin?"

"I don't think so," Kate said. "But I'm pretty sure they had horses in ancient Rome."

Sean dropped the broom and plugged his fingers into his ears. "Do we hafta hear all about it?"

"No," Jackson said. "Not unless you keep dawdling with your chores and don't eat all your dinner and 'forget' to put your plates in the dishwasher."

Way-Ray dropped the sponge, snapped his heels together, and saluted. "Aye aye, Master and Commander. We will make it so."

"Master and Commander," Evie huffed. "Don't let that go to your head."

Jackson grinned and held out his empty glass. "Refill, sailor."

Way-Ray snatched the glass and hustled for the pitcher on the counter. Sean dragged the broom at triple-time, raising a swirl of dust.

Kate sneezed and batted at the air. "Enough, Sean. That's good enough." She opened the oven and pulled out a deep casserole dish bubbling with chicken stew and topped with dumplings. "Way-Ray, take that sponge off the table and get the plates on."

223

Twenty minutes later Rhea drove up with three containers of ice cream and two minutes after that the boys careened across the porch intent on filling a pail with blueberries ripened by the heat.

When the screen door whapped closed, Evie smacked her hands on the table. "What's going on in town? I want to know what wasn't on the news."

"The part about police having no leads is pretty accurate," Jackson said. "The guy who owns that private campground put more money into bark mulch than lighting and the goons wore masks, so the only descriptive words are 'big' and 'strong.' The campground is between two roads that connect to the highway and it's surrounded by trees, so they had good cover for their escape and only a few hundred feet to run to where they left their vehicles. They came in from both sides—eight or ten of them, maybe more."

"If they knew about those roads," Evie said, "maybe they're from around here."

Jackson shrugged. "Or they scouted the camp."

"Well, at least one of them was smart enough to recognize the value of the terrain and use it," Kate said. "And to set up an attack from two directions. Maybe he was in the military."

"The chief and I thought about that." Jackson rubbed at a smear of grease on his cheek. "We wrote out a list of everyone we knew who'd served, on up to a World War II vet who's legally blind. Not one person on the list felt right, but the chief is doing a little checking anyway."

Evie drummed her fingers on the table. "Maybe one of those goons knows someone who was in the service. A friend. Or a relative."

"They wouldn't have had to tell that person what they were up to," Kate said. "They could have claimed they were staging a paintball war or something harmless."

"And that doesn't narrow it down one bit." Rhea mashed the tines of her fork on the crumbs of a dumpling and mopped up the last bit of chicken stew in her bowl. "Almost everybody around here knows somebody who was in the military—or knows somebody who knows somebody. But nobody I know would do something like this."

"Yeah, we've got a pretty small scum population and they're not that hard core." Jackson nodded at Rhea. "I helped the chief pare down the list by paying a visit to a few of them, including those clowns who ripped off your signature sheets. After a little discussion, they denied having anything to do with this."

"Well of course they'd deny it." Rhea pushed her plate aside and yanked a green and white mint from her pocket and tore at the wrapper with her teeth. "They're stupid, but they're not brain-dead."

"They went on denying it after I mentioned that the guy who jumped them could be persuaded to pay them a return visit should it turn out their claim of innocence weighed in on the minus side of honest."

"Oh." She turned the mint and gnawed at the dry side of the wrapper. The candy shot out, bounced on the edge of the table, arced to the floor, and rolled beneath the refrigerator. "Dang it! Figured if I got this new kind in the sealed wrappers I'd eat less. But they get me so irritated trying to break them out that I end up eating more of everything else."

225

And yet calories never stuck to Rhea's lanky frame. Kate hooked a thumb toward the refrigerator. "There's more stew, and we have a bowl of fresh grapes."

"Stew was tasty, but it's not what I'm craving. And grapes are too . . . grapey."

Kate stood and got a shallow bowl from the cabinet. "Corn chips with melted cheese?"

Rhea rubbed her hands together. "Now you're talking. Got any sour cream? Maybe some green onion?"

"You'd think this was a damn diner the way people drop by and put in special orders," Evie groused. "Let's get back to the point. I'll bet those guys who started the fight at the first protest were in on this. The driver's still on the loose, isn't he?"

"Yeah," Jackson said, "but Chief Lowell is pretty sure he's with his brother in California. And the other guy was pulling an all-night shift on the front desk of a motel down the coast."

"Crap." Evie kicked the table leg, setting ice tinkling in Rhea's lemonade.

"That sums up my feelings," Jackson agreed. "I spun my wheels all day."

Kate slid the bowl of chips smothered with grated cheese into the microwave and dug a container of sour cream and a couple of green onions from the refrigerator. "How's the girl they tried to rape?"

"Bruised, scraped, mad, terrified, in shock. They're keeping her in the hospital another day. Turns out she's the one who came out here with that boy who got tossed in jail."

Evie paled. "Cassie? The girl from New Mexico?"

Jackson nodded.

226

Kate stared through the glass door of the microwave at the bubbling cheese. The shark was from New Mexico. An image of that yellowed fingernail and space-alien-skin turquoise ring rose in her mind. She snatched a knife from the drain board and chopped the onions, then yanked on the door handle, releasing a cloud of steam scented with toasted corn and sharp cheddar. A few moments earlier she might have bent over the bowl and filled her lungs, but now the aroma made her gag and she tossed on the onion bits, scooped a mound of sour cream on top, and rushed the snack to table.

"Did she get a piece of one of them?" Rhea asked. "Scratch him? Get some skin under her fingernails like they do on those crime scene shows?"

Jackson shook his head. "The others say she tried to run, but when they caught her she curled up and didn't fight like the other women did."

Kate thought about women who'd come to the domestic violence shelter she ran back in Arkansas. Sometimes fighting was the right thing to do. And sometimes it earned you a harder beating and more verbal abuse. She wondered if Cassie had experience with abuse—had suffered herself or seen a relative or close friend abused physically or emotionally.

"I hope she gets past it," Evie said. "Cassie looked like she led a pampered life."

Looks could be deceiving, Kate thought. Sometimes pampering was part of the cycle. It appeared to be atonement for abuse and lulled a victim into believing that this time the abuser would change.

"What about the rest of the kids?" Rhea mumbled around a mouthful of chips and cheese. "They going home?"

"The last I heard they were putting out a call for reinforcements."

"Bert and Sandi and the others will love that," Evie snorted. "A mobilized mob of kids wanting to change this little corner of the world."

"Chief Lowell can't think much of it either." Kate slipped into her chair and gazed at Jackson. "He'll have to protect them or it will look like he's leaving them at the mercy of vigilantes."

"And while he's protecting them, Bert and the others will scream about overtime and wasting manpower," Evie agreed. "Poor guy can't win. How many days does he have 'til he retires?"

"Too many," Jackson said.

They were all silent for a moment, then Evie smacked her palms on the table again. "I should have talked with those kids." She raised her hands, fingers spread. "It might have been a waste of breath, but we don't *know* that. I should have tried."

She scowled, jumped to her feet, and headed toward her bedroom. "I'm going down to that campsite now. Right now."

"And say what?" Kate asked.

"I'll say . . . I'll tell them . . ." Evie held her hands out as if pleading. "I'll tell them people who live here—people I know—are good people."

"I'm going with you," Jackson called.

"No. I'm perfectly capable of going alone!"

"I'm aware of that. But I'm going with you."

Evie frowned. "Are you afraid there will be another attack while I'm there?"

"Not tonight. The camp will be on red alert."

228

"Then what?" Her frown deepened. "You think I need a babysitter?"

"No, a driver," Jackson said. "It will be full dark by the time you head home."

Evie puffed out cheeks mottled purple. "Are you saying I'm a bad driver?"

"No, I'm saying your night vision sucks. Daylight's no problem, but you're a hazard to others—and yourself—after the sun goes down."

"That's a load of manure." Evie's eyes flashed with fury. "I was driving these roads while you were sitting in a high chair eating strained fruit and pooping in your diaper."

Jackson grinned. "I rest my case."

Evie raised a fist, her arm shaking with rage.

"Ding." Rhea waved her arms. "Round over. Back to your corners."

She stood and pushed in her chair. "And the decision of the judge is that 1) you both zip it, 2) Jackson stays here with the boys, and 3) Kate drives Evie to the camp because she's got to pick up some milk anyway."

Jackson shook his head. "That's—"

"Fine with me." Kate jumped to her feet and put a hand on Jackson's shoulder. "I'll take my cell phone and I'll keep the motor running in case we have to make a fast getaway. But we'll be fine. You said the attackers wouldn't be back tonight."

"Unless they figure that's what everybody's thinking." He frowned, then nodded. "In which case they'll wait until later in the night, close to dawn. That's what I'd do."

Kate bent and kissed him, tasting ice cream on his lips. "I'm glad you're on our side."

229

Fifteen minutes later, she and Evie turned down the rutted gravel road that led to the campsite.

"There's Curtis." Evie pointed to the deputy's car backed off the road but perpendicular to it, ready to roll in either direction. He raised a hand in greeting and then snapped on the dome light and made a note on a clipboard.

"He's taking our names." Evie stared at him as they passed. "Why would he do that?"

"Maybe he's keeping a record so he knows who's here if there's trouble."

Evie grunted. "Let's hope we're gone if trouble turns up. These old bones won't take much of a pounding."

And there are those who would like to pound on you, Kate thought. Starting with your son.

A hundred feet farther on, a grove of oaks arched tangled branches above the lane, creating a tunnel of darkness. At the end of it, the road circled an open central area with extra parking spaces, a bit of scruffy lawn hosting four picnic tables, and a hut containing showers, sinks, and toilets. Campsites spiked off from the outer edge of the circular drive and flames guttered in bamboo garden torches stuck into the ground between tents and camper trailers. The flickering lamps made the grove beyond the reach of the light seem even darker, more ominous.

About thirty people gathered around a fire pit in the center of the lawn. All heads turned toward Kate's SUV as she stopped.

"They look like they're expecting trouble or planning to go out to meet it," Evie said. "Those aren't paring knives on those tables."

Kate noted knives with wicked points and wide blades. "And I bet at least three of those men have guns strapped under their shirts."

"I shouldn't have been so quick to run my mouth to Bert and Sandi. But I never thought things would go this far down the road to lunacy. Except for that psychopath who came hunting you last summer, this has always been the kind of dull, boring little town where nothing ever happened." Evie unbuckled her seatbelt. "And, damn it, I liked it that way."

A man strode toward them, his hair bunched under a black ball cap, the left side of his face a swollen mass of cuts and bruises, his left arm in a sling. Kate recognized Abel Moorhouse, the boy who had come out to Evie's place. But this was no longer a boy. He was leaner, harder, a walking streak of rage.

Evie opened her door and stepped down. "Evening, Abel. How are you?"

His eyes flared with reddish light. "You here to talk us into leaving?" he mumbled through split lips.

"I doubt I have enough breath in me for that." Evie moved around the door and swiveled her head. Kate followed her gaze, taking in the men closing ranks behind Abel, the women hanging back, arms crossed, shoulders hunched. That body language seemed to indicate that leaving this place soon was something they'd at least like to discuss. "It seems you've set your course."

"*They* set the course. We don't advocate violence."

But you courted it, Kate thought. You flirted with it, danced with it.

231

"We're not looking for a fight, but we *will* defend ourselves if they come back."

"For Cassie," a woman at the back called out.

"For Cassie," a few others echoed with more tentative loyalty.

Kate leaned from her open window. "How is Cassie doing?"

"How would you be doing?" A stocky man with a blond beard snarled.

"Not well," Kate answered in a clear voice. "That's why I asked."

"Well, it's none of your—"

Abel raised his right hand and the man grumbled into silence and stomped off past the perimeter of quavering light. "Thanks for asking. Cassie's hurting bad and she's scared and pretty messed up." He put his fingertips to the sides of his head. "Mostly I think she can't believe that it happened—that it *could* happen."

Was Cassie such an idealist? Did she believe wealth and position exempted her? Or was she simply naïve?

Evie glanced at Kate as if thinking the same thing, then turned her attention to Abel. "I'm sorry about the attack, sorry about what happened to Cassie. When I heard, it was like a punch in the gut. People in Castaway Beach don't do things like this."

"They did last night."

"*Somebody* did last night. When Chief Lowell catches up with them, I think we'll find they get their mail in another town. A long way from here."

"Chief Lowell." Abel spat again. "He and that kid deputy parked out by the highway couldn't catch the flu in an epidemic. They probably know damn well who beat us up. And if those jerks come back, I

232

bet that kid cop will conveniently be munching doughnuts miles from here."

A rumble of agreement swept through the crowd.

Evie's shoulders squared and her hands rolled into fists. "Chief Lowell is one of the most honorable men I know. And Curtis—yes, he's young, but he's dedicated to his job." She aimed a finger at Abel's chest. "No matter what you think, they know their duty. And no matter what they think of you, they'll do it."

She stalked to the SUV, levered herself inside, and slammed the door. Taking that as her cue, Kate rolled, following the drive around the patch of lawn, conscious of heads turning to watch their progress, of two women gazing with longing at their retreat.

When they were out into the tree tunnel, Evie groaned. "That was as easy as plucking the eyebrows on a cat."

Kate snorted back a laugh. "Have you ever done that?"

"No. And I don't know why I ever would." She brought her fist down on the console. "Damn it, they're cooking up a recipe for disaster. And there's not one thing we can do about it."

CHAPTER 23

When the phone rang as she poured their first cups of coffee the next morning, Kate exchanged wary glances with Evie and Jackson.

"Can't be good news," Evie muttered without moving from her chair. "Good news would wait until I had my ration of caffeine."

"My turn to get crapped on." With a hand planted on the table, Jackson levered himself to his feet and hobbled to the desk. "Wildlife center."

Kate couldn't make out words or identify the caller but even from across the room, the agitation in the voice was clear. She set the pot back on the warmer and eased to Jackson's side.

"Calm down," Jackson said. "I can't understand you. Start from the beginning. Who are you? Why are you calling here?"

He punched the speaker button as the caller shouted, "This is Abel Moorhouse. Cassie's gone. They took her from the hospital last night."

Kate put a hand on Jackson's arm. "Abel, this is Kate Dalton. Evie's here, too. Who took Cassie? The people who attacked your camp?"

"Yes. No. I don't know. Nobody will tell me anything. Her room's empty."

"Maybe a nurse took her downstairs for an X-ray or—"

"No. She's gone. Her clothes are gone." He paused for a few seconds and then his voice grew puzzled and uncertain. "And her earrings and watch and rings. They're gone, too. So is the book I brought her yesterday. And her toothbrush and makeup."

Kate gnawed her lower lip. Allowing Cassie to gather her clothing and jewelry and bring along a book didn't sound like the work of someone in a hurry, someone bent on harming her. "Have you called the police?"

"No. But they won't care."

Jackson pressed the phone into Kate's hand and headed for the door. "I'm going down there."

"Call Chief Lowell," Kate ordered Abel. "Right now. Then stay there. I'm coming."

With a squeal of brakes, Jackson slid his truck into a parking space near the hospital's emergency entrance. Kate leaped out and trotted to double glass doors that slid open as she approached. On the far side of the broad receiving area, Maureen O'Bannion looked up from behind a tall desk. Her graying hair stood up in tussocks as if she'd been twisting at it.

"Chief Lowell's up on the third floor talking to the nursing supervisor," she said when Kate was still two yards from the desk. "But that boy who called you left ten minutes ago."

"Going back to the camp?" Jackson asked.

"I don't know." Maureen seized a spike of hair and twisted so furiously Kate expected part of her skull to pop off. "I was on the phone when I heard his van rattle past. By the time I got to the window he was out of sight."

"And Cassie is definitely gone?" Kate asked. "She's not in another room or in X-ray or—?"

"She's gone. Sometime before 5:00 a.m."

Jackson scowled. "How did she leave in the middle of the night?"

Maureen released the tuft of hair and wheeled on him. "This isn't a prison. It's a hospital. We don't have concertina wire around the parking lot and guards with machine guns on the roof."

Jackson took a step back and raised his hands. "What I meant was, people have to sign forms if they leave before the doctor releases them, don't they?"

"And what about the financial stuff?" Kate asked. "Insurance?"

Maureen leaned across the counter, looked both ways, and lowered her voice to a whisper. "You didn't hear this from me, and I haven't seen it with my own eyes, but it's all over the hospital that the administrator found an envelope pushed under her door when she came in. It was stuffed with money to cover that girl's bill. Big money. More than the charges might have run to."

They paid to spring Cassie from the hospital. Hardly something kidnappers would do.

Kate thought about the day she met Abel and Cassie, about his rusty van and unkempt appearance, her sculpted nails and jewelry. She

236

recalled her impression that Cassie had been born to money while Abel either had far less or shunned the trappings of wealth. Then she remembered he said he wouldn't put up bail after the fracas on the beach because he didn't have the money. So the cash in the envelope didn't come from him. Unless it belonged to Cassie and he'd brought it to her and was now only pretending to be alarmed that she was gone. But if that was the case, why would he call Evie?

"And no one saw her leave?" Jackson asked.

"No one who's mentioned it yet," Maureen said. "But there's only a skeleton staff at night. It would be easy to walk out."

"Or walk in and persuade someone else to walk out?"

Maureen shrugged and pointed to the emergency room doors. "The front doors are locked, but those stay open. And there's a stairwell door at the end of each wing. Folks go out for a smoke and leave a door propped open, especially this time of year."

"Security cameras?"

"Chief Lowell's all over that."

"Then we'll try to find Abel." Kate turned to Jackson and put a hand on his arm. "Before he finds trouble."

Jackson's eyes glinted with what Kate took to be the thrill of the hunt and ten minutes later they pulled up beside the hut at the protesters' campground. A few of the camping spaces were empty, but a dozen people sat at the picnic tables on the scraggly lawn, mugs and tin plates in front of them. They sagged like rag dolls and their faces were gray and puckered. Kate guessed few had slept last night.

237

"I don't see his van." She pointed to a slice of packed earth beside a pair of plastic chairs and a red ice chest. "It was parked there last night."

"Maybe he's been and gone already." Jackson killed the engine and they got out. The aroma of frying onions and potatoes wafted over them, making Kate's mouth water.

"What's your problem now?" The stocky man who had been so vocal the night before came forward, hands rolled into fists, jaw thrust out. The corners of his mustache glistened with egg yolk, and toast crumbs speckled his beard.

"No problem." Jackson wrapped his fingers around Kate's arm and squeezed. "We're looking for Abel. Evie Hopkins wants to talk with him about potential legislation."

Jackson squeezed again and Kate wove her own thread into the fabrication. "And the county commission race. If there's new blood after the election, they might be able to put some pressure on the legislature to change the rules about driving on the beach."

The stocky man's shoulders relaxed. "Abel's not here. He went to check on Cassie."

"Thanks," Jackson said. "Sorry to interrupt your breakfast. We'll try to catch up with Abel in town. If we don't, please ask him to call Evie right away."

With a grunt, the stocky man turned and marched back to his place at the table. The others nodded and signaled with raised thumbs that he'd handled the situation well.

"I didn't want to be the one to tell them about Cassie," Jackson said when they were on the other side of the grove.

"That's what I figured." Kate glanced over her shoulder. "I forgot to tell you last night. Some of them have guns."

"Four. That I saw," Jackson said with a snort. "Amateurs."

"I'll call Evie and bring her up to speed in case Abel calls or goes out there." Kate slid her cell phone from her purse. "I can't imagine where else he might be."

"Let's see if the video from the hospital tells us anything."

"Guys knew the camera was there and kept their heads down and their backs to it." Chief Lowell pointed to the computer on his desk. "Look if you want, but I guarantee all you'll learn is that they were wearing black suits, size XXXL."

Kate drew in a hissing breath.

Lowell turned. "You know them?"

"Not their names." She slid her hand into Jackson's. "I've seen them. They drive a black car with windows tinted deep gray. They stopped me on the street last week and their slimy boss told me it was in my best interest to urge Evie to make the 'correct' decision about the future of her property."

Lowell scowled. "Who's this boss?"

"A New Mexico developer pushing the golf course project," Jackson said.

Kate frowned. "Why would his thugs take Cassie?"

"His name is Hernando Castillo. I'm guessing he's a close relative, probably her grandfather."

Kate shuddered. Young and beautiful Cassie, sharing the same family tree with that repugnant man.

Lowell grunted. "Think he's behind the attack on the camp?"

"It's possible. Maybe he didn't know she was part of the group." Jackson's eyes hardened. "Or maybe he thought she needed a lesson."

"Hell of a lesson," Chief Lowell said.

"Yeah. But if he wasn't behind it, her injuries gave him an opportunity to interfere. Removing her in the night could raise anxiety levels and bring the protests to a halt."

"We've got to find out if she's okay." Kate grasped Jackson's arm. "I talked with her. I made her lemonade. I want to know that she's not hurt—hurt worse."

"My money says a chartered jet took off for Santa Fe this morning and she was on board."

"I'll check that and wake Curtis up and send him out to the camp to talk to that boy," Lowell said. "See if he knows how to get hold of her parents."

"Abel's not there," Kate told him. "At least, he wasn't ten minutes ago. We left word for him to call Evie if he turns up."

"All right. I'll have Curtis check the beaches."

"We'll do that," Jackson volunteered. "Let Curtis catch up on his sleep."

"Can we check while we're eating breakfast?" Kate asked as they climbed into his truck.

"My thinking exactly."

Jackson headed for a drive-through and in a few minutes they were sipping coffee and chewing on breakfast burritos as they made a sweep of the beaches and an extensive tour of the town.

No trace of Abel or his van.

Kate called home and got Way-Ray who told her Evie was talking with a volunteer and the phone hadn't rung since he and Sean got up. Before Kate could tell him to be sure to get a number for Abel if he called, Way-Ray blurted, "Whoa. The geese are going all crazy. Maybe there's a snake. I gotta go see."

"Be careful," Kate told the broken connection.

Jackson raised an eyebrow.

"The geese are sounding off. Way-Ray thinks there might be a snake. I hope he—"

"He'll be fine," Jackson said. "He's all boy, but he's not as foolhardy as you think. He and Sean like to keep plenty of running room between themselves and snakes. I happened to be on the roof working on a gutter when they came across a big one by the garden."

Kate smiled. "Good to know, but I'll let him hang onto his pride and pretend I don't know that." She slipped the phone into her purse and wadded the greasy paper wrapping from the burrito into a sack. "Where could Abel be? Who does he know besides the folks at the campsite?"

Jackson pulled into a parking space in the town lot and sucked coffee from the hole in his cup lid. "He might know the shark. Or at least know of him from Cassie."

That made sense. In the getting-to-know-each-other process Cassie and Abel would have talked about their families, if only in terms of the people

241

and attitudes they were rebelling against. "But did Abel and Cassie know the shark was in town?"

"My money's on a negative answer to that question. They were focused on the beach. They might have heard about the golf development, but I can't see why they'd look into who was behind it. And a man courting local business interests wouldn't want it known that his granddaughter was one of the protesters. If he knew she was here, I bet he avoided contact."

"Until he stepped in and made Cassie disappear in the middle of the night and left a bucket of cash behind."

Jackson rolled his coffee cup between his hands. "If Abel heard about that, then maybe he's gone shark hunting."

Draining his coffee, he revved the engine. "Time for us to do the same."

Kate shivered, remembering that rasping voice, the comment that he wouldn't hurt her that day.

This was another day.

"Where? Where do we look for him?"

Jackson turned the truck south. "Where all the sharks stay." He pointed at the sloping hills bunched against the flanks of the Coast Range. "The most expensive resort hotel on this stretch of the coast."

242

CHAPTER 24

Thirty minutes later they chugged to the top of a ridge and pulled into the drive skirting an emerald lawn spread out before an imposing log structure with a 180-degree view of the coast. A blue-jacketed valet trotted from beneath a portico, his eyes filled with a mixture of purpose and alarm. Jackson waved him off and wedged the truck between two foreign-made luxury cars parked halfway down the lot. The valet didn't retreat, but stood at attention as if guarding the hotel from assault by hoi polloi.

Feeling like a street urchin, Kate tugged at the tattered hem of her cut-off shorts and smoothed her rumpled T-shirt. "I didn't know this place existed."

"People who stay here don't want you to."

Jackson swung out of the truck, checked his teeth in the tinted window of a silver car, picked at something with his thumbnail, then hobbled to the valet, his spine stiff, his chin high. He seemed unfazed by and even indifferent to the opulence of his surroundings. Kate admired that, wished she could see this place only as wood and stone and

243

manicured shrubbery instead of as a shrine to wealth and privilege. Beyond that, she wished it didn't make her feel vaguely inadequate.

"Tell me about the kid who was out here a while ago trying to cause trouble for one of your guests," Jackson said. An order, not a request.

Because of Jackson's tone or because of a desire to see him gone, the valet complied. "The kid in the van?"

Jackson nodded and the valet rubbed the point of his jaw. "Gunned that wreck right to the front door and punched me when I told him to move it. Before I could tackle him, he charged into the lobby yelling for Mr. Castillo, telling him to bring Cassie back."

Jackson nodded again and the kid ran a hand across his crew cut and went on. "Mr. Aldridge—he's the manager—yelled for someone to call the cops but then Mr. Castillo's driver and his personal assistant came out of the dining room and said they'd take care of it."

"And did they?"

"I guess. They grabbed the kid by the arms—he was still yelling—took him outside, and jammed him into Mr. Castillo's car. Then the small guy got in the van and they drove off." The valet grinned. "Small? Huh. They're both huge. We call them G-1 and G-2. G for gorilla."

"You know their names?"

"Nah." He brushed his hand across his hair. "They're in a suite with Mr. Castillo, no names on the register. And those guys, they don't talk to the staff. Heck, they hardly talk to each other."

Jackson grunted. "And that was the end of it?"

"Yeah. Mr. Castillo told Mr. Aldridge the kid was someone he fired and they'd had trouble with him

244

before. He said his assistants would take him to the sheriff's office." The valet's face creased. "Did you have trouble with that guy too?"

"In a way. How's your jaw?"

"Hurts like hell." The valet patted his jacket pocket and grinned. "But Mr. Castillo gave me a hundred bucks for taking the punch."

"You should have asked for two."

Jackson turned and walked back to the truck, leaving the valet rubbing his jaw again, a confused frown on his face.

"Where do you think they took him?" Kate asked as they careened down from the ridge, brakes squealing.

"Any of a thousand places where there'd be no one around to watch them pound him senseless."

Kate shivered once again, imagining Abel's broken body dumped into a grave scraped out between the roots of a Douglas fir, his van rolled into thick brush at the bottom of a ravine. There were places where the undergrowth was so thick you'd be invisible if you walked a hundred feet into the forest.

They were nearly to the highway when her phone rang.

"Finally." Way-Ray's voice was high and he gulped for breath. "I've been trying and trying and trying to call you."

"We must have been in a dead zone."

"Evie says to get here real fast. There's a fire."

"Fire? Where?"

"By the barn."

"The barn?"

Jackson stomped on the gas.

The barn was ancient, its sagging rafters and splintering walls perfect kindling. Hay bales piled

245

high inside would feed the flames. The surrounding trees would catch and then—

"Are the fire trucks there yet?"

"Evie didn't call them."

"Why not?"

"I don't know. She told me not to. She said you'll see when you get here. I gotta get another hose. Bye."

Way-Ray broke the connection, but Kate clutched the phone to her ear for a few seconds, as if the answer to her question might still be in transition. "Way-Ray said there's a fire by the barn."

"*By* the barn? Not *in* the barn?"

"Right." A straw to grasp at. "But he said he had to get a hose. *Another* hose. And Evie didn't call the fire department."

"Must have it under control." Jackson braked and skidded into a turn. "That barn's a pile of tinder, the well out there won't give her much more than a trickle, and the pump's about shot. But she knows that better than anyone."

"That's why I'm surprised she didn't call for help." Kate flipped the phone open.

"She must have a reason."

"She told Way-Ray I'd see when we got there."

"Then let's fly."

Snapping the phone closed again, Kate shoved it into her purse, and stared through the bug-spattered windshield.

The truck's engine growled and something clattered and scraped under the hood. "Not now," Jackson muttered, "don't blow up on me now."

Fence posts flicked past, the field beyond them a blur of gold and green. Then they were in Castaway Beach, sliding onto a side street, running parallel to

246

the highway and its plodding traffic, the backs of shops and houses smeared together by their speed. The truck swayed as Jackson threaded it around a beer truck making a delivery and an RV wrapped in the accessories of vacationing—lawn chairs, bicycles, and a canvas canopy striped like a peppermint stick.

They hit the highway again, engine thrumming, the grinding beneath the hood as shrill as a saw, then slid into the road to Evie's place, canting over on the edges of the tires, chassis rocking.

Kate gripped the seatbelt with one hand and braced the other on the dash. Except for another muttered, "Not now," Jackson gave no indication of concern. He punched the gas the second he straightened the wheels.

Kate's teeth snapped together as they shot along the road, tires slamming into ruts and potholes, struts and shock absorbers squawking, doing little to mitigate the pounding. Blackberry canes raked at the doors and she smelled the acrid scent of smoke and heard herself moan in fear.

Then they shot into the clearing. Abel's van was crunched into a tree, a faint plume of vapor rising from the crumpled front end.

"Damn it!" Jackson stood on the brake.

The back end broke loose and they spun a doughnut. Kate caught a glimpse of Way-Ray swinging a hose back and forth, wetting down the grass between the van and the barn and Sean chopping out a firebreak with a hoe. They looked tall and competent, more like young men than boys.

Way-Ray waved his free hand and pointed over his shoulder to where Evie knelt, her hands moving across something obscured by the tall grass.

247

With a shriek of metal and a dull rip of rubber, the truck came to a halt, steam hissing from around the hood, the front axel dropping to the right with a whoosh and a thud.

"Help Evie." Jackson shoved his door wide. "I'll check the van."

Stumbling over hummocks of tangled grass, Kate ran to Evie's side and saw Abel. He lay on his back, his face streaked with blood, his T-shirt torn, his legs dark with dirt and bruises.

"Someone—he won't tell me who—beat the tar out of this boy, crashed his van, and started a fire," Evie said. "We got him out before he got scorched."

Abel moaned and tilted his head to peer at Kate through swollen eyelids. She dropped beside him and put a hand on his shoulder. "Did you call an ambulance?"

"No. He didn't want me to. Didn't want me to call the cops, either." Evie glanced at the van. Jackson was peering into the engine compartment and Sean was hauling out clothing and bedding and spreading it on the grass.

Abel moaned again and Evie stroked his forehead. "Lucky for him the geese went nuts and Sean and Way-Ray smelled smoke. Double lucky whoever set the fire botched the job."

"I know exactly who set it."

"The people who attacked the camp?"

"No. The ones who took Cassie out of the hospital."

Abel gripped Kate's arm and whispered a mash of syllables through puffed and torn lips.

"Sshhh. It's okay," she told him. "We think she's on the way back to New Mexico. Chief Lowell is checking."

Tears leaked from the corners of his eyes.

"What happened to her isn't your fault," Kate said, fearing that some of it might be. Abel had chosen to light a fuse, chosen confrontation.

"I think we're good." Jackson limped up behind them, bent, and braced himself with a hand on Kate's shoulder. "How's he doing?"

"Well, he took a couple of solid punches to the face so he's not going to win any beauty contests in the near future. And he's bruised up where he tried to defend himself." Evie raised Abel's arm and traced her fingers around a series of dark swellings. "They stomped his legs and back. But it looks like they were in a hurry, so . . ."

What she didn't say, Kate thought, was that those punches could have done damage they couldn't see, that there might be blood leaking in his brain, something ruptured in his gut. "We should get him to the hospital."

Abel moaned. Fear flickered across his eyes. "No."

"Those thugs took Cassie from the hospital," Jackson said. "There's no reason they couldn't take him, too."

"We could take him to another hospital," Kate insisted. "Get him in under a fake name. Or Chief Lowell could guard him."

"The chief wouldn't be inclined to do that unless Abel's willing to testify to the beating he took today."

Abel shook his head and moaned once more.

"That's what I thought." Jackson nodded to Abel. "Right now they think he's dead, so he's not a threat."

"What's he's supposed to do? Play dead for the next twenty years? Hide in a cave until the shark dies of old age?"

"The shark?" Evie sat back on her heels and glared at them. "What are you two talking about? And why haven't you bothered to clue in the old lady?"

Kate winced. "We thought . . . we wanted to . . ."

Jackson made a chopping motion with his hand. "We'll explain after we get Abel to the house. Get your car, Kate."

An hour later they had bandaged Abel's cuts, got him into clean clothes borrowed from Jackson, and settled him on the sofa with a glass of lemonade and a flexible straw. Way-Ray and Sean offered to play a video game with him, but Evie sent them back to the barn with sandwiches, drinks, a bag of potato chips, and orders to watch for smoke and race back to the house if they saw anyone coming.

When they were out of sight, she glowered at Kate and Jackson. "Now, sit. Tell me everything, including why you decided to tell me nothing."

"The shark is a big investor from New Mexico." Kate dropped into a chair and took a long pull on a glass of iced coffee. "Jackson thinks he's a relative of Cassie's. He travels with two 'assistants.' They're the ones who took her from the hospital and beat up Abel. A few days ago they stopped me in town and told me it would be in my best interests—in all of our best interests—to persuade you to accept the next offer that came along."

Evie chewed at her lower lip, then sat and tapped her fingers on the table. "Paul's offer. To trade for that piece of land south of town."

"That's what we assume they meant." Jackson said.

"They scared you." Evie leaned forward and looked into Kate's eyes. "They scared you bad."

Kate wished she could deny that, but it was the truth. "Yes."

"But you didn't lean on me to make the trade." Her voice rose. "You didn't think it would matter that you might get hurt? That Way-Ray—"

"No," Jackson slapped the table. "We knew it *would* matter. We knew it would matter too much. So we kept it out of the equation."

"Well, now it's in." Evie dusted her hands together, went to the refrigerator, and pulled out a tub of cottage cheese and a bag of celery sticks. "Now we know what we're up against."

She got a box of wheat crackers from a cabinet and returned to the table. "And before too long, they'll find out what they're up against. This is my home and the only way I'll leave it is when they carry me out in a coffin."

251

CHAPTER 25

An hour later, Kate and Jackson returned to the barn and sent Sean and Way-Ray to the house to get a lecture from Evie about the importance of keeping secrets about the fire and Abel.

While Jackson changed the blown tire on his truck, Kate checked over the van to see if anything should be staged to support the story they'd tell Chief Lowell. When Evie hauled Abel to safety, he left smears of blood on the steering wheel, the door, and the edge of the seat—smears he might have left escaping on his own. She sorted through the possessions in the grass, fished out a journal that she tossed into Jackson's truck, then stowed everything else back in the van, tipping boxes to make it appear they'd fallen when the van hit the tree.

"Nice job," Jackson said. "Now we roll the windows down, close all the doors except the driver's, and lay a false trail." He pulled Abel's bloody shirt and cargo pants from a paper bag and handed the shirt to Kate.

"Where do we lay this trail?"

"From the van to the spot where Evie laid him in the grass, then across the road, then around the meadow and part of the way down the path to the cove." He walked to the edge of the road, bent, and stuffed the pants pockets with rocks. "It might be overkill, but if they bring in a search dog, it could pay off."

"Our scent won't confuse things?"

"I don't know. Let's hope not."

He walked along the road to a place where a spreading maple kept sunlight from reaching the blackberry hedge and, lifting his feet high, stomped stunted canes to the ground and plunged through to the meadow beyond. Kate followed and they split up in the high grass, wandering in looping patterns, dragging the clothing behind them, meeting at the second band of trees, then going through together, following the trail along the edge of the headland and descending to the steepest switchback.

Waves thrashed below them, breaking over the long tongue of basalt and boiling up the scrap of beach almost to the enormous log at the top of the cove.

"Now what?"

Jackson stuffed the shirt inside the pants and rolled the clothing into a compact package. Cocking his arm, he threw it into the surf. In a second, it was gone, sucked under. "Now we hope the tide takes it out."

Gripping Jackson's arm, Kate leaned out but saw no sign of the bundle. "And if it doesn't?"

"Then we hope the rocks fall out of the pockets before those pants wash up somewhere."

Kate nodded. Things could get complicated quickly when you started to lie. And lies piled up in haphazard ways, teetering so that if doubt was cast on one, the tower might tilt and fall. She crossed her fingers and turned away from the surging tide, willing it to drown all evidence of their fabrication.

"I'll call the chief," Jackson said.

"Go through it again for me before you do."

"Okay. We came back from town a couple of hours ago and spotted the fire. The grass is dry and heat from the engine must have started the blaze. You recognized the van as Abel's and we guessed he was hurt and confused and went looking for help. After we put out the fire, we searched but didn't find him."

Kate nodded. "I'm glad you're the one calling the chief. You're a much better liar."

"I wish honesty was a choice here, but it's not." He kissed her forehead. "If they don't buy that Abel fell in the ocean, they'll come looking for him. Then he's dead for sure."

"I know. I just wish . . ."

Jackson put his arms around her and kissed her eyelids. "Can't be helped. Until he's able to get out of here, that kid's life depends on how well we con everyone, even Chief Lowell."

And Abel's life might not be the only one hanging on a lie, a lie that would be Evie's to tell.

Half an hour later Chief Lowell pulled up beside the barn and got out, hitching at his belt. "Still no sign of him?"

"Not a trace," Jackson said. "At least not beyond where he shoved his way through the blackberries." He pointed to the bent and broken canes. "Once we got the fire out and soaked down the area, we searched the meadow that runs out to the lip of the headland. Deer are through there all the time and if there's a fresh trail I couldn't see it. The path to the cove cuts right along the edge of the lower meadow, but Way-Ray and Sean are up and down it at least once a day—Evie too—and it's packed as hard as concrete. I couldn't see any footprints."

"Well, if you couldn't, I doubt anyone else can. I'll call the search and rescue team and ask them to bring a dog." Lowell scowled. "Probably a waste of time. My bet is he went over that cliff and hit the rocks. He's crab food by now."

Kate stifled a moan.

"Sorry," he told her, "but it's a fact of life. Kid was disoriented, maybe hurt bad—internal injuries or concussion."

He dug a cell phone from his pocket. "Did you check the woods between here and the highway?"

"Probably should have, but after I saw where the bushes were mashed down, I assumed . . ." Jackson twisted his lips in a wry smile. "Hell, you know what happens when you assume."

Chief Lowell snorted. "All too well."

"We'll search there now," Jackson offered.

Lowell glanced at Jackson's bad leg, then waved the offer aside. "We'll leave that to the team. What about around the house? The kid knew the way, seems logical he'd try to get there." He gazed at the trodden hedge. "If he went through those brambles, he might have come back out to the road—there or someplace farther along—and followed it toward the house."

"We thought of that," Jackson said. "Way-Ray and Sean have regular patrols going—the perimeter and all the outbuildings. And the geese will warn us if a stranger shows up.

"Yeah, some say geese are better than watchdogs." Lowell flipped open the phone and punched at buttons with a thick forefinger. "I'll take fur over feathers any day."

Jackson turned and squeezed Kate's arm. "We'll take one more look along the road up to the house. Be back in a few with water and a couple of lawn chairs."

The chief waved his thanks and they started along the road, making a show of peering into the brush and tall grass on either side. In a few moments they were screened by a bend and Kate whispered, "Are you sure we shouldn't tell the chief?"

"If we tell him now he'll be pissed that we didn't tell him sooner. And he won't put on a convincing act." Jackson crossed the road and pulled her against his chest. "Playing for time is our best move right now."

"But it's not really a move because we're not taking action. We're just waiting."

"And you hate waiting."

"Yes, but what I *really* hate is not knowing how long the wait will be."

He tilted her chin and kissed her, sucking her lower lip. The heat of him was warmer than the sun on her bare arms.

"Stillness, Kate. Practice stillness." He kissed her once more, deeper and harder, and gazed into her eyes. "We need to know more about these men. Clear your mind and think back to that day on the street. Imagine you're peering into that car. You see something, you remember something you didn't tell me about."

Kate let her vision slide out of focus, let herself drift, safe within Jackson's arms. "A finger. One finger wasn't there. The driver had his arm draped across the back of the seat and there was a gap. The index finger is gone. Cut off clean."

"Good. What else?"

"I smelled cologne. Strong, musky, but sharp and biting. It made me want to sneeze."

"And . . . ?"

"A tattoo. The other had a tattoo on the back of his neck." She closed her eyes. "It's . . . I don't know what it is. I could only see part of it. Maybe some kind of a bug. A red bug."

"Could you draw what you saw?"

"I think so."

Jackson kissed her eyelids. "Then let's get some paper."

"Abel's in my room," Way-Ray announced when they came into the kitchen. "Evie said anyone who walked by the living room window could see him on the couch, so we blew up the blow-up bed and put it in the corner where the toy box was."

"And then we disguised—uh, camouflaged—him so he looks like a pile of dirty clothes," Sean added. "In case Chief Lowell or Curtis comes and searches the house."

"They won't." Kate turned to Jackson. "Will they?"

"No reason for them to. But we'll want to offer coffee and cold drinks and the use of the bathroom to the search team. And if the bathroom downstairs

257

is occupied, someone might go upstairs." He ruffled Way-Ray's hair. "So that was a smart move."

Way-Ray and Sean beamed at each other. "And we won't tell anyone," Sean said. "Not even my mom. Or my brother."

"We're gonna show you how good we are at being quiet and doing secret stuff and subter . . . subterfuge."

"That's Latin," Sean clarified. "We looked it up."

He and Way-Ray did a fist bump and again Kate was struck by how much older Way-Ray seemed—Sean, too. She'd been with them every day and yet she felt as if she'd blinked or looked away for a moment and missed a crucial leap in their development. Next time she took her eyes off them she might find they'd grown whiskers or were learning to drive or talking about girls. Was this the way it was for all parents?

Jackson put a hand over his heart and snapped to attention. "I stand ready to be awed and amazed by the depth of your furtiveness, by the reverberating noiselessness that will enclose us like a bell jar."

"I didn't say we'd be quiet." Way-Ray rolled his eyes. "Not all the time. We'll just be quiet about this guy and the stuff you tell us not to talk about."

"We know this isn't a game," Sean added. "Evie explained it to us. Some guys beat him up."

"And they might come back," Way-Ray chimed in. "So he has to play possum."

"But not really like a possum does," Sean elaborated. "He doesn't have to look like he's dead or even stay in Way-Ray's room all the time. Just when somebody might see him. Somebody who's not us."

Jackson grinned. "I'm glad you clarified that."

The porch door whapped closed and Evie came in wiping sweat from her forehead. "Don't know if I'm sweating from the heat or because I'm stressing about making that call." She poured herself a glass of lemonade and gulped down half, then went to the desk. "But it's got to be done."

"We'll clear out and give you space," Kate offered.

"No need. We're all in this together now. We all have our lies to tell." Evie picked up the phone and winked at Way-Ray. "It's not often that we declare open season on fibbing. You and Sean enjoy it while you can."

She pulled in a long breath, then punched Paul's number. Without a greeting, she got to the point. "I might have been a little hasty when you were here the other day. I'm not saying yes, but if the offer still stands, I'd like to take a look at that piece of property."

She listened for a moment and then mimed cutting her own throat. "Can't do it tomorrow, got some new volunteers need training. Maybe the day after if there isn't a critter crisis. Okay. Good. Day after tomorrow."

"I woulda believed you," Way-Ray said when she hung up.

"Me, too," Sean agreed.

Evie blew on her fingernails and polished them on her ratty blue T-shirt. "Nothing to it. Even if I never did it before."

Way-Ray's eyes widened. "Never? You never told a lie? Ever?"

Evie pinched her chin, considering. "Well, there was this one time. Last year."

259

"What did you lie about?" Sean bounced on the toes of a pair of sneakers so tattered they wouldn't see out the summer. "Who'd you lie to?"

"I lied to Kate."

Way-Ray gasped and glanced at Kate and Jackson. "Kate hates lies more than I hate beets."

Evie shot Kate a wink and, playing along, Kate shot back a glare and Evie ducked her head as if dodging a blow. "I know she does." She leaned closer to the boys. "But it couldn't be helped. I wanted her to come work here, so I had to lie and tell her that . . . that . . ."

"That what?" The boys yelled.

Evie cupped her hands around her mouth. "That I liked Way-Ray. That I thought it would be nice to have him around."

The boys' jaws dropped and for a long moment there was silence. Way-Ray canted his head and peered at Kate who feigned shock and anger. Then Evie laughed and punched Way-Ray's shoulder. "Gotcha!"

"Good one!" Sean bounced on his toes again.

"Yeah." Way-Ray's face creased with thought and he glanced at Kate again. "You're not lyin' now, are you? You said you loved me the night we made the ice cream sauce. You said you loved Sean, too. Were you lyin' then?"

Kate felt tears prickle behind her eyelids, tears for this orphaned boy who might never be completely certain of love.

Evie gathered both boys into her arms. "Of course I'm not lying. I love you two to pieces. I'll love you even more after you do your chores."

260

"We woulda done them by now but we were busy," Sean said. "Puttin' out the fire and blowing up the bed."

"And watching the fire spot again," Way-Ray added. "And hiding Abel and stuff."

"And you did a great job," Jackson said. "But your regular chores are still hanging fire."

"You can't hang fire," Sean said. "Unless it's like in a lantern or something."

"Is that Latin?" Way-Ray asked with a loud sigh. "Do we hafta get the dictionary?"

Kate slapped a hand over her mouth. Evie bent over the desk, shuffling papers.

"No, it's not Latin," Jackson said. "It's an expression that has to do with antique muskets. I'll explain later."

"That's okay." Way-Ray wrinkled his nose and sidled toward the door. "I'm pretty sure we don't need to know about old muskrats. Come on, Sean, let's go clean up bird poop."

When the screen door slapped behind them, Kate let her laughter loose. Evie collapsed in a chair by the desk, shrieking with glee. "Old muskrats!" She pointed a wavering finger at Jackson. "Is that Latin?"

"Philistines," Jackson snorted.

"That's us," Evie agreed.

Jackson's scowl held for the count of four, then collapsed with a chuckle. "Old muskrats."

For a few moments they stretched out their amusement, savoring it like the last chocolate in a box, then Evie stood. "Now, what do we do with this time we supposedly purchased?"

261

"We find out more about what we're up against," Jackson said. "Who these thugs are and how they operate."

"And how do we do that without telling Chief Lowell about them?" Kate asked.

"Every information network is like a river," Jackson said. "There are the official channels, the shipping channels that are marked with buoys, and then there are all the rest, the currents that sweep close to the bank, the streams and ditches and trenches and sewers that feed the river. As soon as I'm finished pretending to search for Abel, I'll start dredging up the sludge."

CHAPTER 26

All afternoon the search team hunted for a trace of Abel Moorhouse. They sectioned off the woods and the meadows, they walked every foot of beach revealed at low tide, they brought a boat up close to the cove, and they followed the trail from the owl enclosure down to the tidal marsh and slogged along the base of the headland.

Jackson planted himself with Chief Lowell beside Abel's van, prepared to put a spin on anything searchers found that contradicted his theory. With fingers crossed, Kate went about what she hoped appeared to be a normal afternoon's activities—paperwork, laundry, gardening, dinner preparations. Evie, after announcing that cabinets needed cleaning and organizing, disappeared into the medical trailer.

At sunset, with Jackson riding shotgun, Chief Lowell drove up to the house. Stomach knotting, Kate rushed out to greet them, sagging with relief when Jackson shot her a wink as he climbed out of the patrol car.

"We already ate," she told Chief Lowell, "but I have a big bowl of chicken salad and plenty of cheese biscuits if you're hungry."

"Too tired to eat," the chief said through the open window. "Too much misery on my mind. The dogs lost his scent on the trail above the cove, so it looks like what we guessed—he fell in and went out with the tide."

Kate gazed off in the direction of the ocean.

"What . . . what happens now?"

"We wait for the tide to bring him back."

"Into the cove?" Kate heard the edge of anxiety in her voice and rushed to supply a reason other than concern about searchers returning to wait for the body. "Way-Ray and Sean go down there almost every day and . . ."

Jackson slipped an arm around her waist. "The cove is probably the last place he'll turn up. The current will see to that."

"Probably take him south." The chief winced and cursed under his breath. "He'll wash up on a crowded beach near town, the tourists will go nuts, and the media will be on me like vultures."

"That why they pay you the big bucks," Jackson said. "How many days until you retire?"

"Too many!" Lowell smacked the steering wheel with his palms. "I'll see they tow that van out of here tomorrow. Take care of those yellow jackets before those kids get stung."

"Yellow jackets?" Kate asked as they watched Lowell drive away.

"There's a nest in the cemetery."

"A nest? There are no trees in the cemetery."

"It's in the ground, under Amanda's stone."

"*Under* the stone?"

264

"The soil is still fairly loose and there may have been a burrow—mice or moles—the yellow jackets took over. I'll kill them as soon as I get a chance." Jackson kissed Kate's forehead. "But now I'll have some of that chicken salad and half a dozen biscuits before I set off to troll the informational sewers of the nation."

A few minutes later Kate watched him spread butter on a biscuit in a kitchen strangely silent. Way-Ray and Sean had gone home with Rhea, Abel was asleep, and Evie had shut herself in her bedroom. "You don't know their names. How can you find out anything about how they operate if you don't know who they are?"

Jackson grinned, took a huge bite, and smiled. "Best biscuits in the world."

"Don't flatter me, answer the question."

"Pushy, pushy, pushy." He stuffed the other half of the biscuit into his mouth and chewed with a contented humming. "Getting their names should be easy given their size, the missing finger, and that scorpion tattoo you drew for me. If they're from New Mexico like Castillo, they may be local legends." He forked up a load of chicken salad. "And there's always someone who collects information about legends. It's just a matter of finding that person."

"And how do you do that?"

Jackson chewed and swallowed. "I'll start by going to Portland and checking with some people from my past that you'd be better off not knowing about."

Kate glanced at the phone on the desk. "You can't call them?"

"I could if I had their numbers, and if I wanted to take the risk."

"Risk?"

"I'm assuming that if Paul has friends who can turn off our power, these guys have friends who can monitor our phone calls."

"But that's—"

"Illegal?"

"Yes." Kate raised her hands. "I know, I'm naïve."

"Wasn't going to say a word."

Chewing on the inside of her cheek, Kate watched him devour a plate loaded with chicken salad and two more biscuits. She respected the zones in his life that he kept silent about, but she resented them, too. It wasn't an angry resentment; it was more of a forlorn and hungry feeling. She felt that she was somehow wanting, less of a partner to him than she should be, too trusting, too unaware of corruption.

"If I'm lucky, I'll be back in the morning. If I have to work for it, I'll be back when I can." He stood and drew her up against him. "Lock the doors. If the geese raise a ruckus, get into that gun safe. In fact, since Way-Ray's gone, get a gun out now."

"You don't think—"

"No." He kissed the tip of her nose. "Not tonight. Not after that search and Evie's call. We're safe for now."

For now.

Those two words kept sleep at bay.

For the first few hours Kate read propped up against the pillows in their bed. Every few pages, she checked the cell phone in the pocket of her shorts, fearing she had turned it off by accident and would miss Jackson's call. Then she recalled he never said he'd check in and she set the phone on the nightstand.

It was, she realized, the first night they'd spent apart for a year. The emotional commitment she'd made to Jackson was the longest and deepest of her adult life, and now she recognized the price—this longing to hear his voice, to have him beside her, this yearning to be reassured that he was alive, that he felt the same for her as she did for him.

It was childish. Irrational. Unproductive.

And perhaps selfish?

Was she worrying about him, or also worrying about the shape of her life without him?

Bolting from bed, she paced through rooms devoid of the sound of Jackson's uneven stride, Sean's snuffling snores, and the muffled and intelligible words Way-Ray uttered in dream conversations punctuated by flailing arms and legs. Only the glow of clock faces and the displays on the stove and microwave lit her way.

At first she didn't turn on the lamps. That would reveal her if a lurker had gotten past the geese. Without interior lights, she could peer out into the yard, scanning shadows in search of anomalies. But there were many odd bits of shifting darkness— random breezes saw to that—and her brain couldn't seem to sort and catalog them.

Deciding the geese wouldn't let her down and allow an intruder close to the house, she abandoned all hope of sleep and, with a rifle leaning against the wall, immersed herself in household chores frequently added to lists but seldom checked off as accomplished. She rolled the refrigerator out and cleaned behind and beneath it, pulled the bottom panel from the toaster and dumped a pile of blackened crumbs into the scrap bucket, organized the shelves of the bathroom cabinets.

267

Every hour or so, she checked on Abel, waking him to study the size of his pupils and quiz him about abdominal pain, bringing him aspirin, juice, a heating pad and cold packs, helping him stand and totter to the bathroom. One eye was puffed closed and his swollen lips cracked and bled, but he swore he was feeling better each time she asked. Back on his mattress after the journey to the bathroom, he plunged into sleep like a man swept from the deck of a ship by a rogue wave.

"You look like a zombie bride," Evie said when she came into the kitchen with the first rays of sunlight.

"I couldn't sleep." Kate ran her fingers through greasy hair.

"Not worrying about Jackson, I hope, because there's no point in that." Evie poured coffee. "He's got more lives than a cat. Not necessarily the best quality lives, but lives just the same. He'll come back."

She raised her hands, palms out. "It's not that I don't care for him. He's more like a son to me than my own, but—"

"I know," Kate said. "You two are like oil and vinegar. You go together but you never quite mix."

Evie sipped her coffee. "Makes life interesting. How's that kid doing?"

"Better. I took him some coffee and toast a few minutes ago. His face is a mess—black and blue and red—and he hurts all over, but he doesn't want to stay here any longer than he needs to."

Evie jammed two slices of wheat bread into the toaster. "Where's he gonna go?"

"Seattle. At least for a while. He's got a cousin in college there."

"Let's hope that's far enough. How's he getting there? That van is nothing but salvage and damned little of that."

"He says he'll hitchhike."

Evie sputtered into her coffee cup. "If those goons spot him he'll be nothing but a grease spot on the highway."

"He knows that. I offered to drive him to the airport or a bus station, but he doesn't want to cause us any more trouble. He wants us to cut his hair tomorrow and get clothes that aren't like anything he had before."

Shaking her head, Evie plucked a jar of almond butter from the refrigerator and set it beside the toaster. "Can't see how that's gonna work."

"That's what I thought at first." Kate pushed a jar of honey closer to Evie's place at the table. "And then I thought about those church kids who come around every year on their missions. They all wear the same kinds of shirts and slacks and that's what I see—not their faces, not the color of their hair, not whether they bite their nails, but their clothes."

"Hmmm." Evie poked at the toaster lever, elevating the bread. "Yeah, most people see what they expect to see. Whack off his hair, strap a knapsack on his back, and he might get out of town in one piece."

269

CHAPTER 27

At 10:45, Kate abandoned pacing and time-passing chores, showered, and drove into town for the comfort of Rhea and chocolate.

"You look like crap on a cracker." Rhea stuffed ice cream into a huge waffle cone and ladled hot fudge sauce on top.

"Thanks for telling me. I had no idea. Apparently my mirror needs adjusting."

Kyle stopped rubbing the glass display case with a wad of newspaper and blinked at her. "Huh? I didn't know you could adjust mirrors."

"You can't." With a flourish, Rhea squirted whipped cream on top of the fudge sauce. "She's yanking my chain."

"Oh. Good one, Kate." Kyle tossed the newspaper over his shoulder into the trash can and snatched up a broom.

"Yeah, not bad for a woman who looks like she got even less sleep than I did last night." Rhea handed over the cone. "What the hell's got into Sean and Way-Ray? They've been giggling like little girls."

Kate shot a glance toward Kyle. "Maybe they got hold of some comedy material beyond their maturity level."

"Hey." Kyle let go of the broom and raised his hands in protest. "After the time Sean asked grandma if she liked shopping better than sex, I keep my videos locked up where those two weasels can't get at them."

"Yeah, that was one of the finer moments of family life. I'm still hearing about my failings as a mother." Rhea pinned Kyle with a glare. "I can't wait until certain people get married and have children of their own. There will be major payback then."

"Change of subject." Kyle picked up the broom and attacked a drift of colored sprinkles in the corner. "I heard at the gas station that most of those protesters left this morning."

Kate swallowed a bite of ice cream, feeling its icy burn all the way to her stomach. "Was there another attack?"

"Nah. But they kinda lost traction when that girl beat it out of the hospital in the middle of the night and sent a text that she wasn't coming back. Then that organizer guy drove his van into that tree and fell in the ocean." Kyle brushed sprinkles into a dustpan and dumped them in the trash can. "Where do you think he'll wash up?"

"That's one of many things I *don't* want to think about." Rhea slid the ice cream scoop into a tub of water.

"Change of subject," Kate said. "What's the latest on your campaign?"

"Lois and I decided that we can't guarantee that we'll win, but we *can* guarantee we'll shake things up and break with every stodgy political tradition

271

there is. We're going to run the greenest campaign we can. No billboards or fliers or bumper stickers. And none of those annoying signs people stick in their lawns."

"Interesting." Kate tipped her cone and sucked at chocolate sauce and whipped cream. "But how will you get your name out there without those things?"

"Well, we figure we've got pretty good name recognition right now, so we'll focus on showing up at meetings and events. We'll count on personal contact and word of mouth to get the message out about what we stand for—which is mostly just stopping to think about what we want this county to be like down the road before we jump at projects because someone says they'll create jobs or bring more tourists."

"We're asking people to make their own signs." Kyle twirled the broom like a baton. "Out of natural stuff or things they can recycle. Like cans and cardboard. Maybe they can mow Mom's name in their lawns. Or write it on T-shirts they already have."

Kate crunched a chunk of cone, seeing endless possibilities and plenty of room for creativity and weirdness. Some people would love the idea and get behind it. The more traditional ones, however . . .

"Bert and Sandi already dropped by to tell me homemade signs will make the town look trashy." Rhea grinned and stretched across the display case to wipe at a spot Kyle missed. "That's how I know it's a good idea."

Kate flashed on the day Bert and Sandi visited Evie, their concerns about the protesters' impact on the community. An image of Abel's battered body formed in her mind. Could Rhea's attempt to buck the establishment also have consequences? The sweet, smooth richness of chocolate turned bitter on her tongue.

"Change of subject." Rhea interrupted her dark thoughts. "Do you think Way-Ray can survive a few days without Sean? Jim's sister wants to take him camping with them tomorrow."

"He'll manage." Kate shook off her fears and forced a smile. "But it will be tough on the rest of us."

"Yeah. Kids are like puppies that way. When you have two they chew on each other and give you a rest now and then."

Kate was on the porch, watching the advance of late-afternoon shadows, drinking iced coffee and chewing the loose skin around her thumbnail, when she heard Jackson's truck. She dashed around to the front of the house and saw his bad leg crumple beneath him when he slid from the seat. Forcing herself not to offer a hand, she watched him grasp the door and pull himself upright. "I need a hot shower and a soft bed," he said.

"We just happen to have both."

"And you look like you could use a double dose of the same." He cupped her face in his hands. "You didn't wait up for me, did you?"

Kate looked away.

"Worrying doesn't help either of us."

"I know. But I couldn't . . ."

He pulled her against his chest and she inhaled the scents of fried onions and potatoes, cigarette smoke, and beer. Had he been drinking? She

273

wouldn't ask. It might have been necessary. And he seemed sober now. So he'd controlled it.

"Are you hungry?"

"Only if you've got more of those biscuits."

"As it happens, Way-Ray and Sean were gone all day—in fact, they're still gone—so I have a surplus of biscuits."

Jackson stroked her hair. "If I didn't already love you, those biscuits would do the trick."

"So the way to a man's heart *is* through his stomach, huh?"

Jackson laughed. "Or thereabouts. But you've had my heart since the first day I saw you."

"You mean the day I thought you were a panhandling vagrant out to mug me? The day I decided to fire you?"

"That would be the day." He kissed her, long and hard. "Lord help me, but I love feisty women. And a feisty woman with a supply of cheese biscuits, well that's just icing on the cake."

Arms twined around each other, they walked inside. Kate sliced a trio of biscuits, cut pats of butter from a stick she took from the refrigerator, centered them on the six halves and slid the plate into the microwave. Jackson was on the third half when Evie came in. "Learn anything interesting?"

"That's one way of describing the situation." Jackson stuffed the remainder of the biscuit into his mouth, licked butter from his fingers, and shoved out a chair with his foot.

Evie eyed the chair without moving. "Interesting isn't necessarily a good thing, is it?"

"Not so much. But then, I may not have all the pieces of the puzzle." He dug into his pocket, pulled out a cell phone Kate had never seen before, and laid it on the table. "I'm still waiting for a few calls. Then I'll burn this."

Kate stared at the phone. "Why?"

"I used a false name, but if someone I talked with feeds information both ways, they could track this phone."

"That's possible?"

"It would be better not to find out."

"Agreed." Evie lowered herself to the front edge of the chair. "Lay out the puzzle pieces you have."

"First, Hernando Castillo, the shark, is overextended. He went all-in on the real estate market at the wrong time and he's got major cash-flow issues. He's been trying to sell off properties, but word is his competitors are scaring off potential buyers."

"So he needs to make this deal happen soon," Kate said.

"Right. But it's not just about money. It's about reputation and respect. If he can't pull this off, he's done. He's been at the top of the financial food chain a long time and he didn't make friends getting there—or staying there."

"So other sharks are circling," Evie said, "ready to tear off chunks of his empire."

"Or chunks of *him*," Jackson agreed. "If they see he's weak, there are some who won't stop at just crippling him financially. Which explains the muscle for hire—the Romero brothers."

"But if he's got money problems," Kate mused, "aren't they worried they won't get paid? Or that they'll be sucked down and chewed up with him?"

Jackson shook his head. "Carlos and Felipe Romero offer vital commodities in their dark world. They follow orders, they're amoral, and they're very

275

good at what they do and at staying alive to do it. If Castillo goes down, they'll find a way to jump clear and someone else will hire them. Maybe they're even working both sides of the street now—protecting Castillo because that's what he pays them to do, and because a lot of money could be lost if Castillo doesn't bring this deal to the table."

Jackson laid a hand over hers. "These guys have acquired a taste for 'creative' violence. More than a taste, an addiction. They like their work. I doubt they worry much about possible consequences."

"But they must know there *could be* consequences to sticking with Castillo." Kate slid her hand from beneath his.

"Maybe. But they're twisted—more twisted than you can imagine. And they're distant cousins to Castillo. That makes them more loyal than money alone does."

"They must have records," Evie said. "Maybe they could be arrested here and it would be a third strike or something."

"No such luck." He tapped the phone. "After a couple of juvenile arrests, they've managed to fly under the law enforcement radar."

"What if Abel presses charges and Chief Lowell arrests them?"

With a longing glance at the remaining biscuits, Jackson pushed aside his plate. "Then Abel's a dead man walking. They'll take him down or hire someone to do it."

"I feel like we're being crushed." Kate grasped the knife she used to slice the biscuits. "Maybe we can find something wrong with this property Paul is offering Evie, and maybe we can throw up obstacles

276

for the next one he offers, but with Castillo pushing on him to get the deal done . . ."

"I should have changed my will and taken this place off the table a year ago, after Paul tried to shut me down over the back taxes." Evie knotted her fingers together. "Now my own son has turned into one of those—what do you call them?—the fish that swim with sharks and eat their leftovers and clean their damn teeth?"

"Pilot fish," Jackson said.

"Right. And he piloted that shark right to us." Her face crumpled and she bolted from the chair and ran to her room, slamming the door behind her.

Kate set the knife down and knuckled away tears for Evie's pain. To bear and raise a child, to sacrifice for him, and then have him practically serve you up on a platter for a man like Castillo. She couldn't imagine how deep that must cut. "We have to stop them! There has to be something we can do!"

"There are plenty of things, but they're either futile, foolhardy, or outside the law. A long way outside." Jackson's hand dropped to the gun beneath his shirt. "I'm not saying I won't go there if they drive me to it, but I'd prefer that what I do looks like what a jury would call a clear-cut case of self-defense."

Kate stabbed the knife into the oblong stick of butter so hard the plate beneath it cracked. "So we're caught in a vise."

Jackson grasped her hand, pried open her fingers, and took the knife. "There's a chance that if financial pressure increases enough, Castillo may have to let this scheme go."

277

Kate looked into his eyes. "How much would you bet on that happening before Evie's pushed into dealing away this place?"

"Not much." He smoothed the skin across her cheekbones with his thumbs. "I learned two encouraging things about the Romero brothers—they're impatient and lately they've been overconfident. Castillo's the same. If we can hang on, that might work in our favor."

CHAPTER 28

The next morning, once Way-Ray was off to put fish out to thaw, Evie paced six circles around the kitchen as if building up momentum, then snatched the phone and called Paul. "Sorry to do this, but can I put you off another day? I got a hawk in last night and another owl. They're in pretty bad shape and it didn't help that we've got an electrical short out in that trailer and I keep losing my light."

She listened for a moment than said. "No, I want to see that place. Especially after last night. Seems that every time we fix something around here something else breaks. It might be a welcome change to live in a modern house."

Rolling her eyes, she listened again and then said, "Well, that would be a real treat. Let's make it a date—unless there's another critter catastrophe. 11:15. I'll put it on the calendar."

She hung up and kicked at the floor, head down. "He wants to take me to lunch," she muttered. "At that fancy place on the bay south of town."

Kate opened her mouth, realized she couldn't tell how Evie felt about that offer, and closed it again.

279

Evie raised the hem of her misshapen T-shirt and blotted her eyes. "His dad and I went there every year on our anniversary."

And Paul must know that.

Was he manipulating her? Or trying to build a bridge?

"They make a passable chowder." Jackson shot Kate a smile. "But their biscuits aren't as good as the ones I get around here."

Evie snuffled into her shirt, then stomped to the door. "I've got some sick birds to check on."

"I hate to see her torn like this." Kate seized a napkin and blotted her eyes. "There has to be something we can do!"

Jackson set his coffee cup aside, but before he could speak, Abel called from upstairs. "Is anyone else around? Can I come down?"

"Yes." Kate jumped to her feet and hustled to the bottom of the stairs. Abel stood at the top, gripping the banister with both hands but favoring the left. "Do you need help?"

"No." He lowered his left foot to the step below and grimaced as he transferred his weight. "I've got to do this on my own."

Kate recognized the same pride and determination she saw in Jackson, and turned aside. "I'll get you some juice."

"And coffee," Abel called. "Please."

As his thumping steps echoed from the staircase, Kate cleared away Evie's plate and mug, poured coffee, and set a place for him. "Would you like a waffle?"

"If it's no trouble," he called.

"No trouble," Jackson assured him. "If you don't mind it reheated."

280

"I'll take it any way you want to give it to me." Abel tottered across the kitchen to the table, placing each foot as if he wasn't sure it would hold his weight. "If you're sure you have plenty."

"We have more than plenty," Kate said with a laugh. "Way-Ray misread the directions on the waffle mix box and put in too much milk. Then he had to put in more mix to sop it up. We've got enough waffles for the next three days."

"I'm not so sure about the 'misread' part," Jackson said. "Way-Ray enjoys pouring batter and listening to it sizzle."

"And filling each square with melted butter before he pours on the syrup. When it comes to waffles, he has quite a ritual."

"He's an enthusiastic kid. He and Sean did an amazing job making me look like a pile of dirty clothes. They took a picture and I couldn't find myself in it." Abel pulled his swollen lips into a caricature of a smile and lowered himself into the chair. "Thanks again for hiding me."

"We couldn't leave you to the mercy of those thugs." Kate set a steaming waffle before him.

"I don't think they know the meaning of the word 'mercy.'"

"Oh, they know the definition." Jackson pushed the butter dish and a jug of maple syrup across the table. "But mercy is counterproductive to their profession. And there's no thrill in it."

"They must have gotten plenty of thrills working me over." Abel spread butter on his waffle, hitting every square, then poured a moat of syrup around it.

He's not much more than a kid himself, Kate thought. A hurt and frightened kid.

Forking off a small corner of his waffle, Abel raised it to his mouth and chewed deliberately, holding his fingers against the hinge of his jaw.

"I still think we should get you to a doctor." Kate set a bowl of blueberries and a container of vanilla yogurt beside Abel's plate.

"I don't think anything's broken." He spooned blueberries into the syrup and sliced off another square inch of waffle. "And if I had bad internal injuries or blood leaking in my brain, I'd be dead by now, wouldn't I?"

"Probably," Jackson said.

Abel dredged the chunk of waffle through the syrup moat and slid it between his battered lips. This time he probed the opposite side of this jaw and the soft spot behind his ear. "If you cut my hair and get me clothes and a knapsack, I'll leave tomorrow."

"All right, but I won't let you hitch rides," Kate said. "We'll take you to the bus. Or the train."

"No. It's a long way and I've been enough trouble."

"But you can barely walk," Kate protested.

"All I have to do is stand by the side of the road." He stabbed two blueberries and slipped them between his lips. "The sooner I get out of here, the safer it will be for you."

Jackson waved that aside. "Safer. Not safe. Unless Evie gives up this land to the developers, we're all in danger."

"And she won't give it up. So you might as well stay until you're healed."

"I appreciate that, but . . ."

"We'll see how you are tomorrow. I'll buy clothes this afternoon. And anything else you need."

"Don't buy them in Castaway Beach," Jackson advised. "Print out some kind of form with a checklist and write his sizes on that. If anybody sees you, you're shopping for a charity that helps young men dress for job interviews."

"Ah." Kate studied him for a moment, admiring the cover story and his ability to look down a road and anticipate a hundred twists, turns, and ambushes. Had he been that way as a child, or was it a skill learned in the military? Did Jackson's mind ever truly allow him to accept and enjoy?

"I don't have much money," Abel said. "But I'll pay you back someday. I promise."

"Don't worry about it," Jackson stood and limped to the refrigerator. "Let's get some ice on your face, see if we can reduce the swelling. You'll never get a ride looking like some flesh-craving creature from a horror movie."

That afternoon, armed with a list of sizes, Kate drove thirty miles to a department store in the next county and picked up a knapsack, black shoes and socks, black slacks, a white shirt, and a black windbreaker. Unable to find anything better, she bought a dark green ball cap with a leaping trout on the front to shade his head.

Jackson approved of that choice and suggested they dilute their original idea further by having Abel carry a thick volume of the adventures of Sherlock Holmes. "Not everyone will pick up someone carrying a bible. Some will figure you'll try to convert them or talk their ear off and they don't want the hassle. Stick with Holmes and Watson."

When she returned with her purchases, Abel was on a chair in the yard, geese pecking at clumps of hair Jackson sheared off and tossed aside. Way-Ray stood in front of the chair, hopping from foot to foot and holding up both a mirror and a picture for Jackson to refer to. "We're gonna make him look like this guy from the movies," he informed Kate.

"Really?" She watched for a moment as Jackson squinted at the picture, parted Abel's hair in the middle, combed it out, and went to work trimming it level with the lobes of his ears. "I had no idea you were a hairdresser."

"I'm not. I cut hair. Period. You want it feathered or razored or poofed up, I'm not your guy."

He stepped back to check the cut and Kate eased close against him. "No poofing for me, so you'll always be my guy, right?"

"No doubt about it." Jackson kissed the top of her head. "Now don't distract the barber or Abel will come out as bald as a cue ball."

"What's a cue ball?" Way-Ray asked.

"It's the white ball you use to hit the other balls when you're playing pool," Abel answered.

Way-Ray scratched his head. "You mean like beach balls that you blow up and put in a pool?"

"And we're off," Kate whispered.

Jackson grinned. "Poor Abel. He's never been through the Way-Ray 'Why Wringer'."

"No," Abel said, his tone patient and serious. "Pool balls are small and hard. Pool is the name of the game. It's played on a special table covered with felt cloth, not in a pool filled with water."

"Oh." Way-Ray scrunched up his face. "If the cue ball is bald, do the other balls have hair?"

Kate slapped a hand across her lips to hold back a giggle.

"No."

"But Jackson said you'd be as bald as a cue ball. And if the other balls are bald, too, then why didn't he say 'as bald as a pool ball' instead?"

Abel gripped the edges of his chair. "I don't know. It's just what people say. It's an expression."

"Is it Latin? Did those old Romans have hairless cue balls?"

Jackson glanced at Kate, his eyes bright with amusement, his lips lifted in a smile. With the sun on his shoulders and his scarred leg encased in his jeans he seemed . . . well, like any normal man. In fact, if someone watching wasn't aware of all that had happened and all that could, they would all appear normal.

If normal included a flock of circling geese.

"I don't know much about the Romans, but I don't think they did," Abel's voice tightened.

"But you don't know for sure, right?"

Abel peered over his shoulder with pleading eyes. Kate pretended to find a stone in her sandal and Jackson bent to wipe the scissors on his jeans.

"I'm pretty sure the Romans didn't play pool," Abel said

"Pretty sure is for amateurs," Way-Ray said in a smug voice. "That's what Jackson says. He says pretty sure is how things get messed up and people get into big trouble. He knows lots of stuff about the Romans and old muskrats and important things like that."

Abel glanced over his shoulder once more. "Well, let's ask him, then. Did the Romans play pool?"

"Doubtful." Jackson clacked the scissors and went to work on Abel's hair again. "Everything I've read indicates it evolved from a lawn game played in medieval times, but when we're finished here, Way-Ray might want to get on the computer and check."

"Pffft." Way-Ray poked out his lower lip and blew, ruffling the hair sweeping across his eyebrows. "I don't hafta check. If you say it's true, then it is."

"But I didn't say it was true." Jackson fixed his gaze on Way-Ray. "If you don't listen carefully, you'll always be an amateur."

Way-Ray poked out his lip again, then chewed at it and dug the toe of one sneaker into the dirt. "Okay." He emitted a sigh that seemed to contain enough air to fill a spare tire, then muttered without enthusiasm, "Hurry up and finish so I can look it up."

The next morning, after checking on her patients and dawdling over a second cup of coffee, Evie disappeared into her room to shower and change. When Kate came in from hoeing weeds in the cornfield, she was still behind her closed door, but Abel was at the kitchen table, tilting his head back while Way-Ray smoothed liquid makeup around his eyes.

"We borrowed this from the bathroom closet," Way-Ray said. "You never use it so I didn't think you'd get mad."

Kate touched her suntanned cheek trying to recall when she'd bought that bottle and why. Except for a little mascara, she seldom wore makeup—couldn't remember the last time she had or the reason she decided she needed it. Did Way-Ray think she should? Had his mother worn makeup? Kate couldn't remember.

"I was about to leave when Way-Ray said I looked too scary to get a ride," Abel explained. "But I'm worried that if he puts too much of that on I'll look like a street art project gone bad."

"Not if we blend it in," Way-Ray insisted.

Blend it in?

Kate gawked. Where had he learned that? Not from Rhea and certainly not from Evie. What was behind this interest in makeup?

Evie's door banged open and she stalked out, a beige dress gathered with a black belt at her waist, the skirt sagging like an old curtain to below her knees. Silver flashed in the puckered hem where she'd used safety pins to secure it. "I hated this dress when it was new," she said. "And I hate it more now. But the moths got into the only other one I own."

"You don't have to wear a dress," Way-Ray said. "Kate never does."

Did he perceive that as a failing, or was he simply making an observation? Kate felt off balance, uncertain.

"Kate's a lot younger than I am," Evie snapped. "She could go to a fancy restaurant wearing a cardboard box or a roll of toilet paper."

"I'd pay to see that." Jackson limped in from the porch lugging a gallon can of wall patch and a putty knife.

"How much?" Way-Ray asked.

"As much as I have." Jackson grinned, set his gear on the end of the counter, and studied Abel's face. "Nice job."

"It's camouflage." Way-Ray screwed the top back on the bottle. "I'm getting good at this stuff."

Kate felt herself relax a little. If Way-Ray thought of makeup as a substance to be used for camouflage, perhaps his comments about her were due to heightened powers of observation, not criticism.

"Well I wish you could camouflage me so I'd be invisible." Evie kicked off a pair of low-heeled red shoes with pointed toes. "My feet are killing me already and I feel as ugly as a stomped possum."

Way-Ray scratched his head. "How do you stomp a possum?"

"Never mind." Kate took Evie's arm and tugged her to the staircase. "Let's go see what's in my closet."

"We don't have time."

Kate tightened her grip. "We have an hour."

"I can't wear your things. They won't fit."

"You know my blouses fit. You wore one a few weeks ago." She nudged Evie up the first few stairs. "We'll find something to go with those slacks you bought when you went before the county commission last winter."

"The black ones? It's summer."

"On TV they say black is always in style," Way-Ray called. "And it makes you look thinner."

"Don't go there," Jackson warned. "You don't want to use the word 'thinner' when you're talking to a woman. Even a woman who's thin as a whip like Evie."

"Is that kind of like the rule where you don't ask them how old they are?"

"Exactly like that. Now wash your hands before you smear that makeup all over the house. Then

288

we'll drive Abel to the edge of town so he has a better chance of getting a ride."

"Then I'll put makeup on Evie. After she's dressed."

"I don't wear makeup," Evie yelled. "I've never worn makeup."

"I know," Way-Ray said.

"What does that mean?" Evie turned, glowering at Kate and the kitchen beyond her. "Where's he getting this stuff?"

"I hope it's because he's so bored without Sean that he watched one of those makeover shows."

"Lord love a duck," Evie said. "Makes me long for the days before cable, even the days before television. The price of progress is getting to be a lot more than I'm willing to pay." She bent and called down the stairs. "Goodbye, Abel. Take care of yourself."

"I'll try, Evie. Thanks again for pulling me out of the van and saving my life after all the nasty things I said to you."

Evie waved that aside. "Well, see that you use the rest of that life wisely. Don't go courting trouble unless you want a marriage made in hell. And if you spot those thugs, run the other way as fast as you can."

"That's not too fast, beat up as I am right now."

"Then you better hope you see them before they see you."

Chapter 29

Forty-five minutes later, Evie rolled her eyes as Way-Ray considered the pale blue cotton sweater, freshly ironed slacks, and not-too-worn black sandals Kate discovered in the back of the coat closet and set Jackson to polishing.

"You don't look like you," Way-Ray said. "I mean, you don't look like you usually do. Are you gonna put on lipstick and eye stuff?"

"No lipstick. I already look like a complete fool with my hair sprayed down," Evie snarled. "How long before Sean comes back from that camping trip and you're back to playing video games and running around the countryside like wild animals?"

"Too long. Tomorrow. Or the day after."

"Well, in the meantime, read a book or do some extra chores or run laps around the pasture, but stay away from those TV shows with hairdressers and makeup artists." Evie leaned close and gave him a conspiratorial wink. "Not that there's anything wrong with knowing a little about style. But Jackson's right, most women don't want you to mention their weight or suggest how they could improve their hair or makeup. Unless you're dishing out a compliment. Got it?"

Way-Ray pooched his lips in and out. "Got it."

"Then let's have that compliment." Evie straightened and tugged at the sweater.

Way-Ray glanced at Jackson who raised his hands and shook his head. "It's all on you."

"Kate?"

Kate took cover behind the refrigerator door. "I'm packing lunch to take to the cove as soon as Peggy Cortland shows up. You can come up with something on your own. Concentrate."

Sucking in a breath, Way-Ray looked Evie up and down again and then cleared his throat. "Um, you um, you look way better than a stomped possum."

Evie's jaw dropped, but then she let loose a laugh. "I'll take it. It's honest and—you know what?—I think it's just about the way I'd describe myself."

"No point in setting the bar too high," Jackson said. "Or setting it at all."

Evie narrowed her eyes, then spun about. "Is that a car?"

Way-Ray raced to the porch and pressed his nose against the screen. "It's big and black. And there's a man inside."

Kate's hands shook, rattling the bag of corn chips. "Just one?"

"Yeah."

"It's Paul," Evie said.

"Your son Paul who was here the other day when you told me to go inside? Paul the guy you fibbed to?"

"Yes. But that's a secret, remember."

Way-Ray ran his index finger across his lips.

291

"He's taking me to lunch." Evie tugged at her sweater once more and raked her fingers through her hair, undoing the work of the hair spray. "Where's my purse?"

"Right here on the desk." Jackson scooped up the black bag Kate had loaned Evie and looped it over her shoulder. "There. You're good to go."

But Evie stood for another moment, gazing at them. "I hope I do this right. I hope I don't make him mad. Or get mad myself."

"You'll be fine." Kate set a jar of mayonnaise on the counter and gave Evie a hug. "Just count to three before you speak."

"Make it ten," Jackson advised.

Evie pulled from Kate's embrace. "Sometimes I get so fired up that counting to ten thousand isn't enough. But I'll count until I run out of numbers and then bite my tongue in half if that's what it takes." She fiddled with the clasp on the purse. "I should be back by 3:30, 4:00 at the latest."

"We'll be back before that," Kate said. "The tide will be coming in and I don't want to leave Peggy alone here too long. She's pretty calm, but she doesn't have much experience with injured birds, and she was hoping to spend the afternoon making calls to businesses looking for donations to the auction she's planning for the fall."

"You could go to the cove later." Longing tinged Evie's voice. "We could all go together."

Kate pulled her into another hug. "I promised Way-Ray we'd have lunch down there. But there's no reason we can't go back for a marshmallow roast this evening if the tide cooperates."

"I'll be counting on it." Evie squeezed Kate, then trudged across the porch.

"Everybody says having to spend money makes Paul mad enough to spit," Way-Ray counseled her. "So if he makes you mad, just order the most expensive stuff so he gets mad, too. Order two desserts! Bring one home for me."

Laughing, Evie went out the door and plodded to the long black car. Paul leaned across the seat and opened the passenger door for her.

"He shoulda got out and opened the door for Evie. That's what you do when you have good manners." Way-Ray crossed the kitchen and peeled a slice of Swiss cheese from the package in the sandwich assembly line. "Didn't he learn that when he was little?"

Kate struggled for a neutral answer, but Jackson fielded the question. "Maybe he didn't. Evie was pretty busy running a dairy farm when he was growing up. Or maybe he learned and then forgot. If you don't use a skill—any skill—you lose your edge, you get rusty."

"I don't want to get rusty. Especially not at hiding and camouflaging and stuff." Way-Ray folded the cheese in half and then in half again. "Rusty is for amateurs."

"Right," Jackson agreed. "Go get the camouflage gear you've been working on and we'll practice at the cove."

"They'll be sitting down to lunch about now," Kate said as they emerged onto the lower meadow, walking single file with Way-Ray in the lead. "I hope Evie's not so nervous she can't eat."

293

Jackson grinned at her over his shoulder. "Evie's not the type to waste food, especially if she's not the one paying for it."

"Hey! I'm goin' over there and put on my stuff and hide." Way-Ray pointed to the cemetery. "Tell me if you can see me."

"Hold it," Jackson said. "Don't go inside the fence. There's a nest of yellow jackets in the ground. If you get too close, they might come after you."

"I thought you were going to exterminate them," Kate said.

"Didn't get to it yet. Maybe this evening."

Way-Ray turned and tugged at the front of Jackson's T-shirt, tightening it, revealing the outline of the holster clipped to his belt. The sight of it jolted Kate and reassured her as well. Until the shark moved on to other waters, this was a fact of life.

"What's exterminate mean?" Way-Ray asked. "It comes from Latin, right?"

"Probably. We'll look it up when we get home. It means to kill off, to destroy."

"Ooow. I wanna help kill yellow jackets!"

"No," Kate said.

"Maybe," Jackson said.

"No," Kate said again. "Yellow jackets are nasty. They're not like bees; they can sting more than once. You can get sick—or worse—if you're allergic to them."

"Am I allergic?"

"I don't know."

Had Wayne been allergic? Would Justine know? Should she write to her and ask? Should she open that door?

As if reading her thoughts, Jackson shook his head. "Let's not find out the hard way," he told Way-Ray. "If you get stung and you're allergic, you'll swell up. You won't be able to breathe."

"Then I'll watch out for them and won't get stung."

"I admire your confidence." Jackson tugged at Way-Ray's hair. "But the only way to make sure that doesn't happen is to stay far away from the nest during the daytime when they're active, especially if you've been drinking something sweet or if you wear perfume."

"Duh. I'm a guy. I don't wear perfume"

"Aftershave then."

"Double duh. I don't have any whiskers yet so I don't have to shave." Way-Ray rubbed his cheeks. "So can I help you kill the yellow jackets?"

"We'll see," Jackson said. "Let's go have lunch. I'm hungry."

"Oooookaaaay." Way-Ray puffed at the hair hanging into his eyes.

"I see a haircut in your future," Kate said.

"Not until school starts."

"That's not too far off," Jackson said. "Less than six weeks."

"Noooo." Way-Ray slapped his hands over his ears and raced off.

By the time they reached the lip of the headland and paused at the battered duck decoy on its post, he was skidding around the final switchback before the trail turned toward the cove. Kate sat, gripped tree roots, and swung herself about, letting go when her toes touched the spot leveled by thousands of such landings. "When life gets back to normal, we've *got* to build steps here. Or rig up a rope ladder."

295

Jackson grunted as he made the descent—not a grunt of concentration, but a sound jagged with pain. "Might be something Way-Ray and Sean could manage."

Kate blinked, but hid her surprise. Whenever this topic came up in the past, Jackson insisted he would build the steps. Handing off the project was either a sign that he had developed faith in the boys' abilities, or had less confidence in his own strength and stamina. Was his leg that much worse?

Turning aside, Kate gazed out at the ocean. "The water looks higher and rougher than I expected." She adjusted the knapsack straps and eased down the trail. "I wonder if I misread the weather forecast."

"We'll make it a quick lunch."

When they reached the end of the trail at the tumbled rocks, Jackson halted, hitched the blanket across his shoulder, and drew the cell phone from his pocket. "Time to get rid of this." He pried open the case, flipped out the memory chip, and bent it. "Should have cooked it in the microwave before we left."

"Really?"

"That's what they recommend."

Who were "they"? And how did "they" know this?

Kate watched him crush the phone under the heel of his running shoe, pick up the mangled remains, and hurl them far out over the surging water. Then, with a glance at his bad leg, she turned and went down the rocks, facing away from him, allowing him privacy for his struggle.

A band of squalls staggered along the horizon, and the breeze off the ocean raised goose bumps on her bare arms. She spread the blanket in the shelter

296

of the mammoth log and Way-Ray anchored it with chunks of wood. In a few minutes Jackson joined them and, sipping at a cola, lay back on the sand, his bad leg elevated by a chunk of driftwood. Way-Ray dug into the pack and made short work of chips and sandwiches, tossing his crusts to circling gulls, then raced in the shallow surf in search of a whole sand dollar. Gulls chased along, plucking finds from the shallow surf. Way-Ray yelled and shook his fist at a bird making off with a prized white disk.

"He's got to get ahead of those gulls if he wants more than pieces of a sand dollar," Jackson observed. "He's got to get deeper into the surf."

"Don't tell him that." Kate gave Jackson a sharp look. "If he loses his footing or takes his eye off the in-coming waves, he might be swept away."

Jackson sat up and shook sand from his faded red T-shirt. "We'll hunt them together. When he's a little older."

"If that leg lets you. You *have* to have surgery."

Jackson closed his eyes and set his jaw.

Kate felt a flash of anger. "You have to think about—"

"I think about it all the time, Kate." He pounded a fist on the sand. "I think about scalpels and rods and screws, about being unconscious while they cut. I think about being laid up, helpless, asking you do to every little thing."

Anger seeped away and Kate took his hand. She would feel the same, would be anxious not so much about the pain as about having to rely on others, about asking, asking, asking. It would be worse for Jackson with his physical strength, his deep reservoir of confidence and pride. "But if—"

297

"I know, Kate, I know. More pain. Possible paralysis." He jerked his hand from her and, crablike, got to his feet. "That could happen if I go under the knife, too."

"It won't!"

He turned so she couldn't see his face. "It might. It's a possibility."

"And it's also a possibility that Way-Ray will ask for spinach for dessert." She touched his bad leg, drew her fingers along it. "Nothing will change the way I feel about you."

He was silent for a long moment, then spoke in a choked voice. "I know." Turning, he reached down and tucked a strand of hair behind her ear. "I'm working my way to it, Kate, but—"

"Come on, you guys," Way-Ray yelled. "Let's go. I want to show you how still I can be."

Kate squeezed Jackson's hand and kissed his knuckles, then stood and called to Way-Ray. "Why don't you show us how *fast* you can be first? Evie wants to come down this evening to roast marshmallows. We've got plenty of big chunks for a fire, but we need kindling."

"On it." Snapping off a salute, Way-Ray dashed along the dark strip of debris at the high-tide mark, scooping up sticks and bits of bark. Jackson watched, kneading his fists into the small of his back, then pressing his palms against the log and stretching his bad leg behind him.

"Next summer you'll be moving as fast as Way-Ray." Kate ducked her head so he wouldn't see the fear in her eyes. "Next summer I'll race you to that rock on the other side of the cove—the one where we saw all the starfish."

"And back."

298

"Huh?"

"To the rock and back. A race, not a sprint."

"You're on." She bent to fold the blanket, wiping her eyes with a corner.

Way-Ray returned with an armload of kindling and dumped it on the high side of the ring of stones laid in the sand. "The tide's coming in really fast. And hard. Think it will move this log today?"

"Could be." Jackson pointed at the squall line and rows of waves piling up as they approached the shore. "It's a spring tide and the wind will help push water up the beach."

Way-Ray scratched his head. "How can it be a spring tide when it's summer?"

"Spring tides can happen any time of year when the sun and moon are aligned."

"What's aligned?" Way-Ray's eyes narrowed. "Is it Latin?"

"You'll find out when you get home and look it up." Kate swung the knapsack to her back. "Now get your hiding clothes on and let's go."

With another salute, Way-Ray dumped out his pack and pulled on a beige T-shirt streaked with mud, and festooned with bits of green and brown and yellow cloth, lengths of twine, and bits of vine. The shirt had once belonged to Jackson and hung to Way-Ray's knees, sleeves dangling past his elbows. "I made this myself."

"Not bad," Jackson said.

"And here's my hat." Way-Ray pulled out what had once been a cloth shopping bag but now looked more like a bird's nest torn apart by a storm. Blobs of yellowed glue held clumps of grass, twigs, leaves, dried berries, and feathers. "It took me three days to get all the stuff and make this." He smiled up at them as he pulled it on and peered through a rectangular slice. "I learned a whole lot about being patient."

Jackson held out his hand and they slapped and then fist bumped. "Go on up to the meadow and we'll see if we can spot you when we get there."

"But don't go near the cemetery and that yellow jacket nest," Kate cautioned.

"I won't." Way-Ray splashed through a few inches of water sluicing across the tongue of basalt, leaped to wedge his fingers in a crevice high on the boulder at the bottom of the trail, then climbed hand-over-foot up the jumbled rocks.

"He looks like something out of a science fiction movie," Kate said. "Like a pile of old hay come to life."

"That's the idea. If he doesn't get too anxious and move too fast, he'll blend right in on the meadow."

Way-Ray turned at the top of the rocks and yelled back, "Bring my pack, okay?"

Kate picked up the pack, slung it over one shoulder, and waded into the foaming water. "We're getting out of here just in time." She anchored the toe of her right shoe in a cranny, the rubber sole squeaking against the rock as she stretched her arm high for a handhold. "This seems to get harder every time. We ought to pound in some spikes or go buy whatever those things are mountain climbers use."

"I saw a few old railroad spikes in the barn. Kinda rusty but they'd do for a start. I'll get them the next time I drive past."

Kate hauled herself up and wedged her left toe into a crack. "It would be cheating in a way, messing with Mother Nature, but . . ."

"We'll rationalize our way around that." Jackson grunted, a sound pitched high enough to be more of a gasp.

Kate forced herself not to turn her head or ask if he was okay. Bent like an inchworm, she angled her way up the jumbled boulders, reached the packed earth of the trail, and stood. Way-Ray was out of sight, probably already on the meadow. Stooping, she tied a double knot in her shoelace, peering through the hair that fell across her eyes. Jackson was still near the base of the tumbled rocks, his mouth twisted into a grimace of painful concentration. Another jolt of anger sizzled in her brain. If he'd had surgery in the early spring, he—

"I'm not gonna hide until those two guys are gone 'cause they might spoil it."

Way-Ray's words drifted to her on the wind, faint but clear.

Two guys?

Kate snapped upright and spotted him a few switchbacks above her, his hat off.

Dread, like an icy winter fog, wrapped its tendrils around her gut. She put a finger to her lips, then crooked it, gesturing Way-Ray closer.

301

CHAPTER 30

Way-Ray jogged down the sloping trail and halted a few feet away, the twine and vines on his ghillie suit fluttering in the breeze. He cupped his hands around his mouth and said in an exaggerated whisper, "Why do we hafta be quiet?"

Kate breathed in until her lungs burned and clenched her trembling hands.

Calm. Stay calm.

It could be anyone. Hikers. Birdwatchers.

She pulled her cell phone from the pocket of her shorts and snapped it open. "Jackson said we had to be quiet to practice better. Where are those guys? What do they look like?"

"They're way back by the trees and I couldn't hardly see them." His brow furrowed. "They have all black clothes on."

Kate felt her heart compress to a lump of ice. "No," she whispered. "No."

"Who are they?"

Killers.

She breathed in, the air like needles in her lungs.

Should she lie? Feign ignorance?

No. Way-Ray was in on their conspiracy to fool these men. "I think they're the men who hurt Abel."

"How come they're here? Everybody thinks he fell into the ocean and drowned—even Chief Lowell."

"What's going on?" Jackson dragged himself across the final boulder and stood beside Kate, his weight on his good leg, his breathing a series of gulps.

"Way-Ray saw two men on the meadow. They're wearing black."

Jackson's eyes tightened. "They're hunting us."

"You don't know that."

But even as she spoke, Kate was certain of it, certain they knew Jackson had been asking about them, certain they planned to accelerate Castillo's deal. Had they gone to the house, questioned Peggy, perhaps tortured or killed her?

Jackson nodded at her phone. "Do you have a signal?"

Kate shaded the screen with her hand. "No."

"I coulda told you you wouldn't," Way-Ray said. "You have to be up on the meadow. But not by the trees. The other side of the cemetery is the best. I know 'cause one time when you and Rhea were talking and talking and talking, Sean and me took your phones and experimented. That's the only place unless you go back by the house or to the barn."

Jackson squinted at the phone. "You're sure?"

"Totally." Way-Ray grinned. "I'm a professional."

"That's good, because right now we need a professional we can trust with an important mission."

"I can do it." Way-Ray's eyes shone with excitement. "What is it? Tell me. Tell me."

303

Jackson put his hand on Way-Ray's shoulder. "Without letting them see you, sneak around the far side of the cemetery and get to the spot where you can get a signal. Call Chief Lowell and tell him the men who took Cassie from the hospital are here. Tell him we're in the cove and he should bring all the help he can find."

"On it." Way-Ray saluted. "Don't let them see me. Call Chief Lowell."

"Good. Give him the phone, Kate."

Kate felt the frozen lump that was her heart compress. She jammed the phone into her pocket. "You're not serious. He'll walk right into their arms."

"I'll be crawling," Way-Ray said. "Not walking."

"He's dressed for it and he's been practicing for weeks. These are city guys. Chances are they'll never spot him." Jackson yanked his shirt up and unfastened the safety strap on the holster. "I'll cover him from the top of the trail."

"I can do it," Way-Ray insisted. "Easy."

"No. I'll go."

"You don't have camouflage stuff."

"I'll wear yours."

"No fair." Way-Ray backed away, gripping his hat. "I made it. And you never practiced sneaking and being still."

"That doesn't matter. I won't risk your life. I can't."

"His life is at risk whether he tries to make a call or not." Jackson seized Kate's arm and aimed his chin at the towering cliffs around the cove. "With the tide coming in, we can't get around the headland to the tidal marsh and follow the creek trail out. They're blocking our only escape route."

Kate studied the jut of the headland. "Maybe we could work our way around the cliff face to the marsh. Or at least get far enough from the trail that they won't see us. Maybe we'll be able to get a signal out there."

"Too dangerous," Jackson said. "I took a look over that way when we laid the false trail with Abel's clothing. There's a long raw scar where rock sheared away recently and I wouldn't bet on the rest of that face being stable."

"All right, but they have to come down the trail to get at us. Way-Ray and I can hide behind those fallen rocks at the top of the cove. If you're on the slope where you hid before, you could shoot them when they come looking for us."

Jackson considered. "That's a good idea—in theory. But it doesn't provide for help being on the way. If I can't get both of them . . ."

He let that hang and Kate considered the possibilities. She had no doubt that Jackson could take one of them off the board. But to do that he might expose his position and then—

Way-Ray peered over his shoulder at the lip of the headland. "We gotta decide fast."

Choking back a sob, Kate dug the phone from her pocket and handed it off. "Be careful. This isn't a game."

"I know. It's like when my mom tried to keep my uncle from finding me, right?"

And died in the attempt.

Kate squeezed her eyes shut for a moment.

"Yes," Jackson said. "It's a lot like that. After you call the police, get to the barn and hide until you see Curtis or the chief or someone you know and trust. Don't go near the house. Don't let anyone see you."

He laid a hand on Way-Ray's shoulder. "And don't come back here. No matter what you hear, don't even look behind you."

"But what if—?"

"Don't look back. That's an order."

Way-Ray swallowed and nodded.

"Stay down and move like a snake."

"A snail," Way-Ray corrected. "Snakes go too fast. They're amateurs."

"Right." Jackson grinned. "Move like a snail."

Kate sniffed back tears. "A professional snail."

Way-Ray raised the T-shirt and tucked the phone in the rear pocket of his shorts. Then he bent low and scurried up the trail.

Jackson drew the gun from the holster and followed, using his good leg to pull him up the slope and his bad leg as an anchor. He punctuated each step with a sharp intake of breath that made Kate almost gasp herself. She thrust her hands out to steady him if he lost his balance but kept them low so he wouldn't notice.

As the trail swung back and forth, Kate glanced out at the squall line, closer now, a gauzy curtain of rain hanging beneath the clouds. Whitecaps dotted the gray-blue ocean and the tempo of the thrashing waves in the cove grew faster.

They reached the base of the sharp incline just below the rim and crouched there, gripping the branches of a few determined shrubs to keep from sliding back, and peering through high grass rippling in the rising breeze. Halfway along the meadow, the shark's thugs stood back to back and about twenty feet apart, studying the terrain. Sunlight shone on their glossy black hair and suits, making the cloth appear iridescent. At this distance, their faces were tan smudges with dark dots and lines for eyes and mouths.

"They're almost even with the cemetery," Kate whispered. "Where's Way-Ray?"

"I don't see him." Jackson shifted, turning side-on to the slope, his good leg lower, acting as a buttress. "The sun's in their eyes. Way-Ray's got that in his favor until he passes them. And, as strange as it might appear, that's a good suit he put together."

Kate chewed at her lower lip, her eyes measuring the scant distance between the cemetery and the southern edge of the headland. "If they go into the cemetery, they'll be almost on top of him."

"Can't be helped." Jackson brought the gun up and sighted along the barrel. "Wish I had the rifle. A handgun's not my weapon of choice at this range."

"You can't hit them?"

"I can hit them, Kate, but probably not where I'd like to. It may take several shots to put them down so they stay down." He tilted his chin toward the thugs. "They must sense this won't be a walk in the park. See how they spaced themselves? When I shoot one, the other will have time to hit the ground."

And then he'll shoot at us.

"And they could be wearing vests. We have to let them get closer."

Closer means more danger.

Trembling, Kate stared at the curving slice of meadow between the cemetery and the edge of the cliff. Way-Ray was there. Somewhere.

The swelling breeze combed the grass and Kate breathed a thank you to the sun and sea that created those in-coming squalls and the gusts they generated. She urged the clouds to move faster, to dump rain that might send the thugs running for shelter in the trees and provide a wider margin of time for help to arrive. But from a year spent watching sea and sky, she knew the clouds were farther out than they appeared, knew those squalls could hang offshore for hours, or rain themselves out before they made landfall.

One of the thugs, perhaps an inch taller and twenty pounds heavier than his brother, called something, then veered toward the cemetery, gun held before him, arm sweeping left and right.

"No," Kate whispered. Every nerve ending felt like the burning wick of a candle. She wanted to leap from hiding and offer herself as a target. Shedding Way-Ray's pack, she inched one strap of her own down her arm.

"Don't," Jackson cautioned.

She shrugged the pack strap up and dug her fingernails into crumbling earth, eyes straining to track the thug's progress.

A year ago she'd faced this same horrible choice— remain hidden and hope to escape and get help, or reveal herself, let Way-Ray know he wasn't alone, and draw a killer's wrath.

A year ago she'd come out of her hiding place.

She rubbed the scar on her leg. The pain of that bullet wound was nothing compared to Way-Ray's life. She'd do it all again in a heartbeat.

The thug reached the cemetery fence. He looked back at his partner who trained his gun on the gravestones.

"That's Carlos going into the cemetery," Jackson whispered. "He's the oldest, the one with the missing finger. It was chopped off in a gang fight."

308

Kate forced herself not to think about that and riveted her gaze on the meadow beyond the cemetery. Was Way-Ray there yet? Could he see this man? Was he frightened? Or, worse, was he too confident?

Carlos swung the gate wide and stepped through. He moved in a lazy circle, counterclockwise, pausing once to kick at something Kate couldn't see—flowers perhaps, or the notes Way-Ray often left by his mother's stone.

Anger blazed through her brain and she jammed her fingers tighter into the ground. How dare he desecrate Amanda's grave!

Carlos kicked again, then swatted at the air in front of his face.

"Yellow jackets." Jackson breathed the words like a prayer.

"Cologne," Kate whispered. "They were wearing a lot of cologne the day they stopped me."

"Let's hope they splashed on a double dose this morning."

Jerking like a puppet on snarled strings, Carlos spun and swatted at his face and chest with his free hand.

His brother shouted something. Trotted toward him. Halted.

Mouth stretched into a scream, Carlos beat at his head with both hands, his gun flashing in the sun. He took a few steps toward the gate, then veered away toward the opposite fence, flailing at wasps that glittered like metallic confetti as they swirled in a macabre halo around his head.

Kate heard a sharp pop and then another. "He's shooting."

309

Eyes straining for a sign of Way-Ray in the breeze-ruffled grass, she leaned forward and shifted her weight to her left foot. If Way-Ray leaped up and ran, she would vault to the meadow and draw the thug's fire.

"Not yet." Jackson gripped her shoulder, bearing down until she bent her knees for balance. "Not until you have no other choice."

No other choice.

How would she know when she reached that point?

Carlos Romero jigged sideways, tumbled over a gravestone, staggered to his feet, slapped at his face again. Felipe gaped, gun hand dropping to his side. His brother spun about, his weapon at shoulder height. The barrel swung in his direction. Felipe ducked.

Another shot popped.

Then two more.

Jackson fired.

Screaming, Felipe fell into the tall grass.

Whipping toward them, free hand swatting at the whirling yellow jackets, Carlos fired off a string of shots.

Jackson squeezed off another shot.

Carlos beat at his chest and fell against the fence. For a long moment he leaned there, his gun pointing at the sky, then the fence collapsed and he crumpled to the ground.

Kate breathed out, relieving the ache in her chest and the pounding behind her eyes. "You got them! I'll find Way-Ray."

"Not until I secure their weapons."

He leaned up the slope, putting his weight on his uphill leg, the bad one. Jaw clenched, he pressed

310

his gun against the incline and reached with his free hand for the gnarled roots at the top of the trail. Kate stretched out her hands, not touching him. He brought his good leg around, planted the foot on the lip of the meadow, and lunged.

A blur of black drew Kate's attention.

Felipe Romero hauled himself to his knees and raised his gun.

CHAPTER 31

"Look out!"

Kate hooked her fingers in Jackson's back pocket and pulled.

Romero fired.

Kate braced herself to take some of Jackson's weight, but his bad leg twisted beneath him and he slammed into her full force.

In a tangle of arms and legs, they crashed through vines and ferns and lupine between the zigzags of the trail. Thorns tore at Kate's blouse and ripped her skin. Then, with a crackle of broken branches, she thudded to the path below.

Wheezing in shallow breaths, she sprawled there for a few seconds, gazing up at a spinning dome of sky, the plastic containers in the pack digging into her back. Then she flexed her ankles and knees, turned her head, and rotated her shoulders.

Nothing broken or dislocated.

At least nothing she could feel just yet.

"Get up," Jackson ordered, his voice gritty. "Get down to the cove and hide."

Kate rolled onto her side, drew up her knees, and rolled again, dizzy. She closed her eyes, fighting nausea.

"Now," Jackson said. "Get down there."

Kate swallowed, opened her eyes, and ripped a length of blackberry vine from her hair. She struggled to her feet and saw Jackson, his back to the slope, pushing himself erect. His face was scratched and his T-shirt ripped along one side, but she saw no spurting blood, no spreading seep.

"I lost my gun in the fall," he said in a flat tone.

"I'll find it." She flung herself at matted foliage, tearing at curling fern fronds, their scent green and cloying. "I'll find it."

"There's no time."

"You shot him." She clawed through a mass of decaying leaves. "He went down. He's hurt."

"Not bad enough. He won't come fast, but he'll come. If we're lucky he'll check on his brother first."

Kate pawed at dead vines, thorns ripping her flesh. "Way-Ray must have called for help by now. He must have. He's okay. He has to be."

She told herself she was shouting to be heard above the faint wail of wind and crashing waves, not in panic. "Way-Ray wasn't hit. I didn't hear him scream. He called Chief Lowell by now. Someone will come. They'll come."

Jackson pulled on the pack, yanking her off the slope. "Forget the gun. Forget thinking someone will rescue us. Get down to the cove. Bury yourself in the sand behind that log."

She stopped digging, faced him. "Where will you be?"

"Right behind you. My leg's . . . not cooperating." He kneaded his back. "It will come around in a minute."

Like the leg of an antique cloth doll, his hung loose from his hip, the foot pointed in. Kate closed her eyes, then forced herself to look again. "It's done this before?"

"Once or twice."

"You never told me. You—"

"Get to the cove."

"No." Kate seized his arm. "I won't leave you. We go together or we don't go at all."

He scowled and twisted about, trying to break her hold. "Leave me, Kate."

"I'll never leave you." She dug her nails into his skin, ducked under his arm, and got it across her shoulders. "Lean on me."

Jackson stood like a stone.

"Then we'll both die right here. And Way-Ray will be orphaned again."

"Forget emotional blackmail, Kate. Your only chance is to get into that crook of the beach and hide before he sees you. You'll never make it if you wait for me."

"We'll both make it if you stop arguing."

"You promised you'd follow my orders."

"If they made sense."

Jackson's left eye twitched. "To hell with it."

He let her take some of his weight and they hustled down the trail, Jackson hopping on his right leg, the left one swinging out to the side. In less time than Kate thought possible, they reached the jumble of rocks. She peered up the trail. No sign of Felipe Romero.

314

"Turn so I'm facing the slope and help me get started," Jackson said. "My arms are okay and there's enough water to break my fall if it comes to that."

Kate peered at the thrashing foam. "Too much water. I'm not sure we can get to the beach." She bent her knees and lowered him, her shoulder and back muscles pinging with the strain.

"We'll get there." Jackson flopped on the edge of the first rock, anchored his palms, and swung his legs over the side.

For a moment he hung there, the muscles in his forearms bulging, then he grunted, swung like a pendulum, and grunted again. In a moment, he slid his left hand along the rock and found another hold. "Piece of cake."

With a glance over her shoulder, Kate dropped to all fours and skittered across the rocks a few feet to the side, wanting to be ahead of him at the final boulder when he'd drop into the surf. If he went down, the tide might pull him off the tongue of basalt and into deep water. With only one leg, could he battle the current and get to shore? Would she have the strength to help him?

She reached the vertical drop and slid over the lip, body close against the rock, her loose shirt peeling up over her stomach. Water sloshed around her feet, her calves, her knees. She dangled from her fingertips, seeking depressions with her toes. The tide fought her, shoving her feet toward the cove, pulling them back toward the ocean. Her toes bumped over a ridge, then into a hole. She twisted her foot to lock it in place, let go with her right hand and dug her fingers into a vertical crevice, then released her left and kept it free to help Jackson.

315

"Come down when you're ready," she called. "The surf is strong but I have a good hold."

Bad leg flopping, Jackson let himself down beside her and they made for the cove. When water surged in, his weight worked in their favor and they plunged forward. When it rushed out again, Kate struggled to keep them upright.

It seemed an hour before they were out of the surf and fighting another battle. With each hop, Jackson sank ankle-deep into loose sand and leaned harder on Kate. She staggered, knees buckling, to the log.

"I got it from here." Jackson bent and grasped a length of driftwood with forking branches at one end. He bashed the branches against the log, snapping them off, then wedged his arm into the V. "Let's get into the brush."

"I'll bury you in the sand. That's what you told me to do."

"No time. And I'd rather be where I can see him." He set off, hitching past the fire pit and then around heaps of hauled-out driftwood and into the scree and brush at the base of the cliff.

Kate followed, turning her gaze in the direction of the meadow, reaching out with her mind, hoping for— For what?

Shaking her head, she trudged through loose stones slick with dry sand. She was too practical to fully invest in the idea of ESP, but she also recognized that her lack of belief didn't mean it was impossible to send and receive mental messages. If Way-Ray—

"Don't," she told herself. "Concentrate on this. Here. Now."

"Get into the undergrowth, get low, and scrounge up some stones," Jackson ordered. "The size of

316

baseballs. Small enough to throw without straining, but big enough to do some damage."

He lowered himself behind a rock the height and width of an executive desk. An icy winter storm had pried it from the cliff and sent it hurtling to this spot. "Set the stones on the top of this. It makes good cover and I can move around it to stay out of sight and brace myself against it to stand."

Kate scuttled to the base of the cliff, gathering stones as she went, tying the long tails of her blouse together to make a sack. In a few minutes, she had two dozen fist-sized rocks piled where Jackson could reach them if he stood.

If.

His skin was a sickly yellow-gray, his jaws were locked together, and his breath came in tortured gasps. Kate couldn't begin to imagine the depth of his physical pain and emotional upheaval. He defined himself as a rescuer, not one who had to be rescued.

"I just need another few minutes to rest, then I'll be good to go." He shot her a grimace she guessed he intended for a smile, and leaned back, arms taking his weight.

"Lie down," she urged.

"This is all right."

Meaning that it was? Or meaning that if he let himself relax any further he might not be able to rise again?

Don't think about that!

"Where do you want me?"

"Not too close. Off to the side. Not in the line of fire behind me."

She rose to a crouch and scanned the rim of the cove and the hillside above it. No movement except

317

the pulsing tide and the ripple of leaves as the wind curried them. Turning her head, she spotted the crease in the base of the cliff that pointed to the spot where they'd hauled the carcass of the buck. The cairn was off to Jackson's right and a few dozen feet away—as far as she could get without leaving the shelter of the bushes.

"He'll have his brother's gun, but I'm hoping they didn't carry extra clips and his wound won't allow him to go back for one. If we can break his concentration and keep him firing, if we can take the gun out of the equation and if I can get in close, we'll be good."

If he misses with every shot.

He flashed the grimace smile again. "We'll be home for dinner, Kate."

If we survive, you'll be in a hospital, in surgery.

Without glancing at his useless leg, Kate asked, "How many bullets does he have left?"

"That depends. With his brother's, at least a dozen, maybe more than twenty. As many as thirty if he found the one I lost."

Thirty might as well be a hundred, a thousand, ten thousand.

"Kate!" Jackson slid his gaze toward the headland, flopped to his side, and pressed himself close against the rock that shielded him. "Hide. Now!"

Her gaze locked on at the man shuffling along the final thrust of the trail, Kate crawled backward, parting thin brush with her toes. Stones shifted and grated beneath her, sounds she knew would be lost in the noise of the wind and buffeting waves.

318

"Remember the first rule is to stay hidden and watch for an opening," Jackson said. "Don't move until you see it. Or until you have no choice."

"I won't." She crawled backward another foot.

"Look at me, Kate."

Turning her head, she peered into his eyes, saw love and pain, pride and regret. "You're strong. You're smart. You took a killer down before. Do what you need to. But whatever you do, make it count."

Whatever you do.

Kate blinked away tears and forced a smile. "Is that an order?"

Jackson smiled back, a true smile this time. "I'm all out of orders."

There were a thousand things she wanted to say, but the man in the black suit was at the rocks. She swallowed, and said only, "I love you. Nothing will ever change that."

Jackson touched his useless leg. "I love you too, Kate. If we get another shot at things, I won't be such a mule-headed jerk."

"If we get another shot, I'll hold you to that promise every day for the rest of my life."

Blinded by tears, she scrabbled to the burial mound they'd built over the dead buck. It seemed thick enough to stop a bullet and there was a depression behind it where she could flatten herself. But for now she hunkered partway into trench, shoulders hunched to keep her head below the level of the stunted shrubs.

The man in the black suit worked his way down the jumble of rocks, pausing every few feet to scan the cove.

319

When he halted at the top of the final boulder, she shifted her gaze to the hillside above him.

No one there.

Hope flickered, dimmed.

Romero squatted, studying the ebb and flow of the tide, then tucked his gun in his jacket pocket, turned to face the rock, and lowered himself over the edge. His feet disappeared into the churning water, his calves, his knees.

Kate crossed her fingers, hoping the force of the tide would throw him down and carry him off the basalt shelf.

No luck. He gripped the rock as she had and, hand over hand, pulled himself along.

He reached the scrap of beach and, too late, she saw what he must see—their footprints, leading to the log and beyond. She should have swept the sand with a branch.

Too late for that now.

Too late for so many things.

Chapter 32

Turning her head by millimeters, Kate found a gap in spiky branches thick with slender gray-green leaves and peered at Jackson. He was sitting in the shadow of the rock with his legs stretched out in a *V*, leaning forward and to one side, rubbing his back.

Romero plucked the gun from his pocket. Following the impressions in the sand, he advanced without hurry but without hesitation.

He reached the log and came around it, his gaze moving left and right, his gun doing the same.

As Romero turned his head, Jackson stretched his right arm up and snatched a rock from the supply she'd scavenged.

Kate's fingers curled around empty air.

She'd scooped up none for herself.

Romero passed the fire pit and halted, inspecting the tangles of driftwood they'd hauled above the tide line. His wet pants stuck to his knees and shins; sand plastered his cuffs and black leather shoes. A gust of wind peeled back his jacket, revealing a holstered gun, another wedged in his belt, and a wide splotch of blood on his right side. The stain started a few inches below his armpit, the top smudged, as if he'd explored the wound with his fingers or pressed his hand against it. Lower down, the blood blended into the black fabric of his slacks.

The words "walking wounded" formed in Kate's mind. How serious was his wound? How much longer could this man keep walking?

"I know you are hiding here." His voice was deep and rough, yet his syllables rolled, rising and falling, almost lilting. "I have your weapon, Mr. Jackson Scovell and I do not think you have another. So, you are trapped. If you come out now, I will arrange a quick death."

He used no contractions and his choice of words and sentence construction were oddly formal. She imagined him as a boy about Way-Ray's age, lugging a heavy book along a sun-scorched street, calling to his brother to wait.

Don't think that. Don't think of him as human.

He was a monster, hired because of a resume written in the blood of others.

"If you do not come out voluntarily, I will find you and hurt you just enough so you are helpless but aware while I take my time with your woman." He smiled, his thin moustache twitching, his eyes squeezing almost shut. "That will be even more pleasurable than killing the boy."

Way-Ray was dead.

Kate's heart pounded in her ears, and her field of vision narrowed to a dime-size circle.

Way-Ray was dead.

She felt her heart stutter, felt numb to the bone, empty.

Soon Romero would kill her too.

Well, she wouldn't be a compliant victim. She wouldn't bargain or plead. She would fight until the last drop of blood drained from her body.

Unclasping icy fingers, she felt at her sides for a rock small enough to lift and throw, wondering how she'd manage to hurl it with her arm trembling like it was. Even on the best of days, her aim was erratic, her range pitiful.

Keeping her movements small and slow, she combed through chunks of driftwood slick and silky to the touch, through shallow pockets of sand and clusters of twigs and leaves.

Something sharp scraped her right palm.

The point of an antler, whitened by sun and wind, protruded from the sand.

Sliding until her feet were anchored in the depression behind the mound, she shrugged off her pack, then probed the buck's grave, tracing the antler to the skull.

Romero put a hand to his ear. "I cannot hear you, Mr. Jackson Scovell." He ran his tongue across full lips. "What is your decision?"

Jackson said nothing.

Canting her head, Kate peered through a weave of branches and saw him massaging his bad leg, his face locked into an expression she'd never seen before, an expression of doubt and despair. She felt her stomach roil with a hopeless sickness. If Way-Ray was dead and Jackson was helpless, then—

Don't think that!

She dug faster.

"I cannot hear you," Romero taunted. "Tell me your decision or I will make that decision for you."

Jackson shifted his weight and pounded at his bad hip with the side of his fist.

With an elaborate shrug, Romero aimed at the bushes to Jackson's left, and fired a single shot.

Kate dug harder, touched bone.

Frowning, Romero stepped closer and swung the gun to Jackson's right, toward her. Kate halted her excavation, slithered deep into the depression behind the mound and held her breath.

A bullet thumped into the mound a few inches from her head.

"So now I know where you are not." Romero fired again, the bullet whining off rock to Kate's left, somewhere close to Jackson.

Three shots. Four counting the one he fired at Jackson on the meadow.

Two dozen bullets remaining. Or more.

Keeping her head down, Kate belly-crawled up the mound and attacked the debris around the antler with both hands, making room to wiggle it, snap it from the skull.

"It was not wise to make those calls, Mr. Jackson Scovell. The people you spoke to have good sense and value their lives and so they passed along your interest in us. We were told you were not a stupid man, that you were an opponent who deserved respect, but . . ." Romero shrugged once more, turned his palms outward, fired into the brush to Jackson's left, then swung his arm across his body and fired again.

The bullet sizzled through the bushes above Kate's head.

She gasped and let go of the antler, slipping back into the depression with a clatter of rock.

324

"Ah," Romero said. "One of you is there. Not Mr. Jackson Scovell, because he would not squeak like a mouse. So, it is the woman, or the boy."

The boy?

Kate felt her heart swell with joy. Way-Ray wasn't dead!

At least not by this man's hands, not to this man's knowledge.

Still, he might have been hit by the shots Carlos Romero fired from the cemetery.

No.

She wouldn't believe that. *Couldn't* believe that.

Pushing with her toes and towing the pack, she inched up the slope of the depression and slid the pack straps over the antler.

Don't look at Jackson. Don't look for help coming down the trail. Don't think about anything but this.

"If you will not come out and face me like a man, Mr. Jackson Scovell, then you will watch like the coward you are while I kill your woman and the boy. Then it will be your turn. When I have finished and you have disappeared, Mrs. Hopkins will trade this land for the life she has remaining."

Never.

If we disappear, Evie will never let go of this place. You'll have to kill her, too.

Kate shoved at the antler, then jerked on the straps, pulling it toward her.

It rocked.

Or was that her imagination?

Romero fired again, the bullet thudding into the mound level with Kate's eyes.

She choked back another gasp and yanked at the straps.

The antler rocked again. More than the first time.

325

Not her imagination.

She pounded at it with the heel of her hand, then wrenched it toward her, hanging her full weight on the straps.

A shot plowed the top of the mound.

With a crack, the antler broke loose.

Kate fell back, shielding her head.

Two more shots sizzled through the brush.

Shoving the pack aside, Kate gripped the antler. Nearly a foot long and slightly curved, it had a ragged inch of broken prong jutting near the base. She fitted her thumb inside the notch and jabbed at the sandy bottom of the depression with the long point. The antler slid in a satisfying distance and emerged unbroken.

It would do. But she had to get close, had to stick Romero where clothing wouldn't keep the point from reaching flesh or where she'd strike bone immediately and blunt the strike. She hooked the broken prong in the waistband of her shorts. It dug into her flesh, but the pain was the pain of possibility.

Rocks clattered on the other side of the mound and then a shadow stretched across the depression. "Such an uncomfortable resting place, Miss Dalton."

Kate raised her gaze to the gun pointed at her head and the man looming behind it.

"I advise you to come out and walk to the beach before you get a cramp." He traced the length of her body with the shadow of the gun. "Or worse."

Telling herself not to glance toward Jackson's hiding place, Kate stood and brushed sand and leaves from her legs, then tugged at her blouse, making sure her weapon was covered. "Thank you so much for your concern."

"You have an attitude, Miss Dalton." He laughed, a slick and sinister sound, a laugh like that of a villain in an old melodrama. "I will enjoy seeing you abandon that along with your pride. Before too long you will beg me to allow you to please me so you might live a few minutes longer."

Beg.

Eighteen months ago Wayne Jessop predicted she would beg him to kill her quickly. A minute later he fell on his own knife and died.

But lightning didn't strike twice.

And this man had a gun.

Still, Wayne Jessop died because he lost control and concentration. He died because she goaded him, enraged him, rattled him.

Perhaps she could create mental turmoil in this man as well.

Perhaps that would draw the lightning.

She plucked a twig from her hair. "And if I don't beg?"

He shrugged, unfazed. "Then you may die more slowly and painfully. Where is the boy? Where is Jackson Scovell?"

Fearing he would see the lie in her eyes, Kate hung her head, fixed her gaze on the toes of her sneakers, and mumbled. "I'm alone. Way-Ray . . . fell coming down the rocks after you shot at us. Jackson tried to get to him. The tide pulled them out to sea."

Romero grunted, spun, and snapped two shots into the brush.

Kate clenched her fists, kept her head lowered. How many bullets left?

He fired again and laughed. "You are a bad liar, Miss Dalton. They are here, hiding as you were. And

327

I will find them. Or perhaps they will come out in a vain attempt to help you as we conduct our . . . business."

Business.

She hated that word. Hated that all of this was about money.

"Is that all this is to you? Was your brother's death just part of a business deal?" She spat the words. "Was it what the man you work for would call an acceptable loss? Will he offer you financial compensation? Stock options?"

Felipe's eyes darkened and his lips compressed, but for only a second. "Your words do not sting me as you hope, Miss Dalton. My brother and I had a contract to do a job. I will fulfill it."

"And what about what you intend to do to me before you kill me? Is that a bonus? An incentive?"

"It could well be both. I will see. Now, walk to the sand by the water. Remove your clothing as you go."

Kate hesitated a few seconds, then inched up the center of the mound, the steepest part. Pushing back with her feet and flexing her ankles, she flipped stones and driftwood with the soles of her sneakers. Pretending to slip, she grasped at bushes and fell to her knees.

"You are trying my patience, Miss Dalton, and merely delaying what is inevitable."

"The slope is steep. The sand makes the rocks slippery." Wobbling, Kate got to her feet and brushed off her knees.

"Then come around." He gestured with the gun toward the edge of the mound where the slope was more gentle. "Now!"

Toying with the bottom button on her shirt, Kate sidestepped to her right—hoping to keep his

328

attention focused on her and give Jackson time. Would he recognize what she was doing and take advantage of the minutes she was buying for him? Was he able to move or was he in too much pain? Worse, had one of Romero's bullets struck him?

Don't think that!

Concentrate on what you can do.

You, alone.

She undid the button and sidestepped again. "What are you going to do to me?"

"Let us consider first what you might do for me. Things you have done for other men, perhaps even for Mr. Jackson Scovell."

A wave of revulsion swept over her. She leaned forward, hands braced on her thighs, and vomited. When her stomach was empty she stared at the half-digested lunch spattered at her feet, inhaling the sour stench of it, retching.

"If you believe I find that disgusting enough to excuse you from our activities, Miss Dalton, you will be disappointed."

Kate tilted her head to look at him, letting drool run from the corner of her mouth. "Can I get some water from my pack?"

"Are you begging?"

"I'm asking. For water. To rinse my mouth."

"The ocean is filled with water."

"Salt water. It will make me sick."

He laughed. "Not before you will be dead. Go down to the sand."

Kate swiped her tongue across her teeth and spat, then wiped her mouth on the back of her wrist and tucked her hair behind her ears. On numb feet, she eased along behind the mound to the slight slope at the far end, poking the second button through its hole.

As she advanced, Romero moved backward down his side of the mound, the gun aimed at her chest. His torso and shoulders—all she could see from her position—twisted a little with each step.

She reached the low end of the mound and saw he was working each heel left and right to plant his shoe in the scree before he took the next step. A few yards and he'd be on the sand; he'd have firm footing.

Kate slid her hand under her shirt and gripped the antler. Batting at bushes as an excuse for not coming straight out, she eased to her left up the spine of the mound. She kept her gaze locked on Romero, willing him to lose his balance, to stumble and look down. Better yet, fall.

Too much to hope for.

Romero swung his left leg back, searching out another foothold. As he did, he raised his right arm higher. The gun pointed at Kate's head.

"Don't shoot her! Shoot me! Shoot me!"

Not Jackson's voice.

Kate tore her gaze from the gun.

Romero spun about, staggered sideways, arms windmilling.

Brandishing a chunk of driftwood, Abel Moorhouse charged along the rind of beach between the mammoth log and the surf.

CHAPTER 33

Romero got his footing, took aim.

Kate ripped the antler from her waistband, lunged to the top of the mound, and launched herself.

Abel veered left.

Romero fired.

Abel spun about, fell sideways, hit the sand.

Kate smashed into Romero's broad back, riding him to the ground, gouging the side of his neck with the point of the antler.

He bucked and twisted, jabbing with his elbows.

Stay close.

Don't let him use the gun.

She wedged her left hand beneath his neck, clawed for a grip on his shirt, probed for a soft spot with the antler, found one beneath his jaw, shoved with all she had.

Romero squealed and heaved, flipping onto his back, onto Kate.

Air huffed from her lungs. Stones gouged her shoulder blades and hips. Her fingers uncurled, releasing his shirt and the antler. The red scorpion

331

tattoo on his neck pressed against her mouth. She smelled the sweet, oily scent of his hair, the acid funk of sweat, and the sharp sting of cologne.

Romero torqued his left arm about, tried to reach the antler. Kate clawed at his wrist and he pulled away, then knotted his fingers in her hair, and yanked. Fire blazed across her scalp.

His right hand came up, the gun aiming at the sky, arcing toward her as his elbow bent.

Kate raked at his eyes with her nails, got a grip on the antler again and worked it like an awl, driving it deeper into his neck.

Romero shrieked, jerked his head up, slammed it back against her face.

Something cracked.

Pain arced across both eyes like electrical current.

Her field of vision narrowed until she saw only the tattoo and the bloodstained collar of his white shirt.

Her lungs flamed.

Romero twisted to his left, broke free, rolled clear.

Kate choked down a breath and touched the flattened ruin of her nose. Through a haze, she saw Romero come up on all fours. The antler hung beneath his jaw, blood streaming along it, splashing onto the tangled kelp at the tide line.

Bright blood.

Lots of it.

She'd made it count.

Felipe Romero wouldn't live to leave this cove.

With a rattling gasp, he rocked his weight onto his left arm and raised his right hand. The gun flashed in the sun.

Kate dug in heels and elbows, squirming backward toward the surf.

332

Romero tilted his chin up, shook his head, squinted, aimed—

Went limp.

Went down.

Supported on one elbow, legs splayed out behind him, Jackson held a jagged rock above Romero's head.

"You okay?" he asked.

Kate coughed, cleared blood from her throat. "Most of me."

"Good."

Jackson raised his arm to the sky, then brought the rock down with a dull, wet thud.

Romero's legs jerked twice and were still.

Kate turned her head and watched the surf foaming across the sand. In a moment she got to her knees, rinsed Romero's blood from her fingers, and cupped cold salt water to her face until her eyes burned and her nose went numb.

"He was a rabid animal," Jackson said. "I've never seen one get better."

"I know."

Her voice, distorted by her broken nose, sounded comical, but her thoughts were bleak. All this death. For money. For greed.

Stones scraped and clattered. Panting with the effort, Jackson belly-crawled to her. "My left leg's dead, Kate. And the other one's going."

His voice was flat, the short sentences simply statements of fact.

"Leave me here. Go find Way-Ray."

Way-Ray!

She lurched to her feet, trying to blink concern and pity from her eyes before she faced Jackson. He wouldn't want that, would reject it. Perhaps, in his

333

pain, even reject her. She needed to be confident, certain, needed somehow to be strong before fear crushed all that out of her.

"Sure, make me do all the work while you lie around." She bent and canted her head to look him in the eyes. "If you're thinking of using the paralyzed-leg excuse to call off our wedding, forget it. I'll drag you down the aisle by your hair if I have to."

Jackson rewarded her effort with a trace of a smile. "When are you planning to do that?"

"Any day you want. Tomorrow. Next Saturday. Halloween."

"Halloween?"

"Sure. Then I can wear a mask." Kate touched her squashed nose. "Now, let's get you out of the reach of the tide so I can find Way-Ray and bring help."

"Way-Ray's at the barn," Abel said. "And help is on the way."

Kate spun about and saw him leaning against the log, one hand pressed to the side of his bloody shirt, a thick book in the other. "But— He shot you. I saw you go down."

"He shot Sherlock Holmes."

Abel came closer and held out the book to display a hole drilled on a slant from cover to cover. "If Sir Arthur had written fewer stories or if this was a paperback or if it hadn't been in the right spot in my pack, I'd be dead instead of just nicked a little."

He removed his hand from a bloody patch on his shirt and smiled. "Heck, the beating those two gave me hurt worse than this."

"How did you find us?" Jackson rolled to his side and levered himself up on one elbow. "Why did you come back?"

334

"Pure chance. I waited an hour before a couple of fishermen picked me up. We went a mile, then I saw those guys turn down your road and I got out and ran as fast as I could. Way-Ray flagged me down and told me they had guns. He said the police were on the way, but then I heard a shot and I—"

"—saved our lives," Kate said.

Abel's knees buckled and he sat, breathing in great gulps of air, hands shaking, sweat beading his brow. Expressions of pain and confusion and wonder chased themselves across his face.

"Adrenaline rush crash," Jackson told him. "Close your eyes and try to relax. You'll be okay in a few minutes."

"I'll get some water from my pack." Kate stood and discovered she was shaking as badly as Abel.

"Take it slow," Jackson advised.

Placing her feet as if she was walking on new ice, she made it to the mound, retrieved the pack, found the water bottle, and rinsed the sour taste from her mouth.

"Don't drink too much," Jackson called. "You'll chuck it right up."

Kate felt herself flush, grateful that he hadn't seen her vomiting, retching, drooling. Or had he?

Sipping, she retraced her steps and handed the bottle to Abel. He sucked at it and blotted his forehead on his sleeve. "I'll go up the trail in a minute and tell them you're alive."

"You won't have to." Jackson pointed to the hillside.

Rifles ready, a string of men approached the jumble of rocks at the end of the trail.

Kate waved her arms and, knowing they couldn't hear above the wind and tide, shouted, "We're here. We're here."

Chapter 34

"And then they put you in that helicopter and it went out over the ocean and tipped its nose down and I thought it was gonna fall but it zoomed off."

Way-Ray bounced in the chair beside Jackson's bed, using his hand to demonstrate the flight. "And Kate and Evie were hugging and crying and Paul kept saying he was sorry and he didn't mean for anyone to get hurt or dead and he was gonna tell the development people to go to hell and call that woman from the TV who always wears red and get a bunch of people in big trouble. But first he drove Peggy to the hospital 'cause she got knocked out and the ambulance guys were all busy with you."

"Not my finest hour," Jackson told Kate as Way-Ray hauled in a breath.

"But before that Curtis got stung by the yellow jackets in the cemetery just like that bad guy, only not as many times and he didn't shoot off his gun. That was kinda scary when that happened because I was really, really close, but I held still and he didn't see me. And Chief Lowell told me I should get a medal and Kate promised I'd get two new video games and more TV channels. And one of the trooper guys said my ghillie suit was better than any he ever saw and Abel told me I could keep the Sherlock Holmes book with the bullet hole in it when it's not evidence anymore."

He paused for another huge breath and pointed at Kate. "And then one of the guys from the ambulance grabbed Kate's nose and smushed it back the way it should be and she only screamed a little and now she looks like a raccoon."

He gave a final bounce and flopped back in the chair, flinging his arms to his sides. "It was the most exciting day of my whole entire life."

Jackson made a sound that was half grunt and half snort, a sound that didn't involve the use of muscles below his shoulders, didn't pull at the scaffolding of rods and screws in his spine. This was as close to a laugh as he could manage for now, so Kate laughed for two, even though, as Way-Ray said, her swollen nose made her sound like a goose playing a kazoo.

Jackson shifted his legs beneath the sheet and Kate laid a hand on his knee, felt him flex it in response, and blinked back tears. The three of us have a way of ending up in hospital rooms, she thought. But that's okay, as long as we end up together.

"I bet Sean's sorry he missed it," Jackson said.

"Oh, yeah." Way-Ray bounced and pounded the armrests with his fists. "When I told him he got so mad he kicked his mom's car and left a big dent and now he can't watch TV for a week. He says he's never going camping with his cousins again not even if they pay him a million dollars."

He leaped from the chair and jammed a hand into the pocket of his jeans, jingling a stash of coins. "Can I go see what kind of snacks and candy bars they have in the machines? In case there's something they don't have in Castaway Beach, maybe something special that would be good for when you get married."

Jackson snorted and Kate giggled. "Every wedding planner agrees that nothing says haute cuisine like a snack from a machine."

"Hoot quizzing?" Way-Ray wrinkled his nose and raised one corner of his upper lip. "Is that Latin? Do I have to look it up when we get home?"

"Not this time. The rules are suspended until Jackson can chase you down if you try to weasel out of dictionary duty."

"How long will that be?"

"Not as long as you wish, you upstart cub," Jackson said with a growl.

Way-Ray grinned and Kate reached up and brushed a hank of hair from his forehead. If he didn't get a haircut soon, he'd need some of Rhea's hairclips. "Go on and check out the snacks before that money burns a hole in your pocket."

"Money doesn't burn. At least not metal money. That melts." He dodged a second swipe at his hair and darted to the doorway. "When you get married, are you going to be Mrs. Scovell?"

Kate dropped her gaze and stared at the ring finger of her left hand. She hadn't thought of changing her name. Hadn't thought of wearing a ring, or filing joint tax returns, of talking things over before she made financial decisions.

"She's not going to be Mrs. Anybody." Jackson took her left hand, weaving his fingers with hers. "She's Kate Dalton to me and she always will be."

"So she doesn't *hafta* change her name?"

"She doesn't have to change her name or wear a dress or a wedding ring. She doesn't have to do anything she doesn't want to do."

Way-Ray pondered that, lips pushing in and out, coins jingling in his pocket as he sifted through them. "What about me? What last name do I hafta use if I get adopted after you get married?"

"Well," Kate said slowly, "getting married doesn't change what we talked about before. You could use any last name you want."

"And you won't be mad if I don't pick yours?" Way-Ray shifted his gaze to Jackson. "Neither of you?"

"There's nothing to be mad about," Jackson assured him.

"Okay then, I'm gonna be Way-Ray Blake 'cause that's what my mother's name was."

"Then that's what you'll be," Kate promised.

"Cool. Then we'll each have our own names." He leaned against the doorjamb, jingling his coins again. "Those yellow jackets were living right by my mom . . . right by where she is. Do you think she sent them to sting that bad guy? To protect us?"

Kate tamped down her doubts about an afterlife and the possibility of spirits crossing over to help the living. Way-Ray wanted certainty. And if any spirit had the power to make that crossing, it would be the spirit of a woman who gave her life for her son. "I'm sure she did."

Way-Ray nodded. "I bet she wants us to stay by her and be all together. You and me and Jackson and Evie."

"Good plan." Jackson squeezed Kate's fingers and flashed a thumbs-up at Way-Ray. "We're on it!"

Also by Carolyn J. Rose

An Uncertain Refuge
Hemlock Lake
Through a Yellow Wood
A Place of Forgetting
No Substitute for Murder

With Mike Nettleton

The Big Grabowski
Sometimes a Great Commotion
Drum Warrior

Carolyn J. Rose grew up in New York's Catskill Mountains, graduated from the University of Arizona, logged two years in Arkansas with Volunteers in Service to America, and spent 25 years as a television news researcher, writer, producer, and assignment editor in Arkansas, New Mexico, Oregon, and Washington. She founded the Vancouver Writers' Mixers and is an active supporter of her local bookstore, Cover to Cover. Her interests are reading, gardening, and not cooking.

Author Website: www.deadlyduomysteries.com

www.ingramcontent.com/pod-product-compliance
Lightning Source LLC
Chambersburg PA
CBHW071305200626
46813CB00015B/155